THE CENTER CANNOT HOLD

AARON STANDER

WRITERS & EDITORS

INTERLOCHEN, MICHIGAN

© 2018 by Aaron Stander

Cover photo by Jeff Smith.

This is a work of fiction. Names, characters, places, and incidents either are the products of the author's imagination or are used fictitiously. Any resemblance to actual events or locales or persons, living or dead, is entirely coincidental.

Publisher's Cataloging in Publication Data
Stander, Aaron.
Deer Season / Aaron Stander. – Interlochen, Mich.: Writers & Editors, 2009.

ISBN: 978-0-9975701-3-7
1. Murder–Michigan–Fiction. 2. Murder–Investigation–Fiction.

Printed and bound in the United States of America.

FOR BEACHWALKER

WHO HELPS THIS ALL HAPPEN

1

~

Toby Osmann moved out of the shadows of the forest and lumbered up the steep hill. He paused to catch his breath, allowing the two plastic gas cans he was lugging to settle into the snow. He slowly scanned the area, listening intently as he turned his head from side to side. All he could hear was the roar of the wind moving in the leafless trees and his own panting. He trudged on, trying to lift the heavy gas cans above the thick blanket of snow, his arms and legs too short for the task. As he sucked in the frigid air and forcibly expelled it, his jaw moved up and down, marionette-like. Nearly inaudible ramblings began flowing from his mouth—scatological obscenities and foul oaths.

Reaching the old farmhouse, he stopped for a moment, again looking and listening for any signs of life, any movement. There were none.

One at a time, he pushed the cans onto the deck, then, grabbing a railing, he pulled himself up. He trudged along the exterior wall of the house, avoiding the deep drift that had formed on the outer edge of the porch.

He stopped at the kitchen door, taking in its features in the dull blue light reflecting off the snow. He peered into the window in the upper half of the door. Frost on the interior of the glass partially obstructed his view.

Pulling off his gloves, he ran his hands over the cold smooth surface. A sharp chill ran through his frame.

"No one here. No one to hear. I'm in control. Pick the lock, leave the window." He worked a tension tool into the cylinder on the doorknob, then raked the key pins. The cylinder slowly yielded to his clockwise pressure.

Moving in largo time, the rhythm of his life and the speed of his cognition, he pushed the door open, the rusty hinges protesting with a dissonant moan. He set the gas cans down inside the door, switched on a small flashlight, and ran the yellowish beam around the rubbish-covered kitchen. Every horizontal surface—counters, the kitchen table, the sink, the top of the refrigerator—was stacked with dishes, pans, yellowing newspapers, empty food containers, and other assorted trash.

He moved through the rest of the refuse that filled the rooms on the ground floor. Gazing at the smudged mirror in one of the bedrooms, he was startled by his reflection in the dim light—large eyes, magnified by thick glasses, peering from a round face bound by tangled, shaggy hair.

He felt his control slipping away. With a sharp left jab, he shattered the mirror. The flashlight slipped from his hand, hit the floor, and the world fell into darkness. He fished around on the cold floor, his fingers sifting through the glass splinters. He wanted to push against the sharp edges until he felt the unique joy of rubbing his fingers in warm, slippery blood. "Stay in control," he said. "Toby hears you, Dr. Schulte. I'm not a cutter, not a cutter anymore."

He searched his pockets for his headlamp, filling the silence with a singsong of mumbled obscenities until he located it. After struggling to get the headband in place, he stood for a long moment as his eyes adjusted to the brilliant white beam.

Finding the door to the basement at the back of the kitchen, he climbed down the open staircase, controlling his descent by tightly clinging to the handrail. At the bottom he stood for a long moment, moving his head in a clockwise motion as he poured the light over the decades of detritus that choked the area: beat-up paint cans in one corner, a workbench littered with tools nearby. Tattered suitcases and cardboard boxes, some with clothing spilling from them, occupied much of the floor. A narrow trail through the debris led to a door at the end of the room. He followed it, his headlamp like a spotlight on the large hasp bolted to the doorframe and the brass padlock that secured the door. He carefully lifted the lock, tipping his head to put the beam of the light on the keyway. "Lucky, lucky little lock waiting for the tickle of Toby's steel cock," he intoned as he began to work the mechanism with his delicate picks, his hands starting to tremble in the cold. After several attempts, he was able to turn the tumbler and pull the lock open. He considered the prize briefly, then tossed it to the side and pulled the door open.

When he stepped into the room and the beam from his headlamp illuminated what was inside, words tumbled from his lips, a mixture of religious awe and profanities.

Shelves lined the walls, each holding neatly stacked boxes of ammunition. Rifles and shotguns stood sentry-like in a long floor rack. Pistols, barrel ends facing right, were carefully aligned on a board above the long guns. A large automatic rifle occupied the one table in the room. Behind the weapon, near the wall, were piles of cartridge boxes. He picked one up—Winchester .30-06.

After filling his backpack with cartridges, he lugged the heavy rifle up the stairs, repeating the mantra, "Lucky, lucky me. Lucky, lucky Toby. The game will soon be on."

Back on the main floor he fetched the gas cans and tipped one of them at the top of the basement staircase, listening as the five gallons of gasoline splashed down the stairs. Then he poured the second container around the house. Finally, he pulled a corrugated paper box from the front pocket of his backpack and placed it on the floor of the kitchen. He opened the top and looked into the interior at the time clock, batteries, igniter, and explosives. Toggling the switch from off to on, he smiled as the seconds on the digital face began rolling forward.

2

ᵕ

Ray Elkins, Cedar County Sheriff, ducked under the police line at the bottom of the drive and clambered through the deep snow up the steep hill toward the fire engines. He looked over at the smoldering ruins. What had once been a house had been reduced to a pile of smoking rubble. He saw a flicker of fire rise from the pile, wavering against the backdrop of the snowy woods.

Ray hated fire scenes. Too often they were the site of great violence—uncontrollable death and destruction. And while the fires were seldom started with criminal intent, the devastation they caused brought heartbreak and suffering to the victims' lives.

Too many times he had stood with the survivors as the fire crews tried to control and then extinguish a blaze. Woodstoves, kitchen fires, electric heaters, and old wiring were usually the suspected causes when the old houses and trailers of the rural poor went up in flames. And the victims usually asked a variation of the same question, "What do I do now?" as they struggled with the almost incomprehensible losses.

"As it turns out, Sheriff, we couldn't do much of anything," said Tom Butler, the township fire chief, as he stopped at Ray's side. "The access road is seasonal. It was drifted entirely over. The first crew on the scene couldn't get up the hill from the highway. We needed an end loader to clear a path. While we were waiting, a couple of the young guys huffed it up the hill. They reported back that there was no rush. The structure appeared to be unoccupied and was fully engaged. We eventually got a rig and a tanker close to the fire. It was getting light by then.

"Just as we were starting to deploy the hoses, one of the guys runs over and starts yelling at me about the popping. I couldn't hear it from where I was standing near the idling diesels."

"Popping?"

"Yeah, ammunition starting to cook off. Sounds like popcorn on steroids. Once you've heard it, you know what it is. Some yahoos need a few thousand rounds stashed around the house to feel secure. When we hear ammo popping, our SOP is to just pull back until things go quiet. The loose rounds don't do much damage. They just burst, the bullets don't go anywhere. Loaded guns, that's a different matter. Guys with piles of ammo have lots of guns, loaded, of course. That's what happened here. Bullets were whizzing around for a bit.

"After things cool down, if someone bothers to rake through the ruins, they will find a collection of guns with spent rounds in the chambers."

"What happens now?" asked Ray.

"We'll wait until the fire mostly burns itself out. Then we'll cool the hotspots. But we're going to do it from a distance just in case. You should probably get the State Police arson investigator. Here's a vacant building—no power, no heat—that suddenly goes up in smoke. Someone did something.

"When I first got up here, I thought I smelled gasoline. I bet that someone poured a lot of fuel around the interior. You know this house belonged to your predecessor, Orville Hentzler?" said Butler.

"People have pointed his house out to me over the years," Ray acknowledged.

"He was one mean piece of work. Someone must have been carrying a grudge for a long time."

"When you arrived, were there any tracks in the snow leading up to the house? A snowmobile, snowshoes, tracks of any kind?"

"Well, if there were, I didn't notice any. Our focus was getting to the fire. Like I said, the drive was impassable, and we were getting heavy lake effect snow."

"Did you talk to Mike Ogden?" asked Ray, his eyes glued to the computer screen at the center of his desk. He continued to fill in the incident report as he waited for Sue's answer.

"He was just finishing up when I arrived."

"How's our favorite arson investigator?"

"He seemed upset. There's a possibility that he's going to be transferred to State Police Headquarters in Lansing," said Sue.

"A promotion?"

"Doesn't sound like it. More a funding issue. They're cutting personnel. Ogden would be filling a couple of slots."

"Bad news if that happens. We've depended on his expertise. What did he say about the fire?"

"Arson. Said we can take that to the bank. And he added that it was a novice job or the arsonist didn't give a rip if his crime was discovered. Mike found a plastic gas can in the yard near the structure. He showed it to me. It was melted and partially burned, but there were still traces of gasoline. He also said he was divorced."

Ray looked away from the screen. "What?"

"Ogden said he was divorced," continued Sue. "I never knew he was married. He never hinted at it. No wedding band. I mean, we've worked together a lot over the last few years."

"And he was talking about his marital status as he was looking over a possible crime scene?" asked Ray as he turned and gave Sue his full attention. He noticed she was wearing her hair differently, a style that enhanced her natural attractiveness.

"No, that was later when we went to catch a burger at Art's. We were sitting there doing small talk, and the divorce thing came out of nowhere."

"So what's the big deal?"

"I don't know. There were times in the past when he was lingering. You know how guys hang around if they're sort of interested. He's a nice guy and all, but I think I've always made it quite clear that I wasn't interested. You know, I was involved with someone."

"Did he ever hit on you?"

"Never. So, did you know the house once belonged to Orville Hentzler?"

"Yes. My memory is that it was a dilapidated old farmhouse. I'm wondering about motive."

"PREVECT," said Sue.

"What?" Ray gave her a look.

"Aren't you glad you sent me to FBI and FEMA continuing education courses?" said Sue, finding an open space on the whiteboard. In a neat hand she wrote:

Profit
Revenge
Excitement
Vandalism
Extremism/Terrorism
Crime Concealment

"REV," said Ray. "I'd bet on some combination of those three: revenge, excitement, and vandalism. And vandalism and excitement are probably one and the same. We haven't seen much arson lately."

"It's been a few years. Maybe we have a budding pyromaniac."

"Now that's a happy thought. Revenge?"

"You tell me. How does torching a house inflict harm on someone who's been long dead?"

"Perhaps it's a poetic gesture? Sort of like telling someone you're divorced," said Ray.

"I don't see the fit."

"Neither do I. That was just a segue in case you needed to talk about the divorce info some more," said Ray.

"No, I'm over it. And I'm not interested. I'm going to stick with canines, specifically Simone," said Sue. "She's always happy to see me, and there's never any unwanted drama in our relationship. Don't worry, I'll continue to share her. You need a dependable relationship, too. Maybe we should go to a biweekly schedule—equal time. But she's going to get fat, Elkins, if you keep feeding her lamb chops."

3

Ray guided his guest from the brilliant afternoon—the sun reflecting off the snow—into the tenebrous interior of the Last Chance, a favorite local bar and grill. Narrow rectangles of light projected from the small windows near the ceiling, illuminating the dark knotty pine paneling and worn black and red asbestos floor tiles. Most of the regular lunch crowd had already departed. There were just a few scattered tables where people were lingering over coffee or beer in quiet conversations.

"I wish I could have seen it while it was still in flames or at least smoldering. That would have been very cleansing," said Gretchen Witherspoon, the daughter of Ray's predecessor as Cedar County Sheriff.

"For safety reasons, the firefighters on the scene had to stand clear and allow the fire to burn itself out. They reported ammunition burning off and some gunfire coming from the building, shells in loaded guns exploding due to the heat."

She gave Ray a long look. "That's not surprising. You never knew my dad, did you?"

"Only by reputation," said Ray. "When I was a kid growing up here, I knew that Sheriff Hentzler was to be avoided at all costs. And after I moved back here and became sheriff, well, I heard lots of stories. But you know how stories change over the years."

"Yes. Stories and legends, and as the years go by, it becomes harder to separate the grain from the chaff." Gretchen inhaled deeply and chewed on her lower lip. She wiped away a tear.

"Lots of memories," said Ray.

"Yes," she said. "Lots of memories, most of them painful. It was a weird marriage. He was decades older than my mother. His first wife had died years before. There were no children from that marriage. When I was growing up, he seemed more like other kids' grandfathers than fathers." She paused, tears welled up in her eyes. "I learned to be a survivor. That was my mother's greatest gift to me. That said, we both were scared of that SOB. Mom protected me and absorbed most of the damage. My brother, on the other hand, my poor sensitive brother, he didn't make it."

Gretchen went silent, turning away from Ray, slowly gazing around the room. Then she looked back at him, her eyes locking onto his. Ray could see a wave of sadness spread across her face.

"He rammed his car into a tree along M22 during the spring of his junior year in high school. It was a clear night, the road was dry, there were no skid marks, no braking. I was away by then, living in Ann Arbor. People up here said it was a tragic accident. It was tragic but hardly an accident. Dylan had been subjected to seventeen years of constant humiliation. He was depressed, crying for help, and all he got from my father were insults and abuse. I think Dylan just needed out. He couldn't take it anymore. And after Dylan's death, my mother decamped. She moved to the other end of the country and worked at restarting her life. Sadly, the damage was done. She died a few years later—uterine cancer. I know it's not rational or scientific, but I blame her death on him, too. His hate and anger were toxic. He harmed the people around him at the cell level. I mean, he was very handsome and could be friendly and engaging. He knew how to court his public. He knew how to get votes. He also had lots of prejudices, but his voters shared many of those. He knew how to manipulate people's fears to his best advantage. I was the lucky one, escaping before I was permanently damaged."

She paused as the waitress arrived with the menus. After they ordered, Gretchen continued, "Let me give you the backstory. My father went off to fight the Nazis in 1942 or 1943. He was maybe seventeen. He came back a big hero, with all the medals to prove it. As he told it, he'd killed a lot of Germans to make the world safe for democracy again. And I suspect he was brave and heroic. He was a man's man.

"Not long after he was mustered out of the service, the sheriff at that time immediately latched on to him. Nothing like having a young, handsome war hero on the force. Anyway, the war hero stuff was an important part of my father's character. Our home was filled with lots of relics of the war: guns, bayonets, shells for I don't know what. On top of that, he was a gun collector. There were handguns and long guns of every type. He called his man cave in the basement 'the powder room.' There were no-smoking and no-trespassing signs on the door. Whenever he got something he was especially proud of, he would make me go down there and admire it. I couldn't have cared less. All those guns arranged just so. Shelves loaded with ammunition boxes."

"After your father died, you inherited the house?"

"Yes, by default. And that was a surprise. By his definition, I was living an evil life in Ann Arbor. I assumed he had disinherited me. In fact, I had hoped for it."

"And you never emptied the house?"

"It's a bit of a story. I wasn't in touch with my father for close to two decades. After he died, his lawyer called me. He told me I was my father's sole heir. The lawyer wanted instructions on the funeral arrangements. In truth, Sheriff, I just wanted to walk away, but Ned, my husband, said my looking after my father's final affairs would help to bring closure. So I did.

"After the service, we drove over to the house. We walked around the exterior, looked through a few windows, and left. I couldn't deal with it. Too many bad memories. I hired a local handyman to put the place in mothballs, and I've been paying the taxes with the money I received from the estate. I haven't used a dime of the money for anything else. In truth, I just wanted the place to go away. It never occurred to me to torch it." She gave Ray a wicked smile. "Whenever you're done with your investigations, I'll have the site cleaned up and put the land on the market."

The waitress delivered their food.

"Did you keep the place insured?" Ray asked.

"Yes, there's a homeowner policy. It was more for liability

protection than anything else. I never bothered to check on current market prices or update the policy," she answered.

"As I told you on the phone, this was a clear case of arson. In the past, we've had empty or derelict buildings torched. Usually, they are in remote places, much like your father's home. We seldom find the perpetrators. Thrill-seeking teens or perhaps some closet arsonist are often blamed. Most likely this was a random act. That said, the arson might be connected to something in the past linking your father and—"

"I think I see where you are going, Sheriff." She paused ruminatively. "I'd help if I could. I just don't know. As I said, we'd been out of contact for years before he died."

4

~

"It's just beyond that curve on the left," said Ray. Sue slowed and turned, stopping behind the large battered pickup that stood idling at the entrance to the Grange Hall Township Cemetery. The driver's side door of the pickup swung open before Sue could switch off the ignition.

"Morning, Sheriff. It's been a while."

"Morning, Harlan," said Ray, pulling off the glove on his right hand. He held Harlan's strong, calloused hand in his for a long moment.

"This is Detective Sergeant Sue Lawrence. Harlan Peck, here, looks after the cemetery for the township. His forbearers were some of the first European settlers to the area."

"Nice to meet you, ma'am. I've seen you on TV," Harlan said, extending a hand to Sue.

Harlan turned his attention back to Ray. "Well, Sheriff, I've never seen anything like this before, never."

"When did you first notice the damage?" asked Ray.

"Late yesterday. We had a burial on Saturday. Lydia Randall. She was ninety-seven. I'm sure you remember her and her husband, Stuart. They always had that vegetable stand along 22 just before Esch Road. They did asparagus in the spring and sweet corn in the late summer. Some folks thought it was the best sweet corn in the county, especially the summer people. And they continued with the stand way into their late eighties. Toward the end, the grandkids were running things. Lydia and Stuart, they eventually moved to town after he had a stroke."

"I remember them and the stand," said Ray.

"Those are the kinds of people that still get buried here," said

Harlan. "People who have deep roots to this land. Not many of them left. In recent years I've only done a couple of burials a year. After I'm gone, the township may not even bother having a groundskeeper anymore. They'll just keep the grass mowed a couple of times during the summer.

"No one remembers most of the people planted here, anyway." Harlan made a sweeping gesture from left to right. "The graves are mostly arranged by family. If you walk through here when everything isn't covered by snow, you will find a lot of history—generations of families, wars, epidemics. It's all written on the stones if you take the time to piece it together. The early settlers had lots of kids. There are little stones for the babies and children. The names are mostly worn away now by the weather. The last soldier killed in action was Jimmy Hopkins. Vietnam." Harlan pointed a mitten toward the south end of the cemetery. "Just eighteen. Don't think he was in 'Nam more than a few weeks before he was on his way home in a box. His kid brother, Mike, is there, too. He was buried that same summer, hit while riding his bike on the road near the family farm. Their mother, Ruth, was never the same. Went gray, became just a wisp of a thing. It was like the life went right out of her. A lot of sadness here, Sheriff."

"The vandalism, Harlan, when did you first notice it?"

"Monday afternoon. I covered Lydia's grave on Saturday after the interment. It was getting pretty dark by then. I was working with the headlights. I came back on Monday just to check my work, neaten things up a bit if needed. That's when I noticed it. Sheriff Hentzler's monument had been pulled down, and the brass plate fixed to it was missing. Let me show you."

They followed him up the plowed trail and then on a path through the snow to a large slab of granite lying on its side.

"My thinking is that they brought a pickup and used a winch to pull the monument off the pedestal. You can see the tracks. Biggest monument in here."

"So Hentzler's family had this erected?"

"No, he had this put in place years before he died. That was common back in the day, people arranging for their deaths way ahead of time, buying cemetery lots, getting the granite markers set. Names and birthdates were etched in the stone, death dates to be added later. In Hentzler's case, the marker had to be changed."

"How so?" asked Sue.

"Well," said Harlan, "His wife's name and birthdate were on the stone. After she left him, he had it changed. Not an easy thing to do. The company that supplied the marker suggested that Orville cover the area with a large brass plaque with just his name on it. You know, they'd just bolt it onto the granite. I was here cutting grass the day the guys from the monument company showed up to attach the plaque. They thought it was all too funny, saying 'Written in stone, revised with brass.' Anyway, as I said, the plaque is gone. Probably end up at a salvage yard."

Peck pointed. "His son's grave is just off to the left side. As you can see, it was untouched. Lots of Hentzler's relatives have markers nearby. Nothing else was disturbed." He looked over at Ray. "What are the chances you'll find the people who did it?"

"We'll do what we can. Sergeant Lawrence will make a photographic record of the vandalism. We'll see if we can find a clear tire print to cast or any other evidence that might help us identify the perpetrator. Have you seen any suspicious vehicles or individuals in the area in recent days?"

"Not out here, Sheriff. In the winter no one much is around that doesn't live here. I don't plow out the cemetery unless there's a burial. Usually, the place is protected from November to late March by a heavy layer of snow."

"What are you going to do about the damage?" asked Ray.

"I don't know. I had a brief conversation with the township supervisor. He's checking to see if our insurance will cover this kind of thing. He said he was going to try to contact Hentzler's relatives. In the meantime, I'm just going to bring my end loader over and block the drive with snow. No one is going to be able to get a vehicle in here till spring."

"Harlan, you've been around here a long time. I'm sure you

knew Hentzler. Can you think of anyone who might want to do this?"

"When he was alive, people either loved him or hated him. He and his boys, you know, his deputies, they liked to crack heads. It was a different world back then, Ray. But he's been gone awhile. When I interred him, no one was here, just me, the priest, and the undertaker. No family, no friends. This vandalism, it makes no sense. Like, who cares? Why bother?"

Someone is targeting a dead man, Ray thought as he and Sue walked back to her SUV. He was sure Harlan had had nothing to do with either crime, but it was probably wisest to keep the arson to himself for now. It would be in the paper soon enough.

"Knock the snow off your boots before you climb in," said Sue. "I want to keep my truck looking new as long as possible."

5

When Ray needed background information on things that happened before he became sheriff, he called on Ben Riley, a retired Cedar County officer. When Ray was first elected sheriff, he quickly discovered that Ben was one of the few officers from the old regime on whom he could rely. He appointed Ben his undersheriff. In addition to administrative functions, Ben took the lead in the recruitment and training of new officers. Responding to an early call from Ray, Ben invited him to his home.

Ben placed two coffee mugs on the kitchen table, filled each one from an almost full carafe of coffee, and settled into a chair across from Ray.

"Still take it black, I imagine?" he asked.

"Mostly, but I have started drinking cappuccinos in the morning. I think the milk buffers the acid a bit. Stomach isn't what it used to be."

"On the advice of your doctor, I imagine," said Ben with a chuckle. "Interesting how an old dog can be taught new tricks, especially when a woman's involved. How is Hanna, anyway?" he asked, referring to Ray's current love interest.

"She's looking at a job in California—Stanford. A research job."

Ray could feel Ben studying him closely, despite the casual way he was slouched forward in his chair. "How do you feel about that?"

Ray caught himself shrugging as if to dismiss his feelings. "It's a big career decision," he answered. "I'm trying to give her lots of space."

Ben let Ray's comment hang as he added several spoonfuls of

sugar to his coffee and stirred the mahogany liquid. "So Orville Hentzler. I've seen the news reports. What's going on?"

"I was hoping you might have some ideas as to the perpetrators," said Ray. He watched a playful grin spread across Ben's weathered face.

"As the last man standing from Orville's motley crew of enforcers, I get to offer some revisionist history of the bad old days."

"You were the outlier," said Ray.

"Yup, the proverbial square peg among Orville's assorted male relatives who had been granted lifetime employment as deputies. Do you know how many times I tried to quit? But quitting probably meant moving, and my wife wanted to stay close to her family, especially when the babies started coming." Ben directed Ray's attention to a wall covered in framed photos. "Look at the wall, kids and grandkids. Baby pictures, school pictures, graduation pictures, wedding pictures, with a few remarriages thrown in. I can't keep them all straight anymore."

"It was good that you stayed. I'm sure you did what you could under almost impossible conditions. I know I was grateful to have you."

"Don't pile it on too deep, Ray. I don't know what I can tell you about Orville. The years have been slipping by. And I think you already know that the last ten or fifteen years of his reign, Orville was sheriff in name only—he had lost it. His ne'er-do-well kinsmen—Dirk Lowther and his brother Danny, and Kenny Obermeyer—were running the show. And now they're all gone. All the violence they perpetrated over the years eventually came back to them. Funny how things work out."

"Yes, but getting back to Orville, his house being torched, his grave being vandalized, something is going on. I can't search department records, because, as you know, they don't exist," said Ray.

A late-night fire had conveniently destroyed the history of Orville Hentzler's almost sixty-year career as sheriff.

"Yeah," responded Riley with a chuckle. "It was a cleansing fire, Ray, a cleansing fire. The last act of Orville's regime, although I doubt if he was involved. He was almost beyond knowing then."

"Not cleansing enough, at least for someone," responded Ray. "But who? We all acquire enemies in law enforcement. Orville seemed to have more than most. Anyone come to mind?"

"Lots of folks. Orville didn't like anyone who didn't look like him, share his religious beliefs, or agree with his politics. He didn't like the migrant workers who flooded in in the summer. Their hands were critical to the cherry harvest before the hydraulic tree shakers. Orville said they all carried knives, and he went out of his way to give them a hard time. He didn't like Native Americans. I was never sure why. He was Catholic and sort of begrudgingly tolerant of Protestants. Anyone else was a heathen. I know you're wondering how he stayed in office. Things changed very slowly up here. To a large degree, Orville shared the prejudices of much of the community. And Orville did lots of favors. 'People of substance'— that was one of his favorite phrases—got a ride home in a squad car when they were stopped for impaired driving. I mean, like they were falling-down drunk. Everyone else woke up in a jail cell. If you were a friend of Orville or his gang, tickets for moving violations got torn up, if they got written at all. And the wink-and-nod law enforcement extended to the families of the people of substance. And I'm not just talking about misdemeanors. These were serious cases, possible rapes, domestic assaults, that kind of thing, and the evidence somehow just got lost during the investigative process and never made it to the prosecutor."

"Any special cases or individuals come to mind?"

Ben sighed. "There were so many over the years. And I think it only got worse when he was too dotty to know or care. The old boys were answerable to no one and did their best to keep me in the dark. I'm surprised they didn't try to take me out."

"So other than people of substance . . ." Ray enunciated the phrase in a mocking tone.

"You got it. Other than the select few, Orville was equally

misanthropic to everyone. In my early years, he was frantic about hippies and how they were destroying America. In truth, there were only a handful of kids up here trying to look the part. They were mostly city kids who spent a year or two doing the back-to-nature thing. Most didn't make it through their first winter. Then a commune of sorts sprang up on a farm near Lake Michigan. Over several years he and his boys went out of their way to harass those kids. I think it was more about his daughter than anything else. She was a young teen then and had been spending time hanging out there. Not that anything untoward happened to her as far as I know, I think it was just a preemptive move on his part. In the end, they successfully frightened the so-called hippies off. In a matter of days or a week or two, they all seemed to disappear. And a few months later, sometime in the winter, all the buildings at the old farm burned to the ground. At the time I knew something wasn't right. I was so green then. It took me a while to figure out what was going down."

"The daughter, you mean Gretchen?"

"Yes, come to think of it. How did you know her name?"

"She came up after the fire to see the ruins of the house, and I was able to have a conversation with her."

"I remember her as a spindly little kid, a tomboy. She's got to be fifty-something now."

"Yes, she's grown into a beautiful, sophisticated woman. Lives in Ann Arbor."

"Good for her. She's living in a place her father hated—the pinkos, lefties, pseudo-intellectuals, socialists, queers, Jews, and lots of other derisive words and phrases. Even when he barely knew his name, he could still spew out that kind of hatred."

"So the members of the commune," said Ray, "any of them still in the area?"

"Hmm, it was so long ago." Riley played with his mug for a moment. "Stu Baker, the painter, was there for a while. You know, the guy who does those big, moody landscapes in oil? I don't know if he was there at the end, but perhaps he can help you. He's got that studio in the old store in North Bay. If I had the big bucks, I'd love to get one of his paintings. I'd put it right there."

"What about the family pictures?"

"We'd arrange them in family groupings. One kid and their family per room. It would be a lot easier to keep them straight."

6

Ray stood on the crest of the bluff overlooking the snow-covered fields of long abandoned farmland. In the distance, over the tops of the leafless trees, he could see the big lake, steel gray water reaching to the horizon. He looked over at Stu Baker, late sixties, slightly stooped, a heavy parka hanging on his narrow frame. Ray had been introduced to Stu a few times over the years at art openings but knew little about the man's background.

"It's been a long time—more than forty years—but even now I can't believe that it's all gone, the buildings, the people, a way of life," said Stu. He gestured toward the plateau, a long flatland between the dunes bordering Lake Michigan and the rolling hills on the east. "If I close my eyes, I can see the place, the familiar faces. I can hear the sound of their voices and their laughter."

Stu looked over at Ray, "My kids have been bugging me for years to write about my hippie days. They're afraid when I kick off, this bit of family history will be lost forever."

Stu slowly surveyed the scene. "I drove out here in early October and spent a few hours. I managed to do a few watercolors, but I didn't get any words on paper. It was a warm, sunny afternoon. I ate a sandwich, drank some wine, maybe even napped for a while, but I did zero writing. My career as a painter, that started here. The idea that I could be an artist, I don't think that would have happened without this place.

"Every season had its magic. But the winter here was always special. I'd go cross-country skiing in the late afternoon, just before dark, and I would stand about here in the gloaming and look down at our little village, the soft yellow light coming from the windows, the smoke from the wood stoves floating up in the gentle breeze.

They say that smell is tied to memory, tied to emotion in some powerful way. The smell of those burning logs, mostly red oak, meant warmth, hot food, companionship, and a woman who was very special to me at the time."

"How did you end up here, Stu?" asked Ray.

"That requires a little background history, Sheriff. I had dropped out of college in '67."

"Weren't you worried about the draft?"

"No, I was 4F. I broke my right leg in sixth grade just at the beginning of my growth spurt, and by the time I was eighteen, I walked with a pretty good limp. I showed up for the physical at old Fort Wayne. They didn't want me.

"So I headed west, did the whole Haight-Ashbury thing. It really was the summer of love—at least some of the time. I drifted around the West for about five years, heading to warmer climes during the winter, picking up jobs up north in the summer. I did whatever it took to keep my body fed and my head slightly buzzed. Just wine and grass, Sheriff. I lived in communes, hippie encampments, went solo occasionally.

"I stayed in contact with my parents—postcards and collect calls home. Occasionally, they'd wire me money to get me through some difficult times. When my uncle died, they got me a plane ticket back to Detroit. I stayed at their place in Livonia for a few weeks and then headed north with one of my cousins. He was just out of high school, and I think I was a bit of a role model—to my aunt's horror. Anyway, he had heard about this place and wanted me to go check it out with him. It wasn't like any other hippie place I'd ever been to. I mean, they were tie-dyed and all that, played flutes, recorders, and guitars. They shared the food, and it wasn't hard to get laid, but that's where the comparison ended.

"The commune was organized. Everyone was expected to work at assigned jobs. But if you were unwilling to do your share for the good of the community, you were forced to leave."

"But you stayed," said Ray.

"Yes. At first, I thought I'd only hang around till fall, and then I would head for Arizona. But I got involved with one of the women. My cousin, Josh, he left in August. He thought being a Spartan was way cooler than being a hippie."

"So how long were you part of the community?"

"Two years and a bit more. Then everything imploded. But before that happened, for the first time in my adulthood I carved out kind of a life."

Stu described how the community supported itself by selling crafts, vegetables, and fruit at a stand up on the highway and at the local farmers' markets. They had a big woodlot and a primitive sawmill—their source of lumber for building projects and repair work. There was also woodworking equipment in one of the outbuildings. Stu started making bowls on the lathe, something he had learned how to do in junior high wood shop.

"Nothing elaborate," Stu said, "just salad bowls to hold fruit and stuff. They were cheap to make, we didn't charge much, and they sold like hot cakes. So I became Stu Baker, the bowl maker. That was my job for the rest of my time here. And one of the women taught me how to do watercolors and later oils. That's how I got into painting, my future career."

"How was the place organized?

"It was democratic early on in an odd kind of way," Stu said. "The farm belonged to Marian Patozak. Her great-grandparents had settled on the land early on. During my time here she told me bits and pieces of her family's history. It was probably a mixture of legend and fact," said Stu. "Eventually the place ended up within the proposed boundaries of the National Shoreline. The government gave them use of the land until the death of the last grandchild: Marian."

"The land meant a lot to her, then," Ray said.

"It did," replied Stu. "Marian's love interest was a guy named Rob Habbers. He had a year or two of college like most of the rest of us. He was a theatre major somewhere, totally wacko, post-dramatic stress disorder. You know what I'm saying. He was always onstage. Lots of noise, lots of gestures. Rob was taken with the Robin Hood myths. So our woodlot became Sherwood Forest. Rob assigned nicknames: Little John, The Friar, Will, Much, and so forth. Rob was short of women's names, so he made them up. He just put 'maid' in front of any woman's name, and it seemed to work. Thus, Maid Marian of Sherwood was reinvented.

"Eventually Rob took over the day-to-day leadership of the little community. No one seemed to mind since it meant we could go on about our lives and let Rob work on the details.

"I mean, there were occasional bitches, but they were minimal," said Stu. "Some people talked about spending their lives here, but most of us knew deep down there was a use-by date. We couldn't do the Peter Pan thing forever. As it turned out, Sherwood unraveled faster than anyone expected."

"What happened?" asked Ray.

Stu went silent for a moment. "At the time I never really thought it through, but now I think I understand what went down. Rob was at the center of this, the initial success of the place and its final collapse.

"Rob was enormously charismatic—handsome, smart, extroverted, ripped. In the good weather, he went shirtless at every opportunity so the women could enjoy his very tan body.

"And Marian, she was stunning," Stu said. "I just liked looking at her. She had this sensuality that would leave you panting. She coupled that with a joyful laugh and a great smile."

Stu explained how Rob was suddenly expelled from the master bedroom in the main house and exiled to the bunkhouse. Stu guessed that Marian was fed up with his dalliances.

"After Rob moved to the bunkhouse, he was always on the prowl. We gave him the nickname 'The Ass Bandit of Sherwood.' And there were lots of women in our community who were happy to share his bed. And then other women and girls floated in during the warm months, mostly teens, local girls, daughters of the summer people, some runaways. I think Rob was accepting all invitations.

"And then there was your predecessor, Orville Hentzler, what an asshole. He and his deputies started harassing us. First, Hentzler said we were squatting. Marian hired an attorney and proved that she had the right to occupy the property. Later, some of the deputies dropped by more than occasionally and bothered our women. I think they were hoping for an easy lay. Then there were the raids, three or four, where they pulled the place apart, sometimes in the middle of the night, looking for dope. They didn't find anything. In truth, I'm surprised that they didn't plant a kilo of grass, you know, enough to make a big case.

"And we were almost powerless to do anything about it. We were breaking no laws, causing no problems, but we were outsiders. In the minds of many of the locals, we were the local manifestation of all the scary things they had heard about the youth movement. You know, drug fiends, VD vectors, communists, atheists."

"How long did this go on?"

"It was intense, especially during the summer months. And then they seemed to lose interest in us. And then out of nowhere, we were the target again, with Rob in the bullseye."

"What caused the sudden interest?" asked Ray.

"Women, especially one woman. She was young, maybe just out of high school. She started hanging out that last summer. She was something, Sheriff. She knew it, too. Pretty women are like that."

"Did she have a name?" asked Ray.

"I don't think I ever heard her real name. Rob called her Ginger Snap. Everyone else called her just Ginger. The rumor was her parents had a summer home up the coast. There was another blond that last summer, young, most likely jailbait, Rob nicknamed Platinum. He joked that messing with Platinum could be very costly.

"But going back to Ginger. It's not like she moved in. She'd just come around. But the two of them became a thing, you know. Our women were pissed at Rob for hanging with an outsider. Marian got involved, too, saying Rob and his little whore should leave. I'm not saying the guys took Rob's side, but I think that's what the women believed. And then Sheriff Hentzler was all over us again."

"And you tie this to Ginger?"

"Near as I could figure at the time, it had to do with this girl or with Orville's daughter, who had also been hanging around. Anyway, Orville and his goons came roaring in one night, sirens, lights, it was like one or two in the morning."

Stu remembered the scene vividly, his turning over in his bunk, unsure of what had woken him. Then the door burst open, and a flashlight beam blinding him, and someone yanking him out of bed.

"What's going on? What the hell?" Stu remembered yelling as the Cedar County deputy hauled him outside. There were cars everywhere—as if they'd brought every vehicle in the department. Stu saw other people being forced out of their cabins—everyone; the deputies were marching them all to the barn, where someone had turned on the weak overhead light. Stu saw Rob with Ginger— he had an arm around her and was trying to shield her from the deputy herding them with a billy club.

They were all milling around the barn, surrounded by a circle of deputies, when Orville Hentzler swaggered in.

"Now sit down!" Orville ordered.

Stu had never felt such hatred and disgust for another person. He looked around to see what the other residents would do. Everyone was grumbling, but most of them were sinking down onto the dirt floor littered with straw. Then Hentzler gestured behind him, and a man in a suit stepped out and scanned the crowd. His face was mean and hard, and Stu felt a prickle of fear move up his spine. When the suit saw Ginger, he waded through the residents of Sherwood and grabbed her by the hair.

"Hey!" Stu yelled and started to stand up, but a deputy shoved him back down. Rob rose and took hold of the older man's arm, but he shook Rob off, and a deputy moved in and walloped Rob hard across the stomach with his billy club, doubling him over.

Stu was on his feet again, along with several other young men intending to go to Rob's aid, and the deputies moved in on them, too. Too late, Stu saw a deputy's fist coming toward his face, and then he was staggering backward, pain exploding in his nose.

Another deputy was beating him from behind with his billy club, and as Stu fell to the floor, he caught a glimpse of Ginger struggling in the older man's grasp as he dragged her out of the barn. He lay in the straw and dirt, struggling to breathe. Then his head snapped forward as a deputy kicked him in the back of the skull. He might have lost consciousness for a few minutes, because the next thing he remembered, the deputies had left the barn, and he could hear his friends moaning and some of the girls crying.

Marian was checking on each injured person. "I'll try to get the doctor," she said after crouching next to Rob, whose face had been beaten to a pulp. Blood shone in the dim light on a three-inch gash in his skull.

"It was movie stuff," Stu said. "I've never been in that much pain. The doctor in the village, old Doc Wade, he arrived the next morning and did his best to patch up our cuts and broken ribs.

"They hurt Rob the most. Later that day, Sheriff Hentzler and one of his deputies arrived. They handcuffed Rob, accusing him of assaulting some of the officers. And that was the last we ever saw of Rob. We tried to file a missing person report, but the sheriff wouldn't accept it.

"He and his goons just pushed us out of the office," said Stu. "The bastards had their billy clubs at the ready. As far as I could tell, there was never any record of his arrest. He just disappeared. The sheriff had no explanation, other than maybe it was time for him to move on. But there was one interesting thing."

"What was that?"

"A few days later Rob's truck disappeared. It was a beater, an ancient Jeep pickup with a dented aluminum canoe strapped to the top. Rob had arrived at Sherwood in that truck, and it made sense that if he left, the truck would have been his mode of transportation.

"The one thing I couldn't understand," Stu said, "is why he left Little John behind. They were inseparable, with a lot of history. Rob seemed to be Little John's caretaker, like an older brother looking after a younger brother who's not quite right. One eye wandered. You never knew who he was looking at. He often seemed to be in another world. He reminded me of people I met out west, kids who had done so much dope that they never made it back."

"Little John—was he true to the Robin Hood legend? Was he a big man?"

"No, not at all. That was one of Rob's jokes. John barely made five feet, if that, including a pair of cowboy boots he never seemed to take off. He was powerful, though, lots of muscle. When he wasn't working, he was usually lifting weights. And anytime we needed some real strength for a job, someone would fetch him.

"After the nighttime raid, Rob disappeared, and everyone at Sherwood was terrified. Within days the residents started to drift away. Being there was too risky. I was one of the first to leave. Marian called me a traitor. She made quite a scene, yelling and screaming. I was sad that we parted like that.

"By fall the place stood almost empty. Then I heard that Marian moved forward with the title transfer to the National Park Service. She wanted her money. She wanted out of here. And not too long after that, sometime in the early winter there was a fire. Every building burned to the ground, every one. I'm sure it was arson, but no one seemed to care. I think the sheriff or his goons were responsible for the fire."

By spring, Stu said, the NPS had cleaned up the site. Ray looked out over the scene. There was no trace of the buildings.

"Did you stay in touch with any of your fellow residents?" asked Ray.

"There were a few of us who stayed around the area, but most left. I think I'm one of the last of the hangers-on. The community that Marian and Rob built enabled a bunch of kids with few skills to feed, clothe, and shelter themselves for a few years. We all left knowing more than we did when we arrived. And in truth, most of the kids here were hippie wannabes who just needed a gap year or two before they scurried back to their comfortable bourgeois lives."

"Marian, Rob, do you know anything more about them?"

"I heard that Marian ended up in the southwest, Arizona or New Mexico. Someone else told me she was in Latin America. That was years ago. Some thought Rob had impregnated the girl he called

Ginger and decided the best course of action was to skip out of town. I didn't believe this story at first, but then I saw her a few years later. I was busing tables at that French restaurant just off the big lake, the one that disappeared after a few seasons. She was there with a little girl and an older guy in a suit. I thought the man might have been her father—he looked like the guy who pulled her out of the barn that night. The child would have been about the right age. Our eyes met, but we didn't talk or anything. And I saw her at the grocery store a few times, decades ago. There was a slight hint of recognition on her part, but I think I was part of the world she didn't want to go back to."

"And Rob and Little John?"

"I heard nothing about either one of them after I left Sherwood. I searched the web for them a few years ago—nothing. I don't know if Little John somehow met up with Rob again and they left the country, went undercover, or died. I knew so little about either one of them. Maybe the stuff Rob said about himself was a fabrication—even his name. But try it out, Sheriff. Google Robert Habbers. You will come up empty-handed."

"Did you ever have any further contact with Sheriff Hentzler or his deputies?"

"Not really. As soon as I left Sherwood, I had to get a job, so I cut the long hair and shaved the beard, at least till I started making it as an artist. For a lot of years, whenever I would see a Cedar County Sheriff's car, I would think about vengeance, but it was just a fantasy.

"And then my art started selling. I invented my adult self and left that world behind."

"So there's no one else from Sherwood I might talk to?"

"Not part of the Sherwood community. That said, do you know Alice Barbour? She's a professor at U of M. She might be retired now."

"What about her?"

"She stayed with us off and on for a while. She was doing a

study. She got to know people pretty good. Well enough to write a book about us. I think she's still got a place up here. She bought a lot of my art early on and sent people my way."

"One more thing. Little John, do you know his real name?"

"No, just Little John."

"Do you remember any other names from Sherwood?"

"Sheriff, I'm getting bad with names, like the ones I should know, people I see every day. Don't ask me about names from forty years ago. My kids say I have CRS syndrome. Besides, lots of the kids didn't use their real names. Some people were hiding from the law, runaways and whatever. And others just wanted a name of their own choosing."

7

Alice Barbour—her large frame cloaked in a colorful, flowing dashiki, heavy socks in Birkenstocks peeking through below the bottom hem—guided Ray into the living room of her home, a once avant-garde 1950s piece of architecture—redwood, copper, and glass—now aging inelegantly. Overlooking twin lakes and the narrows that connected them, the building cantilevered out from a bluff high above the water.

"I got a call from Stu Baker. He said you needed some historical background from an impartial observer of the Sherwood Forest community or commune. I'm not sure they ever settled on the name."

Alice pointed to a large painting in a plain mahogany frame. "That's one of Stu's early works. He had just started experimenting with oils and was developing his distinctive style." She moved closer to the seascape. "The lake and shore through the mist. Isn't it amazing, Sheriff, how Stu caught the magic of a steamy summer morning?"

She directed Ray toward one of two Eames chairs facing a wall of glass that overlooked the frozen landscape—snow-draped forests and dunes.

"We're investigating a suspected arson," said Ray. "There is the possibility that this incident may be connected to something that happened decades ago, in the '60s and '70s. At this point, we are searching for motives. Stu Baker told me you were doing some research at Sherwood Forest during that time."

"Yes, I was collecting data for my dissertation."

"What area?"

"Anthropology. I was on my way to becoming the next Margaret

Mead." She chuckled at her joke. "But instead of running off to an exotic locale, I came up to the area where my family has had a summer home for generations."

"What specifically were you studying?"

"The youth movement, the counterculture, the sexual revolution, the generation gap, civil rights, women's rights, the drug culture, et cetera—at least that's where I started. My dissertation chair, who I suspect thought I was a bit daffy, stressed limiting the parameters of my study. Sherwood Forest seemed like a good fit. I spent two years doing an ethnographic study of twenty members of the Sherwood Forest community."

"Stu Baker said your research produced several books."

"Yes, the books were an unexpected result of my work. *Psychology Today* did a profile on me. The article created a lot of interest in my research and a path to publication. With the help of some very skillful editors, my dissertation research was quickly expanded into my first book, *In the Hills and Valleys of the Young: Finding Alternative Pathways to the Future*. A dreadfully pompous title, isn't it? That said, it was a piece of successful pop-anthropology. Fortunately, it's almost impossible to find a copy today. That was one of the benefits of the pre-electronic age. We could still bury our mistakes. But I thought it was quite brilliant at the time, and it paid the bills for a year or two. With age, I came to realize how shallow it was."

"The people in your study, what was the selection criteria?" asked Ray.

"I was looking for individuals who had enough skills, energy, and adaptability to succeed at creating an alternative lifestyle. I was trying to avoid the stoners and hippie wannabes living off checks from dad and mom."

"What data were you collecting, exactly?"

"I had a long list of variables I was tracking. A lot of these communities were volatile and often disappeared quickly. I needed a place that was going to stay around for a few years. When I began my research, Sherwood had already been around for three or four years. It had a stable residential population and a quasi-democratic system of governance. Every community member had a vote. And everyone participated. There were regular community meetings to discuss important issues.

"While there was no formally elected leader, Rob Habbers was the de facto chief of the tribe. He was handsome, charismatic, and an enormously gifted leader. The Sherwood Forest commune only succeeded because he was able to keep people focused and working toward shared goals.

"But by the second year of my research, things started to change. Rob began to make most of the major decisions without consulting the other members. At first, no one seemed to mind too much because he appeared to be infallible. But then his leadership became more dictatorial, more manipulative. There were, by the way, many more women than men. It was something like a sixty-to-forty ratio. While Rob publicly showed great deference to his Maid Marian, he was taking pleasure with a number of the other women. While it all appeared consensual, I thought his behavior was becoming increasingly narcissistic and controlling.

"I could sense, and this was reflected in some of my opinion sampling, the community members were becoming distrustful of Rob and his leadership. He eventually picked up on this. But before things could blow apart, he pulled the community together to meet a common threat, the proverbial Sheriff of Nottingham."

"You are referring to my predecessor?"

"One and the same, horrible Orville Hentzler and his merry band of thugs. Interesting though, there was a kind of symbiosis between Rob and the sheriff. For Rob and his followers, Hentzler was the devil incarnate. Whatever grievances people had with Rob, those issues disappeared as soon as the sheriff and his men arrived for a narcotics search or some other form of harassment.

"And Hentzler got all kinds of good PR with his base by arriving at Sherwood occasionally and cracking a few heads. He was always looking for a reason to take one of the colony men to jail. Even if they were never charged, they all got the Orville Do, a completely shaved head. Hentzler said the haircuts were necessary to prevent an epidemic of head lice. Most of the locals I talked to back in the day believed that to be true. And they would usually tell me their sister or brother-in-law or some neighbor heard that from the sheriff, so it must be true."

"And then Habbers disappears, right?"

"Yes. Rob was a smart guy. He had a good thing going for several years, but he had to know it was coming to an end. This was the perfect time for Rob to 'Get out of Dodge.'"

"But he supposedly left an old friend of many years behind."

"Makes perfect sense to me, Sheriff. Sacrifice a few things and disappear into the night. There's nothing very original about that."

"You don't sound like you were a great fan of Rob Habbers."

"I think he had a special magic for awhile, then things went sour. He exploited and manipulated the members of the commune, especially women. He might have held the place together, but he extracted a heavy toll. I trust he quickly found a new place to use his charm and good looks to his advantage. People like that always land on their feet and create havoc at their next port of call."

"Stu Baker remembers there was a major confrontation with Sheriff Hentzler just before Rob disappeared."

"I heard that, too, from some of the most reliable people in my pool. Unfortunately, that happened when I was downstate."

"Was Marian Patozak included in your study?"

"No."

"Any special reason?"

"She was bright, most attractive, but I thought she was a bit mad. I could see why Rob might have wanted to get away from her."

"Stu Baker doesn't think anyone from the Sherwood Forest community is still in the area. Is that consistent with your knowledge?"

"Twenty years after my original study, I tried to find the original participants for a follow-up study. They had mostly disappeared from the area. I did find seventeen of the original twenty. Stu was the only one still living up here. The rest were residing downstate, in other parts of the country, or internationally. Most of the study's participants went on to lead productive lives, lives that usually were at variance with the norms of their parents' generation. A number of the women went on to grad school or professional school and entered male-dominated professions. Some of the men became stay-at-home fathers, at least for a while. The people who chose to live at Sherwood were outliers at that time. They continued as outliers, and in a very positive way. It's all in my book, *The Way They Were*. I wonder where they are now?" she said. "Maybe I should do one more book?"

"Do you have copies of your books that I could borrow? I would take care of them and return them in a few weeks."

"I don't, Sheriff. But if you're that interested, I'm sure they are available through interlibrary loan."

Alice stood at the window and watched Ray's car disappear down the drive. Then she walked to the bookcase in her study and pulled a copy of *In the Hills and Valleys of the Young* off the shelf. A photo fell out of the book. She stooped and picked it up, then collapsed into a chair.

"Oh, Marian," she said, looking at the faded color print. "You could have been my Maid Marian."

8

~

Sue Lawrence stood impatiently at the open door waiting for Ray to end a phone call. She feigned a cough to get his attention and then hovered as he wound down the conversation.

"What's going on?" asked Ray after he rang off.

"You won't believe this," said Sue. "Totally bizarre."

"I'm waiting."

"Two guys, duck hunters, downstaters."

"So."

"They're in the interview room. You've got to hear this for yourself."

"Sue, I am so far behind on my paperwork . . . I trust you completely to take these men's statement."

"Ray, you've got to hear this with your own ears."

Ray grumbled a bit, then climbed out of his chair and followed Sue to the interview room, grabbing a legal pad from the conference table along the way.

"Sheriff Elkins, this is Tony Didanado and Jared Dent. They live in Wyandotte and are up here to do some duck hunting."

After an exchange of handshakes, the foursome settled on opposite sides of the gray metal table. Ray looked at the pair who he guessed to be in their forties. They were dressed in camo jackets and pants, smelling of cigars and wood fires. Tony, the taller of the two, was balding. A dense stubble covered his face. Jared, also unshaven, had longish brown hair hanging in greasy clumps below a baseball cap. Ray then glanced at a damaged duck decoy on the table.

"Tell the sheriff exactly what you've just told me," Sue instructed.

The two men exchanged glances, and Ray felt a niggling impatience begin to grow.

"Go ahead," urged Jared.

"Okay, so we're up here for a little late-season duck hunting," Tony said. "This guy back home, one of our customers, tells us about this great place. He said there would be no one around. We'd have the whole bay to ourselves."

"Where exactly?" asked Ray.

"It's a little bay on the north end of the peninsula," Jared said, focusing on Sue, who had proven to be the more sympathetic ear. "I'm not sure of the name. The story we got is that the property belongs to some religious order. They have a seasonal retreat house. The rest of the year the place is empty. Besides, we weren't going to be on their property. We were going to be on the lake." Jared looked over at Ray, as if for approval.

Idiots, thought Ray. *Of course you had to drive across private land to get to the boat launch. It's posted no trespassing. Do you think I don't know that?*

"Okay," said Ray, "I know the place. Go ahead." He gave Sue a knowing look.

Jared talked about their multiple misadventures as they confronted high winds, big surf, and cold water.

"By late afternoon we were getting cold, and it's starting to blow. We huddled down below all that camouflage trying to stay out of the wind. But then suddenly there were a lot of ducks."

"About what time?" asked Ray.

Jared looked over at Tony. "Must been half five anyway."

"Yeah," Tony agreed. "We were getting ready to collect the decoys. But we ended up holding off."

"Then what happened," pressed Ray, trying not to show he was irritated.

"So, suddenly we had these little ducks, buffleheads maybe, several flights, coming in. They were flying just above the water. Hard to see, you know, they were blending with the water. So we both pop up blasting away. And then it goes quiet for a second or two as we're reloading, and then there's more firing, but it's not us. We're using pumps. This was coming from an automatic. Three or four short bursts. Bullets are hitting the water around the decoys. Then nothing 'cept for a laugh," said Tony.

"Oh, yeah," interjected Jared, "Tony says there was some weird laughter, like something out of a Stephen King film. I didn't hear nothing like that. My ears were still ringing from the twelve-gauges."

"So you think there was another shooter, a third shooter."

"Tony thinks so."

"Look at that decoy, Sheriff. That got hit by something. It wasn't birdshot," said Tony.

Ray picked up the decoy and rotated it carefully. The hard plastic outer layer of the decoy had a disk-shaped penetration on one side and a ragged, gaping tear on the other. He ran his finger over the torn plastic and peered into the foam interior.

"Anything else hit? Other decoys, your boat?"

"No," said Tony.

Ray looked at Jared. "Did you see bullets hitting the water like Tony did?"

"I was hunched down trying to reload with frozen fingers."

"Anything else?" asked Ray.

"Tony thinks he saw a muzzle flash," said Jared.

"Maybe the last burst. You know, like I was figuring out something wasn't right. I was starting to look around."

"And where was the flash?"

"I was at the stern and Jared was at the bow. It seemed to come from off to my right."

"The flash, close, far?"

"Hard to say," said Tony. "Snow was flying. It was getting dark and blowing. We were starting to bounce pretty good. The flash was high up, but I couldn't make out where. I don't know the terrain. There must be some high ground."

"So let me summarize here," said Ray. "Tony, you heard some automatic fire and saw a muzzle flash. Jared, you neither heard the automatic fire nor saw a muzzle flash. Is that correct?"

"Sheriff, Jared can't hear crap when he's not wearing his hearing aids."

"I think I might of," said Jared. "After you told me about it. I think I recall hearing it."

"And when did Tony tell you about the automatic fire?"

"At the bar last night," answered Jared.

"When you say automatic fire, Tony, are we talking fully automatic or rapid bursts from a semiautomatic weapon?"

"Full, or maybe semi, I think. But short bursts. They were simultaneous with and just after our shots."

"How many rounds?"

"Hard to say. It was over before I figured out what was happening."

Ray jotted some additional notes on the legal pad, then said, "It was bitterly cold yesterday, especially with that wind out of the north."

"You can say that again, Sheriff."

"Did you have anything to warm you up?"

"Thermos of coffee," said Jared.

"Hot coffee, yes," said Ray. "Especially if there was some brandy mixed in."

"Or some spiced whiskey," added Jared.

Ray saw Tony give Jared a look.

"But it was just coffee, Sheriff," said Jared.

"And this happened yesterday about what time?"

"Yeah, yesterday. It was maybe heading toward six."

"Why didn't you call 911?" asked Ray.

"Our phones, they were in the pickup."

"How about when you got to shore?"

"We were freezing by then. You know it took time to collect the decoys and drag the boat in to shore and get it on the trailer. Then we had to tie it down. We were both shivering so much our fingers almost didn't work. We climbed into the truck and just sat there till we started to get warmed up," explained Jared. "Then we went down the road to that bar, The Last Chance, and had a few beers and dinner."

Ray glanced over at Sue and made an almost imperceptible nod.

"By the time we talked things over and decided to report this, well, we weren't, you know. So we thought it best…"

"Where did you spend the night?"

"That motel near the bar," said Jared.

"So how was your luck?" asked Ray. "Did you get many ducks?"

"Conditions, they weren't so good."

"So you only bagged a few?"

"I thought I winged one," said Tony. "It was getting dark. The waves were really kicking up. As I said, we were cold."

"So you had two shotguns in the boat with you?"

"Yes, Remington pumps," answered Tony.

"Did you have any other firearms with you?"

"Tony always has his pistol," said Jared. "He feels naked without it. He was deployed too many times."

Ray looked at Tony. "Were you packing, Tony?"

"Yeah, I can show you the permit."

"Did you fire the pistol?"

"No sir, it was holstered under my jacket next to my body."

"Where is the weapon now?"

"It's locked in the truck."

"Do one or both of you have any friends or relatives up here?"

"No," answered Tony. "We've never been here before. Right, Jared?"

"I was in Traverse City once as a kid. Cherry Festival. Never been up here since."

"And the person who told you about this place? You said he was a customer."

"Yeah. Jay Wasniak. He sells used cars. He's one of our regulars."

"Everything is good between you and this Mr. Wasniak? He doesn't have any reason to be taking potshots at you?"

"Not a possibility."

"Yeah, we're good."

"Okay," said Ray. "I need to take care of some paperwork. Can I see your hunting licenses, please, and your drivers' licenses? We need to make copies for our report."

As Tony and Jared were digging through their wallets, Ray asked, "Did you buy your licenses online?"

"Is there any other way?" said Jared.

"Did you happen to download the Waterfowl Digest?"

"Of course. We got a copy in the truck somewhere. Why do you ask?"

"Two things. The season up here—we are in the middle zone—closed the day before yesterday. And even if the season had been open, the hunting hours ended at 5:12 p.m."

After a long silence Tony said, "Sorry, Sheriff, I guess I screwed up. But we didn't get any ducks. You can check our truck. So technically we didn't break no laws."

Jared looked over at his friend and rolled his eyes.

"I would like you to show us where you were hunting," Ray said.

"So what do you think?" said Sue as she slowly followed Jared's pickup truck through the blowing snow as he led them down the county road to the place where they had launched their boat.

"It's an interesting story," said Ray. "What we don't know is how much the cold and spiced whiskey influenced their perceptions. The decoy provides an element of plausibility." Ray paused for a moment. "The fact that they didn't make a 911 call is troubling. Have we had anyone harassing hunters in recent years?"

"Not during my time," Sue said as she slowly followed the pickup onto a two-track.

They stopped at a small turnaround just above the beach at the end of the trail. Jared and Tony led them down through the drifting snow to the water and showed them where they had set up in the shallows, with the boat parallel to the shore.

"And where do you think the other shooter was?" asked Sue.

"Tony thought it was over there," Jared said, pointing south.

"Yeah, that's where I think I saw the muzzle flash. I can see the terrain a bit more today. I think it was that high spot. I thought I was back in the effing Gulf. The whole thing freaked me."

Later, as Ray and Sue walked the high ground from where the alleged shots might have been fired, Sue said, "It's hard to tell where the shots might have come from." She swept her hand in front of her. "The storm was coming onshore about that time. The waves had been building. Before the storm, there was only a dusting of snow. Now there's more than two feet. If there's any brass here, it's covered. We're left with questions. Did this happen? If so, what possible motive might someone have had?" Sue looked at Ray. "What do you think?"

"I don't know. There are a number of holes in their narrative. That said, given the potential danger, we can't completely discount their story. Make a note of the GPS coordinates. Let's get someone out here with a metal detector to look for brass. Add it to the shift commander's to-do list. Also, let's do a memo about an unconfirmed incident. Ask people to keep their eyes and ears open and use all necessary caution."

They made their careful way back down to their vehicle.

"Apropos of nothing," Ray began.

"Go ahead."

"My grandfather was a duck hunter. I heard this story enough when I was a kid that I think it is mostly true."

Ray had once shown Sue the location of the family farm and what was left of the little village where he and his parents and grandfather had lived.

Sue nodded as she maneuvered the vehicle back onto the highway.

"He grew up during the Depression years. His mother had been widowed young, so one of his jobs was to bring home game for the dinner table, for his mother and his three younger siblings, starting when he was ten or so. Duck, rabbit, squirrel, raccoon, pheasant, and deer.

"There was a general store in the village then. The owner was partial to duck, pheasant, and grouse. Every time my grandfather brought him one, the man would give him two shotgun shells. Gramps said he learned to pull the trigger only when he had a sure shot. He joked how the game helped feed the family. I always helped him fill his bird feeders. He told me he was paying them back. He died when I was six or seven. I was devastated."

Ray could still conjure up the ghost of that feeling, like a hole blown through the center of his body. He considered it for a long time and then said, "I'm thinking about how the world has changed. Starting when Gramps was little more than a boy, he would wander out with a single-shot Stevens twelve-gauge and, according to legend, rarely come home empty-handed." Ray went silent, thinking about Tony and Jared and all their expensive equipment and how it hadn't helped them get even one duck.

9

~

C huck Peterson opened his eyes in the darkness. The only sounds were the breathing of his companions: his wife somewhere on the other side of the big bed, and their too-large golden, between them or perhaps sleeping between the headboard and their pillows.

He looked at his watch, 4:46. He closed his eyes again and worked on his breathing—slow inhalations, slower exhalations, counting, one, two, three, four, five, six, seven, eight. He had a momentary feeling of sliding away, catching a dream. Then he was awake again. Thor, the golden, was pushing his nose against Chuck's face. He lifted the covers so the dog could slide in next to him. A couple of wet kisses and another herding push indicated that wasn't what the dog wanted.

"What is it?" he whispered. "Coyotes, the bobcat, the skunk?" Thor nudged him again, this time with more urgency.

Chuck pulled himself into a sitting position on the side of the bed, his feet touching the cold hardwood. Thor pushed past him and dropped to the floor.

After donning multiple layers of fleece and down, Chuck found the dog waiting for him at the back door. He clipped a leash to Thor's collar, then pulled on boots, a furry hat, and thick mittens. "Stay close, buddy. Don't want the coyotes turning you into a warm breakfast."

Thor led the way, tugging on his leash. The raw wind off Lake Michigan cut into Chuck's face, a chill surged through his body. Suddenly, he was very awake and alert to his surroundings. They trudged through the layer of new snow as they moved down the long drive, their path lit by the spotlights over the garage door reflecting off the undulating terrain. At the end of the drive, Thor paused and marked the pole of the mailbox. Then he pulled hard at the leash, away from the house toward the unplowed road.

"That's enough. Let's go back," Chuck yelled.

Thor lunged forward, jerking free. Then he started bounding ahead in the heavy snow. Chuck's commands to "stop" and "come" went unheeded as Thor disappeared into the swirling storm.

Chuck pulled off a mitten and fumbled for the flashlight in his pocket. By the time he brought the beam of light onto Thor's track, the dog had vanished into the storm. He followed Thor's path, his progress slowed by the deep drifts. He could hear Thor's baying, now becoming more distant.

Chuck trudged along the west side of the road, orienting himself as he passed the mailboxes. Most of the homes were seasonal, their drives covered over.

Thor's barking became muted, then almost disappeared. Chuck considered returning home, getting his truck, and then continuing the search, but he soldiered on. He was startled when the dog came charging toward him, barking. Chuck grabbed at the leash. The dog kept his distance, moving away, leading Chuck on with urgent howling, and then moving forward again, waiting until his master began to close the gap, then dashing off. Finally, he disappeared.

Chuck found Thor in a ditch at the side of the road, standing near the prone form of his friend, Germaine, a Bouvier des Flandres. Chuck slid down the bank to inspect the other dog. As he drew close, Germaine moved a bit, revealing the form of the small child she had been protecting with her body. It took Chuck a few seconds to comprehend the scene, then he moved quickly, lifting the toddler from the ground, opening his jacket and getting her next to his body, scampering back to the road, and retracing his steps.

Thor led the way, barking. Germaine stayed at Chuck's side, nudging him occasionally. The dogs rushed past him into the house.

"Sharon!" he yelled as soon as he was over the threshold. She appeared almost at once, her eyes wide and frightened. Once he had passed the softly whimpering child into her arms, he was keying 911.

"Where's Becca?" Sharon asked.

10

Ray trudged through the deep snow from his front door to the waiting vehicle. Simone was circling him, jumping from place to place. He stopped and reached out to her. She leaped into his arms before he pulled the truck door open.

"Sorry you had to be on duty all night," he said, looking over at Sue.

"I was available. I have a perverse sense of pride in being the last person standing during flu season." She gestured with her head toward the cup holder. "That coffee is for you."

Sue had called Ray just after five a.m. after a 911 call came in reporting that a small child, a two-year-old girl, had been discovered outside and unattended by a neighbor. Her dog was protecting her. The last thing Sue had told Ray on the phone was that the EMTs had been dispatched and were currently on the scene.

"Update?" Ray requested.

"I just checked with dispatch," Sue said. "The child is awake and responsive. She's being transported to the medical center."

"Parents, guardian . . . ?"

"Based on dispatch's conversation with the caller, the man who found the child, the toddler lives with her mother, who has a beach house on Fox Cove. I ran the name. Becca Sterling, age forty-two. The Fox Cove location appears to be her permanent address." She glanced over at Ray.

"Fox Cove," repeated Ray. "Secondary road, gravel. Probably hasn't been plowed yet. I take it no one has checked on Ms. Sterling yet?"

"No. No one was available."

"Busy shift?"

"It was quiet till around two. Then things started going downhill. Several accidents in sector three, sector one was tied up with a medical emergency."

They fell into silence. Ray sipped the coffee and peered out the windshield. The snow swirled in the headlights. Sue occasionally slowed to a crawl as the visibility deteriorated to near whiteout conditions.

Ray was thinking about the little girl, still a toddler. An image of Ashleigh, his daughter, the child he had never gotten to know, flashed across his consciousness. All he had were bits and pieces of Ashleigh's life—a few photos, memories of the things that were said at her memorial service. He thought back on his brief summer romance with her mother, the woman with the golden hair and the loving smile. It was all so complicated and beyond his comprehension. There were other memories, too, grisly images burned into his psyche. He closed his eyes for a few moments and pushed them back down into his subconscious.

He glanced over at Sue. Their lives had become so intertwined over the years that they were beginning to respond to one another like a long-term couple.

"What's happening with Hanna?" Sue asked. "When is she back?"

"Supposedly this evening. But who knows with this weather? She might end up stranded in Minneapolis or Detroit."

"Is she going to take the fellowship?"

Ray was silent for a long moment. Finally, he admitted, "I don't know."

Sue glanced over at him in the dimly lit interior of the vehicle. "Well, you must have some sense. You've been talking and messaging since she's been gone."

"Not so much," admitted Ray. "This is an important career decision. I don't want to muddy the water. She needs to be free to plot her future."

"Sometimes I don't understand you, Elkins. You're not muddying the water. Couples talk about these things."

Ray didn't respond. He could feel Sue waiting awhile. Then she sighed almost inaudibly and turned off the highway onto Fox Cove Road. She followed a deep set of ruts down the road until they turned into a steep drive. "According to the GPS, we continue south for a bit. We're looking for 2077."

She switched on a spotlight and started checking the address on mailboxes, finally coming to a stop, backing a few yards, then turning and stopping just beyond the road at the base of the drive. Snow swirled in the headlights. The drive disappeared at the top of a steep slope.

"No ruts in the drive, no visible footsteps in the new snow." Sue stopped at the top of the drive near the garage and ran a spotlight over the single story building. A door faced the drive. Piles of snow bordered the drive and the walkway to the house.

"Let's get this done," said Ray. He slid the sleepy dog onto the seat as he climbed out of the vehicle. They slowly approached the house, scanning the scene carefully. Stepping onto a porch nearest the drive, Sue tried the door with a gloved hand.

She turned back toward Ray. "Locked."

They started to circle the building, Ray following in Sue's tracks. On the lakeside of the structure, they found a sliding door ajar. Sue thrust her flashlight into the void and slowly moved its beam across the interior, pausing at one point or another, then she stopped. She sidestepped in the snow to give Ray a better view of the interior of the house. He could see two legs and an arm in the circle of light. Sue handed Ray the flashlight and her mittens and pulled on rubber gloves. Pushing the door wider, she left her boots standing in the snow, pulling plastic booties over her socks before she crossed the threshold.

Ray watched her kneel and check the body. Then she emerged from the dark building.

"She's dead, isn't she," said Ray.

"Yes," Sue answered, blowing out a hard breath. "Body is cold. No obvious wounds or injuries. We need to get Dr. Dyskin out here," she said.

Sue stood near the open rear hatch of her truck, suiting up in Tyvek coveralls.

"Dispatch has sent a deputy to pick up Dyskin," said Ray. "Probably thirty minutes or so."

"Good, that will give me time to shoot the scene and have a look around. After Dyskin makes his call, we'll see if there is anything more that needs to be done."

Ray nodded. "Okay, I'm going to wander up the road and see if I can talk to the man who called this in. Dispatch identified the man as Chuck Peterson. Know the name?"

"Not on my radar. What are you going to say?"

Ray was slow to answer. He hated to do death notifications. He usually did his best to pass that duty off to Sue or some other officer.

"I'll play it by ear. Don't know how close they might have been. They were at least neighbors. I guess I can say that Ms. Sterling is deceased, and we're waiting for the medical examiner. Then I'll see what he can tell me."

"Perfect," said Sue.

"Call me if you need anything," said Ray. Then he started down the steep drive in the dull gray light of the snowy morning.

11

~~

Ray reached the foot of the drive and stood, waiting for an approaching vehicle to pass. The truck, with a snowplow attached to the front, slowed and then stopped. The jarring dissonance of the big Dodge diesel diminished slightly as the engine fell to an idle. The driver's-side door opened and the diminutive figure of Ronnie Poole dropped to the ground and approached Ray.

"What's going on, Sheriff?" Poole asked.

"We had an incident we're looking into. Do you plow this drive?"

"Yeah," Poole answered, pulling a cigarette from his jacket. "I wouldn't be here otherwise," he said, lighting the cigarette.

"You know the woman who lives here?"

"Yeah, a bit. I've been doing this drive for a couple of years. I plow the drive and do some hand shoveling around the house. Throw some salt around if it's slippery. No man there, just a woman and a little girl. Most mornings the place is still dark when I come through."

"When were you last here?" asked Ray.

"Yesterday morning. I was moving an accumulation from the last few days." Ronnie took a long pull on his cigarette, then exhaled slowly. "Thought I could sleep in this morning. Weatherman didn't see this coming. You go to bed with moonlight and a cloudless sky and wake to six or eight inches of new snow. You know what I'm saying."

"So the woman who owns this house, Becca Sterling, how often would you say you see her or talk to her?"

Ronnie flicked the cigarette away. "It's not like the old days, Sheriff. The wife, she emails statements once a month. She sends reminders if they don't pay. I don't have to knock on doors anymore and hand out bills. These days, I don't know my customers. I probably wouldn't recognize them if I was sitting next to them at the Last Chance or Art's. All this internet stuff, it kinda makes us working stiffs totally invisible, you know."

"Would you recognize Ms. Sterling?"

"Yeah. Hard to forget a woman like that. She's a looker. I talked to her for a bit in the fall, early November, when I was here putting in those fiberglass driveway markers, you know. She's got a lot of extra paving. There's a guesthouse and a little studio. I wasn't sure if she wanted it all plowed, so I knocked on the door and asked her. We had a walk around and got that sorted. She also wanted me to do the walks close to the house and take care of the porches and decks this year, too. I don't like to do that, Sheriff. I don't like to get out of the truck. It slows me way down. But I do it for the old folks, especially the women living alone. I told her it would be extra, but she didn't seem to mind." Ronnie paused. "What's going on, Sheriff?"

"I can't say anything yet," Ray responded.

"How about that little girl?" asked Ronnie.

"She's all right."

"Sheriff, you want me to plow or no?"

"Hold off for today, Ronnie."

Ray stood and watched the taillights of Ronnie Poole's truck disappear down the road. Then he continued his trek toward the home of Chuck Peterson. He was greeted by a cacophony of barking as he approached the house. The side door nearest the drive swung open, and two dogs bounded into the snow. A seventy-something man followed them out.

"Chuck Peterson?" Ray called out.

"Yes, that's me."

As Ray reached for his identification, the man said, "Don't bother, Sheriff. I've seen you on TV enough to know who you are. Come on in. You guys, too."

Ray followed the man in, the two dogs brushing past him.

"What's happening with Becca? The news can't be good. She would never let anything like this happen to that little girl."

Before Ray could answer, Mr. Peterson started a rambling monologue.

"I should've checked on Becca right away. I knew that, but my first instinct was to get Ava someplace safe. It took a while for the ambulance guys to get here and check her over. My wife had already wrapped her in some warm blankets and all. Ava was awake and asking for her mom. Sharon had given her some warm milk and graham crackers. She was starting to settle down when the EMTs got here. Sharon went to the hospital with them."

Ray waited before responding until he was sure the older man was through. Finally, he said, "You might want to sit down." After Peterson had settled into a chair at the kitchen table, Ray said. "We found a woman. She is deceased. Perhaps you would help with the identification?"

"I just knew it. Becca should never have been living alone, especially after Ava was born. She has a medical condition, epilepsy. We worried about this, Sharon and I, other members of the family, too. But we never made any progress with Becca. She was smart, independent, and strong-willed. We wanted her to put in some cameras so we could check on her. I mean, I understand why she wouldn't want that, you know. But still."

"Did she have seizures often?"

"No, not for years as far as I know. She had it under control. But I witnessed one years ago. It's not something I'll ever forget. Very scary."

"You said family? Were you related to the deceased?"

"Yes. My wife, she's Becca aunt. We retired up here about ten years ago. Becca arrived about three years ago. Before that, she just summered here at the family cottage. Eventually, Becca inherited the place."

"So she lived there alone with this one child, right?"

"Yes, that is correct. Ava was a midlife surprise." Peterson paused for a bit. "That's not right. It was a surprise to us. I think Becca wanted this child. Ava was probably planned for. Not in the traditional way. Becca always did things differently. As soon as she finished college in Ann Arbor, she headed for New York. And we didn't see her in the summer when she was in her twenties and most of her thirties. For Becca, it was the Hamptons, Fire Island, and Cape May. Places that I've read about but never seen. Becca had a meteoric career as a fashion designer, very successful. And right from the beginning, she moved with a very fast crowd, you know what I mean. She made lots of money, then started her own company. She sold out when she was at the top. We were startled when she suddenly appeared and told us she was moving here. It seemed totally off script.

"And now what? Poor Ava. We're like grandparents to her. We've been part of her life from her birth. When Becca sold her business, she agreed to work with the new owners on a consulting basis for two years. She needed to fly to New York every few weeks. We've taken care of Ava for long periods of time when her mother was traveling. Becca gave us power of attorney and guardianship in case there was a medical emergency while she was away."

He looked at Ray, grief in his eyes and in the downturn of his mouth. "I'm seventy-three years old, Sheriff. I just worry that we might not be around long enough to rear this child." The dogs moved close to Peterson, nudging against him. "And how do I tell my wife? I said I'd come to the hospital as soon as I got things settled here."

"We can help you with that," said Ray.

12

"Anything out of the ordinary?" asked Ray, encountering Dr. Dyskin as he descended the drive to the waiting patrol car. He was wrapped in a down coat that hung to his knees, his feet were in unlaced Bean duck shoes, and a red and black checkered wool bomber hat covered his head.

"Elkins, I always admire the way you begin with pleasantries before moving on to the business at hand. There is seldom a 'Good morning, what a lovely gray winter's day.' You're always on task, aren't you?"

Ray held Dyskin's hand briefly, amused by the always laconic and abrupt medical examiner's lesson on social skills.

"Dr. Dyskin," Ray began again, "lovely of you to stop by on this glorious winter's morning. I was wondering if you had any observations on the deceased that you might be willing to share?"

"I thought you'd never ask," said Dyskin. "The woman was wearing a med alert bracelet, epilepsy. That's not the kind of bangle her type would probably wear if it weren't important. Obviously, I know nothing about the victim's medical history, the severity of her condition, or her treatment program. I suspect we will be able to find that. I did note some injuries that may have been caused by a convulsive seizure."

"So she died of natural causes?"

"I didn't say that, Elkins. That's background information. Remember the position of the body?"

"I just saw the body from outside the door," explained Ray. "In point of fact, all I saw were the bottoms of her slippers."

"Yes, you don't like to get close to bodies, do you, Elkins? What are you going to do if Sue ever falls in love and moves away? Pretty woman, Sue. You always have to be thinking about the future before it smacks you in the face."

"You were telling me about the deceased."

"Oh, yes." Dyskin said. "The injury leading to her death was probably caused by her head striking the stone hearth. But there are other interesting findings. There is a contusion on her right cheek and what appears to be a defensive bruise to her right forearm. These are very subtle injuries. I'm not sure what to make of them. Are these injuries the result of thrashing around during a seizure? Could they have been inflicted in some other way? Was an argument or confrontation going on before she fell or was pushed? Go and have a good look around. Initially, you should treat this as a suspicious death and order a forensic autopsy."

Ray stood by as Dyskin deposited his gear in the back of the patrol car. "By the way," said Dyskin, "my wife likes this arrangement, getting chauffeured. She doesn't trust my driving on snowy roads. She doesn't trust me driving at night, either."

As Ray was donning some Tyvek coveralls, two men carrying a stretcher with a body bag on it passed him on their way to the idling ambulance.

"Morning," he said.

"Morning, Sheriff," responded the lead man, his tone quiet and somber. The man at the rear made eye contact briefly and silently marched forward.

Ray stepped into Becca Sterling's house, where Sue had turned on all the overhead lights. He stood a moment taking in the interior before joining Sue in the kitchen.

"You talked to Dyskin?" asked Sue.

"Briefly," he answered. "Walk me through the examination of the body."

"There were a few items that we couldn't easily explain," Sue said. "Nothing as conclusive as a bloody hammer. We might be chasing clouds, or we might have a murder on our hands."

Sue held out her iPad to Ray. "You can see the position of the body." Using the photos, Sue covered in great detail the same ground Dyskin had related to Ray.

"Did he give you a time of death?"

"Yes, in his usual equivocal way. He said sometime between 11:00 and 3:00. He offered a whole list of possible variables that might have influenced the rate of cooling, like the partially open door."

"So where are we?"

"Before Dyskin arrived I photographed and videoed the body and surrounding areas and made a detailed diagram."

Sue carefully gazed at her surroundings. "I need to slow down and start carefully rethinking things. Dyskin found the medical ID bracelet on his first pass over the body. He started to run with the idea that Becca Sterling died from injuries sustained during a violent seizure. He pointed out the overturned chair, the broken wine glass, and the rumpled throw rugs. And I was running with this. The evidence seemed to support the idea of a seizure. Then Dyskin began to dance around his initial theory.

"As he started his second pass over the body, he talked about how easy it is to jump to the wrong conclusion. Then he noted some other injuries and offered an alternative scenario. In the end, he said, 'I don't think this woman had a seizure. Let a forensic pathologist make the call. We will treat this as a possible homicide until it is proven otherwise.'"

"So tell me about the victim," asked Ray.

"Forty something, attractive, even in death." She peered at Ray noting his melancholy. "What are you thinking?"

"If it's murder, a life has been interrupted, a child has lost her mother."

"We'll get justice for her," offered Sue.

Ray nodded. *But we don't fix anything,* he thought.

Looking over at Sue, he asked. "Do you need some sleep? We could seal off the place and come back after you have some rest."

"Are the search warrants in place?" she asked.

"Yes," he answered. "I sat in your truck and keyed in requests after talking with Dyskin. We should be good."

"Okay, let's keep going, a least for a while. I want to go through the main items on my checklist. Did you notice the Cheerios? Over there."

Ray moved around the table in the large kitchen. He could see an open cereal box on the floor. There was also an open plastic milk container, on its side, mostly empty. He moved closer, then gave Sue a questioning look.

"At some point the little girl got out of bed. Was she awakened by the disturbance? Was she hungry? Was she looking for her mother? My mom used to keep Cheerios in a bottom cupboard so we could get our breakfast if we awakened at some ungodly hour. I'm wondering if that's what happened here. The toddler got some milk, too. Notice there isn't any cereal on the floor. The dog probably helped her clean up and took care of the spilled milk, too." Sue paused for a moment. "I've plotted the little girl's possible trail from her room to the Cheerios." Sue traced the route with her index finger. "She wouldn't have encountered her mother. I think she found her mother after the Cheerios, and she heads off to get help."

"Would a toddler know to do that?" asked Ray. "And where was the dog if there was some intruder here, someone possibly harming its mistress?"

"Probably closed off in the bedroom with the sleeping child."

"Electronic devices?"

"A phone, a tablet, and a laptop. They are bagged. I'll check them for prints back at the office."

"Sue, you look beat. Maybe we should go to lunch. Brett's sitting in his car at the foot of the drive. Your scene is protected."

Sue inhaled deeply. "That would be good. After some hot food and coffee, I can probably finish up here. Art's, The Friendly, or The Last Chance?"

"Your call. I'll buy."

"Was all this snow in the forecast?" asked Sue as she started to work through the warren of secondary roads back to the highway.

"Lake effect," Ray responded, not looking up from his phone.

"Damn."

"What's the problem?"

"Whiteout conditions, and now a slowpoke creeping along."

"Maybe they'll turn right at the intersection," offered Ray, looking up briefly.

A few moments later, Sue responded, "No such luck. And no brake lights on the truck or the trailer."

Ray's head came up. "Look at the plate on that trailer. It's got to be thirty years old. And those snowmobiles, ancient."

"Lunch or a traffic stop?" she asked, looking over at Ray. "Okay," she said, switching on the light bar.

"He's speeding up," she said, turning on the siren.

"It would have been an interesting chase," said Ray as the truck slowed and moved to the side of the road. "Those sleds aren't even tied down."

Sue pulled on her hat and mittens, then pushed her door open as Ray climbed out of the other side. The truck suddenly pulled forward, then reversed back toward them.

As Ray dove into the ditch at the side of the road, he could hear the grinding sound of steel on steel and the explosion of glass and plastic. Facedown in the snow, he felt the thud of a heavy object landing near him. He lifted his head and watched as the truck quickly disappeared into the swirling snow. Then he looked around. The mangled remains of a snowmobile were mired in mud just below him in the ditch.

"Sue!" he shouted as he scrambled up the steep embankment and back onto the road. She called out his name, and he followed the sound of her voice, reaching out to her, and pulling her from the gully on the other side of the road.

"Are you okay?"

"I'm soaked. There's water down there." She stood for a little while, taking inventory. "Yes, I'm okay. Just wet. You?"

"I think so."

She looked past him, her mouth hanging open. Ray turned and took in the carnage. The front of her vehicle was crushed. A snowmobile, skis toward the sky, was lodged in the shattered remains of the windshield. The surface of the snow-covered road was littered with debris: metal, glass, plastic, and wood, and the mangled remains of the trailer slumped at the side of the road.

Sue looked at the wreckage. "My truck." A few seconds later she shouted, "Simone!" as she sprinted toward the crushed vehicle.

13

～～

Sharon Peterson wiped her eyes with a tissue and gazed at the floor. Her husband was at her side on the couch. The door to the small visitor's lounge was slightly ajar. Hospital sounds—voices, phones, beepers—seeped into the room. Ray had pulled a chair close to the Petersons. Most of his words were delivered to Sharon, with an occasional glance at Chuck. He delivered the tragic news in a carefully modulated tone, thinking through each sentence before speaking.

"I knew something dreadful had happened. It was hope against hope things would be okay. Becca would never have allowed Ava to be put in danger."

Peterson reached for a tissue box. After wiping away the tears, she continued. "Becca was always a very special child, gifted and loving. She lost her mother, Monique, my sister, just as she was entering her teen years. It was a difficult time for her. I filled that role as best I could, at least during the summers."

"How about her father?" asked Ray.

"Harvey, I guess he was an okay kind of man. Sadly, he had no idea how to care for a daughter. He was clueless, just clueless, to the emotional side of an emerging young woman. He was cold and insular. He and Monique might have had a marriage, but there wasn't much love or friendship. She never complained, but I could read between the lines."

"Harvey Sterling is deceased also?"

"Yes, years ago. Heart trouble. He was a smoker."

"You were telling me about your relationship with Becca."

"Yes. By the time Monique died, Chuck and I had built our cottage here. Monique and Harvey had taken over the family cottage years before. And Monique and Becca would summer here. Monique had a studio where she did her art. Harvey would sometimes drive up on weekends. During August he'd stay for a week or two. Chuck and I did the same thing. Our kids were near in age to Becca. The five of them were a pack. They spent most of their time outside. By the end of the summer, they were as brown as acorns.

"So after Monique's passing, Becca spent the summers with us at the cottage until she went to college.

"Becca and I had lots of good times together during those years. After she started college, we didn't see much of her. Occasionally she'd show up for a week or two during the summer."

"She'd stay at her cottage," said Chuck. "Becca and her bizarre assortment of friends. Artsy types like her, a rainbow collection of kids, if you know what I mean."

"Now Chuck, they were pleasant and cordial. Not once was there ever a problem."

"True," he said, "but this isn't Ann Arbor. Some of our neighbors got rather upset. All kinds of rumors floating around the neighborhood: sex, drugs, rock and roll."

"That was more about the fantasies of a few members of the summer colony than anything Becca and her friends were doing. I mean, her cottage is pretty isolated. And I've never known her to be indiscreet," said Sharon, glaring at her husband.

"And then Becca disappeared from our lives," she continued. "She graduated and headed to New York. I tried to stay in touch, but she usually wouldn't respond to my cards or phone calls or emails. We spent a few days together when her father died. I'd read about her in fashion magazines and would occasionally see her name in the *Times*. And then she went international, mostly living in Paris, with a year or two in Italy. We were seldom in touch during those years. And then, to my surprise, a few years ago everything changed."

"How so?" asked Ray.

"She called one day out of the blue to tell me that she had moved back to the states and was living in New York City. By that time we'd moved north."

"And then out of nowhere one fall day, there's a construction crew at her cottage," said Chuck, cutting his wife off. "They were tearing out most of the interior walls, just saving the basic exterior design."

"Becca had finally called me to say she was having the cottage rebuilt."

"Sheriff, there was nothing wrong with the place," Chuck protested.

"Chuck, it was her house and her money. That's the way people do things now," said Sharon, turning her attention to Ray. "And after the renovation, Becca was in residence for much of July and August for several summers. She was always here with a cadre of beautiful people, New York types. Some stayed the season, and others rotated in and out. One, Jade, was just extraordinary. She's a model. I knew after we were introduced, I'd seen her in the magazines. Jade was striking, African black, with a lilting Oxbridge accent, and an operatic laugh. She and Becca were inseparable. I thought they were a couple. Everywhere they went, they turned heads, and not just because they were two extraordinarily beautiful women. Two women holding hands still catches people's attention up here, if you know what I mean.

"By the end of summer, Becca and her friends would disappear. She would be out of our lives for the rest of the winter. And then one day in late August a few years ago, Becca pops in and tells me she's going to be our neighbor on a permanent basis. She had sold her business, her New York condo, and was moving to her cottage.

"At the time Chuck said she was looking a bit heavy. I dismissed it."

"I was right," he interjected.

"You were," Sharon agreed. Looking over at Ray she said, "Within a month, she wasn't hiding her condition. That was three summers ago. She didn't have much company that year. We started to get close again, like when she was a teen. As her pregnancy progressed, I filled the role of the future grandmother. Not that I'm new to the role—our kids are married and have children.

"Along the way, Chuck wondered about the father and what the child would look like. I guess I speculated on the same, but I kept my thoughts to myself."

"So you have no idea as to the father?"

"No, not at all."

"Did you ever ask her?"

"Indirectly. It was clear that Becca wasn't about to tell me anything about it. When I first noticed that she was pregnant, I wondered if that was wise. You know, she had this problem with her health, epilepsy. But I held it in. Becca was very determined. I was certain that she would have sought out the best medical advice before she decided to go through with the pregnancy. I don't know. Perhaps I should have been more outspoken. Or maybe we should have insisted that she wear one of those alert devices. If she could have signaled us, we would have been there in minutes."

"Had Ms. Sterling had any seizures lately?" asked Ray, wondering if her response would be the same as her husband's.

"No. There was just a horrific one when she was a teen. We almost lost her. Chuck and I, we've never recovered from that. Her epilepsy has been under control for years. But with childbirth and all, you just don't know."

Ray let her comment hang, then said, "At this point, we are treating it as an unexplained death. The medical examiner has requested a forensic autopsy."

"I don't understand," Peterson said.

"The medical examiner is not sure that her existing medical problem caused Ms. Sterling's death," Ray said carefully. "He wants to be very thorough and make sure he reaches the correct conclusion."

"So what are you saying?"

"At this time he doesn't know the exact cause of Ms. Sterling's death. Based on the findings of the autopsy, the medical examiner will advise us on whether or not to close our investigation."

"Do you think Ava…I don't know how to phrase the question. Did she find her mother's body?"

"I'm not sure. My deputy thinks that the child might have moved from her bedroom to the kitchen without seeing her mother. The sliding door was probably ajar."

"Ava, she's been a great escape artist in recent months. That door is usually blocked off."

"You've been talking to Ava?"

"Yes, when we were in the ambulance and here at the hospital."

"Has she said anything about her mother?"

"Just, 'Where's mom?' That's one of her sentences. She also asked for her dog."

"Did she seem anxious?"

"She knows something isn't right, but that might just be all the strange people scurrying about. She's a very smart little girl. That said, her language is quite limited."

A tall, thin man in plum-colored scrubs pushed the door open. "Excuse me. There's a little girl who's most insistent on seeing her nana."

14

Ray had covered much of the whiteboard in his office when Sue entered with a carafe of coffee in her right hand, her left arm secured in a sling. She set the coffee on the conference table. By the time they'd left the scene of the crash the afternoon before, she had been wincing in pain every time she flexed her wrist.

"You didn't have to come in today," said Ray.

"It's just a sprain."

"Did you sleep?"

"Off and on. I'm sore all over, but especially the wrist. They offered me something stronger at the ER, but I just maxed on Tylenol."

"Simone?"

After climbing out of the ditch, Sue had raced across the road toward their wrecked vehicle, Ray on her heels. Then, a flash of tan, and Simone came scrambling out of the wreckage, barking, and jumped into Sue's arms. She must have been sleeping in the back seat during the crash, out of harm's way. She was shaking and whimpering as Sue and Ray took turns holding her until backup arrived.

"She woke me a couple of times during the night," Sue said. "More dreams than usual with lots of little barks and yelps. She must be sore, too. She needed to be close, kept snuggling in next to me, taking up most of my side of the bed. I dropped her off at doggie daycare just now. Thought she needed some time away from police work." Sue paused for a moment. "Come to think of it, we all could. Having snowmobiles tossed in my direction was never part of the job description. Any word on the—"

"Of sorts. We had a report of a break-in at the maintenance

building of the long-abandoned ski resort. A local farmer uses it for equipment storage. Brett checked it out late yesterday. An old pickup and a trailer with snowmobiles went missing. Sound familiar? The man, Howard Rankin, told Brett the sleds had been sitting there on the trailer since the resort went bankrupt, what, close to twenty years ago. The truck, a 1995 Dodge, was Rankin's. He said he just used the vehicle around the farm and hadn't bothered to plate it for years.

"So, stolen truck, trailer, sleds," Ray continued. "Given that we have done so many of these, we can fill in the rest—expired plates, suspended license, driving under the influence of drugs and alcohol, fleeing and eluding, failure to stop at the scene of an accident, and then there will be the outstanding warrants. Did I miss anything?"

"Yes, how about assault with intent to do great bodily harm?" Sue hissed. "Better yet, attempted murder. And then there's got to be a cruelty to animals statute we could nail the SOB with. Ray, we go out every day knowing the possible dangers. But this is off the wall. What do we tell the troops now? We are investigating an unexplained death. Unrelated, be on the lookout for someone with an automatic rifle and use extra caution. And by the way, there's a kamikaze driver at the wheel of a stolen Dodge pickup."

Ray looked across at her. In a long, restless night, the image of the trailer backing in his direction had flashed across his mind more than once.

"Ray, it could have ended there for all three of us. That was done with intent. Someone was trying to take us out."

"I know."

Finally, her tone softening, Sue asked, "You want some coffee?"

"Sure," he answered. "Do you need some time off?"

"No, not now. Brett didn't happen to find the truck or the driver?" Sue asked.

"No such luck."

"So where are we on the Sterling case?" Sue asked, looking at the whiteboard covered with print.

"I did the death notification and learned a bit about Becca

Sterling. And I met Ava briefly. She's a beautiful child." Ray thought about the few moments he held the little girl. He fell silent.

"It was that hard?"

"Yes. Impossible to keep your professional distance when you know there's no way you can fix the hole in this little girl's life."

"But you obviously have a plan," said Sue, peering at the whiteboard.

"Just standard procedure. We'll start by canvassing the neighborhood. Chuck Peterson gave me the names of the full-time residents. The first, Frances Adams, has a cottage near Becca Sterling's. According to Mr. Peterson, Adams is in her early 90s. Then there's a Dr. Shepard. He lives in town. Most of the summer, he stays out here and commutes to his office. In the winter he spends Tuesday evenings and Wednesdays at his cottage. Chuck says Shepard calls it his midweek escape. Since the Sterling incident happened on a Tuesday evening/Wednesday morning, Shepard might have been at his cottage.

"I've also made a list of other people who might have been in the area and had some contact with Becca Sterling. I've already talked with Ronnie Poole, who plows her drive. We need to talk to the following people." Ray pointed to the whiteboard, where he had written:

FedEx
UPS
USPS
Trash and Recycling

"Get the drivers' names and find out if any of them remember seeing anything. Let's put some people on overtime to help you with the legwork. Also, once you get the names, do a background check on the group."

"Anything else?"

"Sharon Peterson. I've keyed my notes on our conversation at the hospital."

"I've read them," said Sue.

"We need to have an in-depth conversation with Sharon, and we should probably try to talk to Chuck, also. I think it would be useful if we could find a way to do these separately."

"Yes," agreed Sue. "That's probably high priority since it appears that Becca Sterling was in daily contact with the Petersons." She approached the whiteboard and, picking up a marker and removing the cap, started a second list:

Phone
Computer
Tablet
Social Media

"I will double check the search warrants to make sure we're totally kosher. I'd like to get user data from her cell provider to see if there's a disparity between what exists on the phone and what might have been deleted."

"Can I interrupt you two?" Brett Carty said from the doorway.

"Sure, what's going on, Brett?" said Ray.

"We just had a call that an armed man is occupying what should be an empty summer cottage on Round Lake. That's within a few miles of where I checked on those stolen snowmobiles yesterday. The caller's name is Ron Klope. He went to check on a cottage a few doors down from his home. The place belongs to an elderly outstate couple and hasn't been occupied in recent years. Klope stopped at the house and talked to the occupant. The guy claimed that he was a relative of the owners. Klope said the man was belligerent, appeared to be intoxicated, and had a pistol tucked in his belt. There's an older black Dodge pickup parked next to the cottage. I've dispatched the cars from sectors one and two, and as soon as I pick up a search warrant, I'm on my way to join them."

"I want a piece of this," said Sue.

"With your arm in a sling?" noted Ray.

"You get to drive," she shot back.

The four police vehicles rolled into position, the first blocking the truck in place, the next two parking at oblique angles, the last closing off the small private road from the highway. Smoke rose from a masonry chimney at the back of the house.

As one officer, Jake Jacobson, moved to the rear of the house, Brett Carty and Rory Tate climbed onto the porch and went to the right side of the front door. Ray and Sue moved to the left side.

Brett knocked on the door. "Police! Open up." A long silence followed. He knocked again, striking the door forcefully.

The door flew open, and a hulking shape exploded through the portal, grabbed Rory by an arm and body slammed him against the wall. Then the man spun toward Brett, a pistol in his hand. Sue pushed past Ray and triggered her Taser, freezing the aggressor for a brief instant before he made a convulsive plunge to the weatherworn porch floor, collapsing face down, his weapon tumbling off the porch into the snow.

Seconds later, Brett and Rory were on the man, pulling his arms back, cuffing his wrists and attaching leg irons. Then they dragged him to a sitting position, his legs dangling off the porch.

"You okay?" Brett asked Rory, and Rory nodded. "What about you?" Brett asked the shackled prisoner. The man remained stunned for a few moments, then poured out a torrent of obscenities.

"We'll take him to the ER before we take him to jail," said Brett, looking toward Ray.

"Perfect," said Ray.

"Looks like a little home cooking was going on here," said Sue as she and Ray looked at the collection of pans, jugs, bottles, and tubes littered across the pockmarked gas stove and the stained sink in the cramped kitchen of the old cottage. "And the place just reeks."

"It doesn't appear that this laboratory is up to FDA standards. Probably a bit of mouse dirt in every batch," observed Ray.

"Artisanal, handcrafted, mostly all natural," retorted Sue. "That said, that guy is not neat."

"You have a name?"

"Bruno J. Schmidt, Flint address. Several outstanding warrants."

"How about the truck?"

"Plated and insured," said Sue. "It belongs to Schmidt. Damn. I was hoping we had nailed the guy."

"That Dodge will turn up," said Ray, "but don't bet on the driver."

15

"You two okay?" asked Dr. Dyskin as he entered Ray's office.

"Bumps and bruises," answered Ray.

"Same," responded Sue.

"And she's got a sprained wrist," added Ray.

"Amazing video on the news last night," said Dr. Dyskin. "That snowmobile came right through the windshield. You could have been killed, both of you."

"And our dog, too," said Sue.

"The dog—" Dr. Dyskin stopped mid-sentence, his eyes wide, his hands frozen mid-gesture.

"Luckily unharmed," said Sue.

"One of our guys was running Sue to the ER. She had them detour to the veterinarian's office," Ray said, "where Simone was pronounced physically sound, albeit a bit traumatized. Then Sue went to the ER. She's mostly ticked about the loss of her new truck."

"I have spent hours getting everything logically organized in my new crime scene vehicle. Now I've got to start all over. Besides, the truck and I, we had bonded."

A look passed between Ray and Dr. Dyskin. The medical examiner nodded and moved away from the topic. "Sorry about the wrist," he said. "Glad it wasn't anything more serious."

"Much ado about nothing," said Sue.

You've read the pathologist's report?"

"No," said Ray.

"Understandable. It arrived a couple of hours ago. The cause of death was a subdural hematoma. The report confirms my suspicion that Becca Sterling's death was not caused by an epileptic seizure.

When you read through it, you'll run into the term SUDEP, which stands for 'sudden unexplained death in epilepsy.' The usual findings for SUDEP include things like tongue biting, incontinence, aspiration of gastric juices, vomiting, and the kinds of injuries one might sustain by violently flailing about. None of those were present. Just to be on the safe side, I asked that the brain be sent to Rochester for forensic neuropathology. Wouldn't want the autopsy findings challenged at trial.

"You will also be interested in the fact that the decedent had intercourse sometime earlier in the evening. There is nothing to suggest that the sex was forced."

"DNA?" asked Sue.

"I don't know how quickly semen degrades under those conditions. I've requested a check for DNA. The victim's bed sheets and panties should be checked for DNA evidence, also."

"Yes, I've got all that bagged."

"I've been puzzling over this case," Dr. Dyskin said. "I want to refresh my memory by reviewing the video you shot at the crime scene."

Sue directed Dr. Dyskin to a chair at the conference table. "Do you want some coffee before I start?"

"No. I'm good."

After they were all seated, Sue started the video. On the large screen mounted on the wall, the interior of Becca Sterling's kitchen appeared. The camera panned the whole scene—the counters, the kitchen table, the floors, and finally the body. On the second pass, the camera zoomed in on each area, capturing every item in detail—the dishes on the counter, the broken wine glass on the floor, the throw rugs pushed out of place, and the position of the body. The camera then focused on the body, moving from head to toe and back again as Sue had carefully circled the deceased.

"I was lying in bed thinking about this," Dr. Dyskin said. "The postmortem confirms some of my suspicions. I'm still trying to come up with a workable scenario. You did a good job of recording the area around the hearth. The masonry is only a couple of inches above the floor. You can see the hard edge of the split stone. I think that had to be the point of contact. The laceration at the back of the skull is where Ms. Sterling's head hit that edge, resulting in a skull fracture and the bleed that killed her."

"How long would that have taken?" asked Ray. "The time between her striking her head and dying?"

"Hard to say. It depends on the size of the bleed. In this case, probably a couple of hours. Becca Sterling was knocked unconscious when her head struck the hearth. That started the chain of events leading to her death."

"Would she have survived if she had received immediate medical attention?" asked Sue.

"It's never safe to speculate in cases like this. But if the planets had been aligned properly—medical attention immediately after the injury, timely transportation to a level-one trauma center, a quick diagnosis, and a skilled neurosurgeon being on hand to do the work—all of the above would have improved her chances."

A long silence followed, then Dr. Dyskin said, "Can I offer you a scenario? I know, I usually restrict my comments to the medical part and let you two puzzle things out. But this case is bothering me for a lot of reasons."

"We'd welcome it, Dr. Dyskin," responded Sue.

"What if there were at least two visitors to Ms. Sterling's home Tuesday evening. First, she had a male visitor with whom she had sex. Perhaps that was an ongoing relationship. Later in the evening, she had a second visitor of indeterminate gender. There was a dispute of some sort between Ms. Sterling and this individual. Then things got physical. A struggle ensued. Hence the overturned chair and the out of place throw rugs.

"The contusions on each arm are consistent with being held very tightly. Ms. Sterling also had a bruise on her right cheek. That's consistent with being slapped or struck in some way. There is also a small bruise on the forehead. I don't know what might've happened there. At some point, Sterling tumbles over backwards, hits her head on the sharp edge of the hearth, and is knocked unconscious.

The other person departs the scene. You two get to figure out the motives and possible consequences, and of course, the identity of the person."

"Thank you," said Sue. "That was one scenario I was playing with. There were two dinner plates and more than enough flatware to provide two place settings in the dishwasher plus whatever she might have used earlier in the day. I found two plastic pouches in the garbage that match a package of wild caught Alaskan salmon in the freezer, an eight portion pack, with six filets remaining."

"That's consistent with the autopsy. Salmon, orzo, salad, and ice cream," said Dr. Dyskin, looking over the autopsy.

"How was the salmon prepared?" asked Ray.

"Elkins, only you would ask that question," said Sue. "And I'm way ahead of you. I think she poached it with white wine. There was a steamer basket in the dishwasher and a pot in the drying rack. Before I met you I wouldn't have even known that was possible."

She continued, "By the way, there were two wine glasses in the dishwasher. And there was an open bottle of Chardonnay in the refrigerator. It was two-thirds empty. A couple of glasses of wine, a light meal, and a romantic encounter . . .'"

"There were trace amounts of alcohol in her blood," Dr. Dyskin noted. "If she had one or two glasses of wine around, let's say 6:00, it would have been mostly metabolized by the time she died."

"So let me keep running this," said Sue. "The first visitor arrived late afternoon or early evening, and the second visitor arrived in the late evening. There's nothing to suggest that this second visitor was an invited guest. The sliding door at the back of the house was open, the other doors locked. This could have been a home invasion, then a physical confrontation. Sterling falls or is knocked to the floor, and the perpetrator leaves the scene. The disorder was caused by the confrontation. There's no evidence of robbery."

"Becca Sterling was still alive, but critically injured. And her daughter, a toddler, was left in a very vulnerable situation. That's what I can't get out of my head. I can't help but see my own children and my grandchildren. This person walked away. Two lives were on the line, and they simply walked away. That's assuming, of course, the intruder knew there was a child in the house."

"With the little girl, Ava, we got lucky," said Sue. "The fact that she was only mildly hypothermic by the time she was examined at the ER suggests she wasn't outside long before Chuck Peterson found her."

"The dog, the Sterling dog," said Dr. Dyskin, "that's the one piece I don't understand. My little dog would tear into anyone who touched me or my wife or the grandkids, especially the grandkids."

"Maybe the dog was shut in the bedroom with Sterling's daughter."

"Possible, I guess. One more thing," said Dr. Dyskin, "make me a copy of the photos of Sterling's prescription pill bottles. I'll talk with her doctor and see if we can determine if the medications were in her system at the prescribed levels."

16

Sharon Peterson greeted Sue Lawrence at the door and led her into the kitchen. Sue noted that Sharon looked exhausted, her eyelids were puffy and red. She watched as Sharon dabbed at her eyes and wiped her nose.

"Is your husband here?" Sue finally asked.

"No, he and Ava went grocery shopping. They're on what Chuck calls a 'French shopping trip.' You know, three or four stops and then someplace to have lunch. People always make a fuss over Ava. She loves the attention."

"I wanted to tell both of you about the preliminary results of the autopsy. Would it be better if I told you two together?"

"It's okay, Detective, I'm tough. Take a seat and have your say."

As Sue waited for Sharon to settle in the chair across from her, she carefully scanned the kitchen, conventionally furnished with everything in perfect order.

Sue took several slow breaths as she collected her thoughts. "We are not convinced that your niece's death was the result of an existing illness. We think that there was someone else in the house that night and that some kind of confrontation took place. At some point Becca fell or was pushed, striking her head on the hearth. The cause of death was a cranial bleed."

Peterson didn't respond immediately. Finally, she asked, "Her death, was it instantaneous?"

"She was unconscious as soon as she hit her head. She would've died sometime later."

Peterson started sobbing. Sue stood, retrieved the tissue box from a nearby counter, and returned to the table.

"Let me get you a glass of water," said Sue as she moved toward the sink. She filled a glass and placed it on the table near Sharon. For a brief moment, she placed her hand on Sharon's shoulder. "Perhaps we should call your husband?"

"Thank you, no. Let them have their shopping trip. We haven't attempted yet to explain to Ava where her mother is. I'm meeting with the child psychologist tomorrow. We're trying to keep things as normal as possible."

Peterson looked away, and then back at Sue. "Who was in the house? With Becca?"

"I was hoping that you could help us with that."

"You must have some ideas. I mean fingerprints or DNA . . ."

"We have processed the scene very carefully. At this point, we have no suspects."

"At some level I suspected . . ." Sharon glanced out the window, and Sue noticed the view for the first time—the snow-covered shoreline and the gray water that ran to the horizon. "But I wanted to believe that she died of natural causes."

"And that's why I'm here, Mrs. Peterson. I know you were very close to your niece."

"We were, especially after Ava was born."

"Yes. Can you think of who might have been with her that evening?"

"We saw them earlier in the day. At night the two of them would settle in, have supper, a bath, and then story time and bed. Becca was not very social after Ava arrived. I can't think of who might have been there."

"There's evidence suggesting that at some point she had a male visitor." Sue held Peterson in her gaze and waited patiently for a response.

"What are you suggesting?"

"Possibly a love interest?"

"I don't know. It wasn't something we talked about. We didn't pry."

"You and your husband were regular visitors to Becca's house. Who else?"

"Her next-door neighbor, Frances Adams. She's quite elderly. Becca checked on her daily and took Frances shopping and to the doctor. Frances often came over in the afternoon to spend time with Ava. In the summer Frances walks over. In the winter she drives her ancient Lincoln. She's afraid of slipping and falling."

"Anyone else?"

"The usual delivery people. Becca got most things online, even some of her groceries."

"Other possible visitors?"

"There's Dr. Brian Shepard and his wife, Olivia. They're the neighbors on the other side. Brian has a practice in town. He often spends a weeknight here."

"How about his wife? You said her name was Olivia."

"Yes. When the Shepards' children were still at home, Olivia would spend summers here. Brian came out in the evening. She's a fine musician, string player, viola. That's her passion. She performs chamber music for various events and plays in the symphony."

"So you've gotten to know them fairly well, the Shepards, over the years?"

"We're friendly," Peterson said.

"The doctor, any particular evening?"

"I'm not sure. Brian takes one day off during the week. I think he comes up the night before."

"Was he a friend of Becca's?"

"Just a neighbor, I think. I never saw them together. He's a nice man."

"How about people from outside the area? In our earlier conversation, you said Becca had lots of friends from New York and other places."

"During the summer, especially before Ava was born, lots of visitors. But since then, Becca's company seems limited to July and August. Now it's only a trickle compared to the old days. And like I said, she has never had guests in the dead of winter."

"Ava's father, what can you tell me?"

"Nothing, really. Becca and I were very close, but she never shared anything about Ava's father. I approached the topic more than once, but she always closed me down. This is all she ever told me. When she decided it was time for her to have a child, she chose the father very carefully. He had to be smart, physically attractive, and kind. She said she told the man that she wanted to have a child with him, but he would have to sign off on any parental rights to the child before they started sleeping together." Sharon paused for a moment. "I make her sound heartless, don't I? She had two sides. One was warm and loving. The other was analytical. In the case of Ava, she wanted a child, but not a man."

"Do you have access to those documents?"

"No. Becca just told me about it. I don't know if they were created here or in New York."

"Do you know if she has a local attorney?"

"Yes, some woman in town. Becca had a medical power of attorney created for Ava early on so that we could do whatever might be necessary in case of an emergency. She was traveling a lot then, and we were taking care of Ava."

"And what will happen to Ava now?"

"She will be with us, at least for the near future. Given our age, we will be putting things in place in case we are not able to continue with the parenting. We've been talking to our children. This is one of those times when you realize the importance of family. It's amazing when you turn to your kids for guidance and counsel. One of our daughters, Yvonne, is a lawyer. She's starting to walk me through the things we need to consider as we plan for Ava's future."

"You're in a difficult situation, I know," Sue said. "May I ask, was there anything about Becca's manner or did she say anything that might have suggested to you that she was apprehensive, or frightened, or worried?"

"No, nothing like that. In fact, I don't think she was ever happier. Becca had completed her commitment to the group who bought her business. She wasn't going to be traveling much. She was thrilled with Ava. Becca kept telling me how every day was special—

new words, bits of joy, the unfolding of a life. Becca said she was so happy that she could spend this time with her daughter."

"Can you think of anyone who might want to do her harm? Anyone from her personal life, a former love interest or friend, or someone from her professional life . . . ?"

"I'm sorry, nothing comes to mind. Becca made friends, not enemies."

"Have there been any unusual comings and goings in your neighborhood, people or cars that are unfamiliar?"

"Nothing like that. There are only a few places occupied at this time of year. We all look after one another. If an outsider were lurking about, I would have heard about it very quickly. Nothing goes unnoticed around here."

I'm sure it doesn't, Sue thought as she said a polite good-bye to Sharon Peterson, who Sue was sure had been less than forthcoming during their interview. This was the part of the job that rankled Sue most: a supposedly beloved woman was dead under suspicious circumstances, and even her own aunt was reluctant to tell the truth.

17

Chuck Peterson was waiting in his car already when Ray parked at the top of Becca Sterling's steep driveway. Ray had asked Chuck to provide keys to the studio and guesthouse on Becca's property, areas Ray and Sue hadn't yet had a chance to inspect. Ray also thought his request might provide an opportunity to interview Mr. Peterson without his wife being present.

"Becca kept all the keys in a cabinet on the landing to the basement staircase," Chuck said as he led Ray through the kitchen to the door that led to the basement.

"She had a key cabinet built into the wall when the interior of this house was renovated. I love the idea. Everything is perfectly organized. Every key is properly tagged. The key with the blue tag is for the studio, the one with the red tag opens the guesthouse."

"Are the buildings winterized?" asked Ray.

"The guesthouse is. When she rebuilt this house, she installed a geothermal system. The guesthouse was rebuilt at the same time and is part of the system. The studio is an old frame building. It's not winterized."

"Would you mind accompanying me on my initial walkthrough?" asked Ray. "I might have a few questions that you could help me with."

"No problem, Sheriff."

"How is Ava doing?" Ray asked as they crossed from the main house to the guest cottage.

"Hard to say," Peterson replied. "She's eating well and playing much like she's done for the past several months. She hugs her dog more than before, I think. She's spent so much time with us almost from the beginning of her life, I wonder if this seems normal. I don't know what she remembers from that night." He stopped at the entry door of the building. "Sheriff, if you'll give me the key, I'll get the place open and the lights on."

The cottage had an open-concept floor plan, the living room divided from the kitchen only by a long island with a gleaming black stone countertop. Windows covered the lake wall, and Ray looked out at the layers of ice pushed up over each other along the beach.

"Does this cottage get used much?" asked Ray as he walked around the interior, looking into the bedrooms and baths. It was tidy to the point of sterility.

"Becca liked to keep all her spaces just so," Mr. Peterson gestured toward the kitchen, where the glass doors of the cupboards revealed neat stacks of white dishes and clear glassware. "Everything in its place, nothing out of place. Just a few years ago, this cottage, the main house, and the studio were awash with characters of every sort, but since Ava arrived, the summer crowd has become little more than a trickle of visitors."

"Why is that?" asked Ray.

"That's an interesting question. I've never really thought about it. But now that you mention it, I think Becca just made a major change of direction in her life. And for Becca, that wasn't unusual. I've seen her do it several times. When she set a new course, she marched forward, cutting off long-held relationships. I mean, she did that with Sharon. They were so close when Becca was a teen and first in college. Then Becca just dropped off the radar. Sharon was worried about Becca and also really hurt. The two of them only remained in touch because Sharon kept reaching out to her. Years went by, and then suddenly Becca was back, just like nothing ever happened. I admit that I was apprehensive, especially at first. I didn't want to see Sharon hurt again."

Ray nodded. "So everything here is just as it should be?"

"Yes. I was probably the last person in here. Becca likes me to check things over at the end of the season. Even though the building is heated, I drain the plumbing on the off chance that we lose power for an extended period."

"So you're sort of the caretaker here?"

"I guess you could say that. I don't mind. It's one of the ways I can help out. Sharon does a major part of the childcare with Ava."

"It appears to me that you and your wife have had a close relationship with Becca over much of her life. You two were people she could count on, even if she did disappear from your lives for a time."

Mr. Peterson shrugged modestly. "Especially Sharon. But there's a long history. Becca's mother, Monique, was a wild child in her teens and early twenties. Monique was the baby of the family, the surprise child. Sharon was the oldest, with two brothers in between. Monique came of age in the '70s, but she was the proverbial '60s kind of kid—drugs, sex, and rock and roll. In her late teens, Monique got pregnant. Her parents, in their late fifties by then, were beside themselves. They had the means to hush things up by sending Monique abroad before the situation became obvious. Monique ended up going to college in the UK. Some years later she returned with a beautiful little girl and an art degree from a British university—Leeds, as I remember it. And a year or two after she returned to the States, Monique married Harvey, joined the Junior League, and become the perfect suburban wife. Harvey was skilled at making money, and Monique did art, something exotic like mixed textiles and paper. It's the kind of art I could never figure out.

"Harvey was an odd duck, not the kind of guy you could kick back and drink a couple of beers with. But they seemed compatible enough. Who knows what goes on in a marriage? And then sadly, about a decade later, Monique died rather quickly.

"Oops, I've probably said too much. Sharon doesn't like these kinds of family details out in the open. When you live in such a small community, people take any bit of information and use it as fodder for gossip."

"Sure," Ray said. "We know that on the night that Becca died, she had a confrontation with someone who we believe came to the house late in the evening. Do you have any idea who that might have been?"

"I've thought about it a lot. Sharon and I have tossed this back and forth. We can't think of anyone with whom she had a contentious relationship. That's not the kind of person Becca was. I never heard her raise her voice at anyone, ever. She avoided confrontations. She was a lovely, peaceful woman. And late-night visitors, no. Sharon and I joked about how Becca went from burning the midnight oil in the old days to going to bed soon after she got Ava settled. I mean, what a change. We learned it wasn't safe to call or drop by after 10:00."

"You said that Becca associated in the past with many different kinds of people. Was there anyone—a former lover or business associate, for example—who might be carrying a lot of anger for something that happened in the past, before Ava was born?"

Chuck Peterson's face contorted as he seemed to search his memory. "That's always a possibility, I guess, but sort of inconsistent with the Becca I knew, as a young woman and even more recently. I mean, yes, she disappeared from our lives for a while, but there was never any animosity."

"Have you noticed anything unusual of late? Someone around who shouldn't be?"

"Nothing like that."

"Did Becca express any concern about her safety?"

"No, not that I can recall. Becca was a little too casual about locking doors. I lectured her more than once."

"Was there ever an occasion where anyone entered her home uninvited through an unlocked door?"

"Not that I know of, and I think she would have told us if something like that had happened. The wife and I, we spent most of our working lives in urban areas. Locking houses and cars is just sort of in our DNA. Becca just felt so safe here." He thought for a couple of moments. "But she did start locking up. I thought it was my influence, but now I'm not so sure. Maybe she wasn't feeling so safe, I don't know. Maybe that's why she got a dog."

"Any change in her manner? Did she seem tense or anxious?"

"If anything like that was going on, I missed it. And, as I said, Sharon and I have been going over and over this. We can't begin to explain what happened. It's eerie living so close to Becca's house knowing that whoever did this to her is still out there somewhere."

"Is there anyone who would profit from Becca's death?"

Ray watched Chuck Peterson closely. His answer was slow in coming.

"I can't see how. Becca set up her estate to provide for Ava in case anything ever happened to her. She worked with an attorney who specializes in this area of family law. Everything is tied up in trusts and other things I don't quite understand. Becca was an astute businessperson. I'm sure there weren't any loose ends. There's nothing else that I know about."

"Do you have plans for a memorial service?" asked Ray.

"Sharon is working on that. Our kids will be arriving over the next few days. Becca stipulated that she wanted to be cremated, which we've already arranged to happen once her body is released. I think there will be a memorial service for family members only within the next week and maybe something later for her friends. Sharon's thinking maybe in spring or summer. Something we could do on the beach. That's where Becca wanted her ashes strewn. She has friends all over the world, Sheriff. It's all very complicated, even contacting people to let them know what's happened, not to mention figuring out flights and housing for our own immediate family."

Mr. Peterson looked over at Ray. "And you want to see the studio, too? I doubt if anyone has been in there since I winterized it."

"Yes, please. I'm just being thorough."

They followed a shoveled path to a small building situated on a knoll close to the lake. Chuck Peterson struggled with the lock, swearing a few times before he managed to turn the key and open the door.

"I need to spray a little WD-40 in the keyhole and get things loosened up. I tell myself that every time I go in here. You know how that goes, Sheriff. The best intention, quickly forgotten."

After Mr. Peterson got the lights on, Ray quickly looked around the building. The floor was a concrete slab painted a dull red. A wall of glass composed of many small windows faced west toward the lake. Two small changing rooms and toilet stall ran along the north end of the building. A bit of dull midwinter light seeped in from an east-facing clerestory above. Outdoor furniture and a large plastic bin filled with assorted sand toys were stored near the door that opened to the shore.

"In the early days, this was a beach house. During Monique's years here, she converted the structure to her studio. Those windows up there brought in the morning light. By early afternoon the light was streaming in off the lake. Monique liked working in the late afternoon and evening. Said that's when the light was best. There's a deck out front facing the lake. Midsummer she liked to sit there, drink martinis, and watch the sun sink into the water. For a few years, it was a bit of a ritual—the cocktail shaker, the crystal glasses. And then it wasn't. Interesting how things change." Mr. Peterson was looking at Ray. His mouth had slackened somewhat, and his words seemed to come from a distant place.

"There was a time when this place was filled with Monique's works. Nothing ever quite finished. Lots of things in progress. In addition to the paper and textile art, she did oils and some watercolors. I liked coming in here back then. Oil paint has a nice smell. Maybe it's just the linseed oil. The old building, the paint, the smell of the shore in summer. There was an earthy aroma. And Monique…there was this sensuality about her. My wife, Sharon, she's not the jealous type. But I could tell she wasn't happy with me spending too much time with Monique."

Ray held Mr. Peterson in his gaze. He said nothing. He just waited and let the silence fill the space.

"You see, Monique . . . I shouldn't probably say this. She told Sharon everything. Sharon told me that Monique said she and Harvey had an open relationship. The open part, I don't think so. I think Harvey was clueless. Most summers she seemed to have a love interest. We'd sometimes speculate on who would be next. She worked her way through the more attractive men in the summer colony. Most were married. Monique told Sharon that she preferred married men because they were discreet. They didn't go around bragging about conquests. And this studio, isolated from the rest of the compound, was probably where most of the trysts took place. And now, as you can see, the place is mostly empty. There used to be a daybed here. I had it hauled out of here a year ago—mildew and mice had done it in. Becca was using the building as a beach house again. Nothing more as far as I know."

"When were you last in this building?" asked Ray.

"Early October. I drained the plumbing."

"And everything is just as you left it?"

Mr. Peterson scanned the room. "Yes."

"Monique's private life, no explosions, no confrontations?"

"No, not that I know of. Life is so interesting. Lots of drama at one time. A few decades out, most of the players are dead, and no one knows or cares."

Mr. Peterson looked over the interior of the house again, slowly. Their eyes met again, and Ray noted the sadness in his gaze.

"Is there anything else, Sheriff?"

"Just one more thing. Would you walk through Becca's house with me? I would like you to look things over very carefully and tell me if anything appears to be missing and if anything is present that shouldn't be there."

"Certainly."

They started in the basement and then moved to the upper level, Mr. Peterson taking time to observe the contents of the rooms. They completed their tour in the kitchen.

"Can we talk outside?" Mr. Peterson asked.

Their extended time on Becca's property had started to affect the older man; Ray could see that he was fighting back tears.

Standing with Ray in the cold wind, looking out toward the dark shadows of the Manitous floating above the gray water and under the heavy overcast, Mr. Peterson said, "I can see Becca in every nook and cranny of that place. There was such economy and order in the way she lived. Nothing extra anywhere. She surrounded Ava and herself with beautiful things—not necessarily expensive things. It was all about design and craftsmanship. Her clothing was much the same—style, fabric, and texture. And never about the name on the label. There was a certain irony there given the fact that she made her fortune in fashion."

"Did you notice anything missing in the house?"

"No, everything seemed to be there."

"Did she have any valuable jewelry or keep a wad of cash anywhere in the house that you know of?"

"Her jewelry was mostly earrings. Very simple, delicate, handmade. No diamonds, rubies, nothing liked that."

"How about cash?"

"Becca never seemed to have any cash. She did everything with credit cards. Our kids are the same way. Cash is so yesterday."

"How about other valuables in the house?"

"Sheriff, the house is filled with valuables, but most people wouldn't recognize them as such. Every lamp, chair, rug, fork, and spoon was selected because of its design and craftsmanship. The flatware was stainless steel. There was no silver."

"And you didn't see anything that shouldn't be there?"

"No. Other than the chaos in front of the fireplace, everything was just as it should be."

Ray started his vehicle several minutes after parting with Chuck Peterson, pondering what he had seen and heard. *Like bits and pieces of an ancient mosaic in the process of being uncovered,* he thought. *I can make out her features, but little more.* He was left with a sense of sadness and loss. "An unnatural death, the interruption of nature," he said out loud as he thought about the meaning of the phrase.

18

Even before Ray touched the doorbell, his arrival was announced by a high-pitched, multi-layered yapping. Once the door was opened, he was surrounded by a pack of small dogs of various colors and body types.

"Say hello to the guys," the petite and sprightly woman ordered in a low gravelly voice, "and they will find you less offensive."

Ray dropped to his knees and scratched ears and petted heads. One by one, the dogs started to wander away.

"I'm drinking Armagnac and espresso with heavy cream. Can I offer you the same?"

Ray inhaled the aroma of strong coffee and spirits. He would have liked nothing better. "No, thank you," he answered. "Frances Adams?"

"I am."

"Mrs. Adams, thank you for allowing me to stop by. We're trying to learn as much as we can about Becca Sterling."

"Well, you came at the right time. I've finally gotten past my hysteria. I've cried myself out. I've cursed the gods, as if that might make a difference. I can't believe this has happened." She briefly cut off the torrent of words. "You sure about the coffee, Sheriff?"

"Okay, coffee with cream, that would be lovely. But, please, no brandy." Ray leaned against one of the counters as Mrs. Adams scurried around the kitchen.

"I assume you've known Becca Sterling for some years?"

"Years, Sheriff, decades. And her mother and grandmother, too. And lots of other relatives from several generations. That's the special thing about an old summer colony." She paused, poured the espresso into a porcelain cup and carefully floated the thick, yellowish cream on the surface with the help of the back of a spoon.

"Let me modify what I just said." She placed the cup on the counter next to Ray. "In the old days, we all seemed to live in two worlds. One was the real world—Detroit, Chicago, Cleveland, Cincinnati, or wherever. The other world was here. Families came for the whole summer. The 'season,' that's what we used to say. We arrived just after school was out and stayed until school was starting again. Dads would come and go. Some were here for weekends, others for a few weeks or more. And when I was a child, this was my universe. This part of my life was the better part of the two. Every day was an adventure, running free from dawn to dusk.

"And we were mixed up in the lives of all the other kids. We were on the beach together, in and out of everyone else's cottages. You usually had a meal wherever you were." She stopped and looked at Ray. "Where was I going?"

"You were going to tell me about Becca."

"Yes, Becca, I'll get to her. I just wanted you to understand how well we all knew one another. And that's all gone away. The world is different. As we die off, most of the places get sold now. The property is too expensive. The taxes are too high. And you've seen what's going up. The McMansions, more like Cape Cod or Maine, or other places where the wealthy gather. And these people, you never see them or their kids outside. There may be five cars in the drive, but the residents are invisible. It's like they don't connect with this place anymore. It's all so different. But, I digress.

"Becca, she was friends with my granddaughters. What a delightful child. She was so artsy, almost from the beginning. The kids would do art on the beach with whatever was about. Shells, bits of driftwood, stones, and sand became imaginary places— castles, villages. And they also did plays—mostly adventure stories, kids being lost and having to look after themselves, that sort of thing. They would make costumes, write scripts, create parts. It was amazing. And we, the adults, the audience, would have to traipse all over to follow the actors and the action. Every scene was in a different location. It was wonderful. Kids today, staring at their devices. It wouldn't happen now.

"And Becca's mother, Monique, always had an easel set up, you know, with brilliant colors of paint and lots of newsprint. Sarah and Jenny, my granddaughters, would wander home with wonderful paintings. We'd put them up all over. That's what you can do in an old building. We'd thumbtack them to the wall."

"This background is useful," said Ray. "Thank you. Do you know anyone who might have a reason to harm Ms. Sterling?"

"No, Sheriff." Mrs. Adams went silent for a moment and took a deep breath. "I'm sorry you didn't know her. Becca was so kind, so thoughtful. I can't imagine she had any enemies."

"When was the last time you saw her?"

"It was last week, a Wednesday. I had a doctor's appointment in town. She was going in to do some shopping, so she worked me into the trip."

"Was there anything about her behavior that suggested she may have been worried?"

"Not at all. Becca was just her same effervescent self. I sat in the back seat with Ava on the way into town. I think most of our conversation was with or about Ava. There was just a lot of laughing and singing. She and Ava, they were always singing. Becca was very musical. What a beautiful voice. I think she could have done musical comedy, maybe even opera, if she had focused on it early on. She had so many talents."

"Do you know much about Becca's personal life?"

"Personal life, you mean with whom she was sleeping? Sheriff, did you share the details of your sex life with your grandmother?" Mrs. Adams shot back. "What are you trying to find out? Ava's father? Current or former lovers? Castoff lovers who might be seeking revenge? We may have lived next door, but, as you might have noticed, there is a bit of a dune between our homes. I never regaled Becca with the details of my sizzling love life, and I think she took that as a signal to be discreet about hers."

"Did Becca ever mention anything about the possible father?"

Frances bobbed her head like she was pondering the question. "Sheriff, it was woman-to-woman stuff. I would be violating the seal of the confessional and revoking a patient-client, lawyer-client relationship. I must take the fifth."

"Frances, may I call you Frances?"

"You may."

"Frances. Becca is dead. We now believe she was murdered. My job is to find her killer and bring that person to justice. I need some straight answers."

"Okay, I did ask her. That's what I do. But we were playing a game. She said there were two possibilities. She called them Princeton and Williams. She said in both cases they were smart, handsome, and sweet. Also, married. Princeton could play the piano and sing. Williams was a poet with a blinding serve and a great backhand. She couldn't decide whose seed to carry, so she had them both at a time she could conceive. Her little joke was 'let fate decide.' Becca told me that neither man knows that they may have fathered Ava. But remember, Sheriff, Becca was a fabulous raconteur. That's a great story, isn't it? There is perhaps some truth in it, but maybe not too much."

"And the Princeton and Williams men, we're not talking about summer people, are we?"

"No, part of her New York set. I have no idea as to whether either one was ever here."

"Was Becca seeing anyone locally?"

"I don't know, but I don't think so. Until recently Becca was making regular trips to New York. That was part of the sales agreement on her business. If she had someone there, I wouldn't know. But she was young and vibrant and beautiful. I certainly hope she wasn't wasting her life."

"Other than friends and neighbors, any people who come to your home on a regular basis?

"You mean like the mailman?"

"Exactly."

"Yes, the mailman, Herb."

"Who else?"

"UPS late in the day, a young guy with a mustache. FedEx in the morning, a woman in her thirties, blond hair tied in a ponytail. Ronnie Poole, the snowplow guy. And there's the woman who reads the electric meter once a month, drives a red Toyota truck. And then garbage and recycling, every Tuesday morning. That's at the foot of the drive. I never see them."

"And Becca used the same people?"

"Most of them. We share information."

"I've talked with you and the Petersons. The other homes look closed up for the winter. Am I right about that?"

"Yes, that's sort of it. A few of the summer people will be up for the holidays, and then they won't be here again until spring. There's one more person who is here occasionally. Dr. Shepard, Brian Shepard. He's got a surgical practice in town. Nice man. I think he spends one night a week here during the winter. He and his dog, a big black Lab. I don't recall seeing his wife during the winter months."

"Any specific night?"

"I wouldn't know, Sheriff. The days, they all sort of blend."

"Anyone else?"

"Not really. People in the other cottages come and go, but not too much."

Mrs. Adams moved close. Ray looked down at her wrinkled face and pale blue eyes.

"I haven't helped you at all, Sheriff, have I? I am so sorry for that. I can't imagine why anyone would hurt Becca. She was so special. And to take her away from that beautiful little girl."

"Do you have any pictures of Becca?"

"Give me a moment." Mrs. Adams drifted away and returned holding a couple of photos. "The first one goes way back. That's Monique, Harvey, and Becca somewhere on the beach out front. As you can see, Becca was just a toddler then. And that little dog, how Becca loved that floppy little pup. I must have snapped that forty years ago. Somehow it doesn't seem that long ago. And here is a new one. Becca gave me this just a few weeks ago, her and Ava. You can hardly see Ava in that funny snowsuit."

"Could I borrow these?" asked Ray. "I'm trying to get a sense of these people."

"No problem," Frances answered, slipping the photos out of plastic frames and passing them to Ray.

Mrs. Adams reached out to be held, and Ray put his arms around her.

19

Ray swiveled his chair in the direction of the window at the back of his office. Lost in thought, he gazed out at the freezing drizzle carried in with the overnight thaw. A thin coating of ice glistened off the pavement and the vehicles in the lot below.

He turned back to his computer, pausing to look at the copy of the picture Frances Adams had taken of Becca and her parents. It was an old print from the late 70s. The colors had begun to fade.

The beach scene was familiar and changed little from one decade to the next. Lake Michigan was in the background, whitecaps rolling toward the shore and dune grass bending in the wind. Monique, Becca's mother, was wearing a short powder blue shift dress with laurel green accents at each side. She held a small poodle in her arms, its ears appeared to be lifted by the wind. Her arms, legs, and face were richly tanned, her flaxen hair styled in a French twist.

Monique was smiling at the camera. Her open shoes in a matching green were partially hidden in the sand.

A man stood at her side—*Harvey*, thought Ray—in a blue sports coat, tie, and gray slacks that appeared to be rolled up a bit, showing darks socks and wingtips. The man's smile seemed forced. A small child, a girl, body facing the lake, head partially turned toward the camera, clung to his hand. Ray was pulled into the scene, a July or August day. He could feel the warmth of the sun and hear the wind and waves.

Ray looked at the photo of Becca and Ava. Focused on Becca he sensed the joy she was experiencing playing in the snow with her daughter. Then he was confronted with his recent memory of seeing the lifeless form stretched out on the floor and the memory of holding her daughter for a few brief moments.

Ray turned his attention back to the report, trying to construct an accurate narrative based on his conversations with Sharon Peterson, Chuck Peterson, and Frances Adams. After completing a draft, he read it through, making minor corrections and revisions, and then saved the file in the Becca Sterling folder, knowing Sue would probably be reviewing it before they met for lunch.

Ray then had to put the Becca Sterling case on the back burner. He called the jail and asked to have Bruno Schmidt brought to the interview room.

"Want me to stay?" asked Todd Maskow, a corrections officer, after bringing Schmidt into the room. "This individual has been nothing but trouble since he was transported in."

Ray looked over at Schmidt, now dressed in a jail jumpsuit, his wrists in cuffs, his legs in irons, his bulky frame filling out the bright-orange jumpsuit.

"Please," answered Ray as he looked over the brooding, angry figure before settling in the chair across from him at the interview table. He switched on the cameras and recording equipment and Mirandized Schmidt. "Do you understand what I've just read to you?"

Schmidt's response was guttural and indistinct.

"Does that mean you understand?"

Schmidt snorted, then wiped his nose on the arm of his jumpsuit.

"The address on your Michigan driver's license, is that accurate?"

Schmidt was looking down at his hands. His massive frame slowly rocked back and forth as he pulled in air. Finally, he answered without looking up. "What's the street?"

"North Saginaw."

"No. I haven't lived there for years. Maybe an ex still lives there."

"So where do you live now?" asked Ray.

The answer was slow in coming. "Here and there."

"So you currently have no permanent address? Is that correct?"

Schmidt briefly met Ray's eyes, then looked back down at his hands. He was slowly working his thumbs one over the other. "Not really. I find places to crash. It's not like I'm sleeping under bridges, nothing like that. I'm not homeless."

"How did you end up at the house on Round Lake?"

"It's a long story."

"I've got the time."

"None of this is what you think," said Schmidt. "Just because I've been inside, you believe…"

"Schmidt, if I believe something about you, I'll let you know. Now just tell me your story. Let's go back to my question. How did you end up at the cottage on Round Lake?"

Schmidt's answer was slow in coming. "I was staying at a place near Buckley, an old deer camp."

"You came up for hunting season?" Ray prodded.

"No. I've been crashing there most of the summer. It's just a couple of old trailers cobbled together. Stayed there years ago when I came up hunting with a friend from the Buick. I was up here this June roaming around, and I remembered the place. It had mostly collapsed now, but better than sleeping in a truck. I could get by there when the weather was good. But by October it was getting worse. No heat. No water or plumbing. The roof leaked. I was talking to a guy at a bar. He told me about the Round Lake place. He said I could live there rent-free."

"Does this man have a name?"

"I think it was Chad, or maybe Chas. Noisy place, that bar, and my hearing ain't so good."

"Did you get a last name?"

"He didn't say, or maybe I forgot."

"So this Chad or Chas said you could live rent-free. That's an unusual offer to make to a stranger."

"Yeah. But here's the deal. Chad said he had some stuff there that needed protecting."

"What kind of stuff?"

"He didn't say."

"Did he come up to the Round Lake place with you? Did he show you around?"

"No. Chad, he just drew a map on a napkin."

"Anything else?"

"Yeah. He gave me some money."

"How much?" asked Ray.

"I don't know."

"Give me your best guess."

"It was a roll. I didn't count it. Said my job was to protect the place. If I did good, there'd be more money. And he gave me a gun. Said I might be needing some protection. Someone was after him."

"When did this happen?" asked Ray.

"Don't know for sure. The days, they kind of blend."

"Give me your best guess."

"A couple of weeks, maybe more."

"So help me understand this. You meet a man in a bar. He offers you a place to stay. Then he gives you a roll of cash."

"Yeah. That's the way it went down."

"So did this Chad character give you a key?"

Schmidt straightened himself a bit in his chair. "Yeah, I had a key. How else could I get in?"

"And when you got to the cottage and had a look around, what did you think?"

"What do you mean?"

"There's a fair amount of apparatus in the kitchen. Didn't you wonder about Chad and what he might have been into?"

"Look, I needed a place. It had heat, a wood stove. I didn't look at his crap. None of my business."

"This morning when we came to the Round Lake cottage, we identified ourselves as police officers, and we asked you to come out."

"Yeah. That's how Chad said it would go down. Some guys saying they were cops would show up. Like I said, that's why he gave me the gun. I thought you guys would kill me. What would you do? Instinct. Trying to stay alive, that's all. And now, because I got a record, you got it all wrong."

"So tell me again, where did you meet this man?"

"Like I said, in a bar. Buckley."

"Are you sure about that?"

"Yeah. Well, maybe Mesick. Little towns up here, they're all the same. And I've been drinking some. Too many days. Life's tough. That's how I get by. It might've been Mesick."

"So Mr. Schmidt, can you tell me what Chad looks like? Tall, short, fat, thin, old, young, white, brown, black?"

Schmidt rubbed the gray stubble on his cheek and chin with his right hand. "Kind of in the middle. He wasn't real white, so he mighta had something other mixed in. You know what I mean?"

"How about age?"

"Fifty, maybe."

"Tall, short?"

"I don't remember."

"Did you see him again?"

"No."

"Did he call you, message you?"

"Don't have a phone. Just my girlfriend—" Schmidt stopped mid-sentence. He moved his head back and forth and mumbled an obscenity under his breath.

"You haven't told me about a girlfriend, Mr. Schmidt. Does she have a name?"

"We're not together no more."

"When you were together, did she have a name?"

"It was someone I just met. I don't feel good. I'm going to be sick."

Ray stood, gave Schmidt one last look, and signaled to Maskow, the corrections officer, using his thumb. "When this man decides he wants to cooperate with me, please give him access to a shower and clean clothes. And then let me know. I may want to talk to him again."

20

Over the course of the morning, the freezing drizzle had turned to a steady rain. Ray, bundled into a down jacket covered with a waterproof slicker, was walking the half-mile trail that circled the Cedar County Government Center. When he stopped for a moment at the crosswalk and waited for a vehicle to pass, Sue pulled up near him in a battered Dodge sedan and lowered her window.

"Nice car," said Ray.

"This is all the county garage could offer me."

She thought back to how she had been razzed by the mechanics at the garage, Billy Moon and John Piedman.

"Lady, we give you a brand new ride and two weeks later we can't even use what's left for parts."

Then they showed her the Dodge that would not die—a decade old four-door sedan, sitting low on the springs, the driver's seat sagging toward the floor, a patina of rust covering much of the body.

"This one here has withstood the test of time," said John. "You will be driving a legend."

"They don't make them like this anymore," echoed Billy. "We give it to the worst drivers on the force, especially those college interns. It always comes back still running. Lot of good miles left in that machine."

"It's kind of thirsty when it comes to gas," said John.

"And oil, too," added Billy. "If the engine starts knocking bad, it needs oil. We put a case in the trunk. Just dump in three or four quarts. It will settle right down."

"My new truck, any word?" asked Sue.

"There's some delay, model changeover, a strike at a supplier.

Don't worry. If need be, this will get you through the winter. And if you do get into a wreck, you got tons of quality American made steel protecting you."

"What's going on, Ray?" she asked, the wipers on the car slapping back and forth, leaving the windshield streaked.

"Trying to get my ten thousand steps in while practicing Ujjayi breathing, mindfulness, and gratitude—all the stuff you've been telling me to do."

"How did things go with Bruno?" Sue asked.

Ray just shook his head.

"That bad. We'll talk. I'm getting wet. I brought you lunch. Don't be long." She gave him a parting wave as her window slid up between them. Then she sped away. Ray stood for a few moments and then continued with his hike.

When he returned to his office, Sue was sitting at the conference table finishing her lunch. She pointed to the bag resting at his usual spot. "Veggie Burger with gorgonzola on a whole wheat bun, aioli on the side, and a half order of sweet potato fries, no salt, and a tall green tea."

"You nailed it," Ray said, settling across from her.

"You took your time. I couldn't wait," explained Sue. "I was hungry. I watched your interview with Schmidt while I ate."

"What did you think?"

"A troubled life. Bits and pieces of truth, maybe. As you would say, 'a farrago of fact and fiction.' Did you see Schmidt's blood alcohol when they brought him in?"

"Yes, 0.21," said Ray. "Most of us would be struggling to walk with that BAC, yet he was still full of fight when we knocked on the door. He's obviously been training for a long time."

"The interview, he gave you an amazing story," said Sue. "I wonder what he could do if he were sober." She paused briefly. "But don't a lot of fiction writers do their best work when they're drinking? That's what I've heard."

"That's mostly a legend," said Ray. "Other than you-know-who, most of the writers I've met spend their time locked away, staring at computer screens, dead sober."

"Did you read my messages while you were out there practicing gratitude in the rain?" Sue asked.

"I left my phone in here. Dead battery. Leaving it behind was the source of my gratitude. I'm into disconnecting. What did I miss?"

"Some interesting news. Put this under the oldies and goodies column. Guess who is back?"

"I'm afraid to ask."

"Rhonda Johnson."

Whenever she was in Cedar County, Rhonda Johnson was a regular blip on the law enforcement radar. Over the years she'd been brought in for a litany of low-level crimes.

"When did she get out?" asked Ray.

"April. And she's already hooked up with a new guy."

"Who's the lucky victim this time?"

"You'll like this, a new twist in an old plot. Rhonda's new main squeeze is none other than Bruno Schmidt." She looked over at Ray. "I can see you have to chew on that one for a while."

Ray washed the last bit of his burger down before responding. "No one will ever accuse her of being a social climber. And how did this bit of intelligence float your way?"

"We had just finished working the Round Lake scene when Rhonda came flying off the highway onto the two-track toward us. As soon as she saw the police cars, Rhonda pulled a fast one-eighty in the snow and mud and sped away. Rory pursued her and tried to pull her over. Rhonda stayed on the throttle, spun out at the first curve, and slammed into a snow bank. That's where Rory caught up with her. I arrived by the time Rhonda managed to climb out of her car. When Rory approached her, she sprang into action, running at him, screaming. Rory grabbed her wrists, and they both slipped and fell. And then I was able to get her in cuffs. Ray, her hair has gone gray, and she looks painfully thin and small in spite of her puffy coat."

"Rory is not having a good day," said Ray. "And you," he said to Sue. "What happened to the sprained wrist?"

"When I don't think about it, it doesn't hurt," she said. "It's not that bad."

"A quick check shows that Rhonda doesn't have a driver's license. The vehicle belongs to a Ruth Vondracek. The tags are more than a year out of date. I have impounded the vehicle. Rory brought her in for fleeing and eluding. I've requested a search warrant so that I can go through her car. I asked her about Bruno. She says she's never heard of him. She just made a wrong turn."

"Yes, that's my memory of Rhonda. She will sit across from you in the interview room and lie about the color of her hair. She was never a very convincing liar and she seemed to know it."

Ray paused for a moment. "So much for that. What did you find in the cottage?"

"Lots of prints everywhere, including some on the meth-making equipment. I'll be able to give you some results fairly quickly, as if there's any doubt. The side door of the cottage had been kicked in at some point. That's probably how he or they initially gained entrance. There were wads of money stuffed into a backpack also loaded with baggies containing a white crystalline powder. Let me revise that, the powder was fifty shades of gray. But given the laboratory in which it was produced, that's probably to be expected. Most of the end users we've encountered are not big on the purity thing. It looked like Bruno's diet mostly consisted of pizza and Reese's peanut butter cups washed down with Bud Ice and Old Crow." She paused for a moment and looked over at Ray. "You are what you eat."

"Anything that places Rhonda there?"

"Not really, not in my first sweep. No women's clothing or anything. Maybe some of the prints are hers."

"Production and sale of drugs has never been part of her MO, but who knows. Does the Chad or Chas mentioned in the video sound familiar?"

"No, but I'll do some checking with Grand Traverse, Wexford, and Benzie. Where are we on the Becca Sterling case?"

"Have you been through all my notes?"

"Yes, but I'd like to go through them again."

"Brian Shepard, he's the only person who might have been at Fox Cove on Tuesday that we haven't talked to yet. I called his office. He agreed to meet me there at 4:00. I'd like you to go with me."

"Sure."

"Any trace of the black truck?"

"Everyone's looking: State Police, NPS Rangers, Tribal Police, neighboring agencies. Nothing."

21

D r. Brian Shepard—dressed in scrubs—led Ray and Sue into his consultation room. "Please," he said, gesturing toward two chairs facing his desk. He settled into his own chair across from them. The whites of his blue eyes were bloodshot, the lines around his mouth deeply etched.

"Thank you for meeting with us on short notice," said Ray.

"Sorry I couldn't work you in earlier. I had a full schedule of patients and an emergency surgery." Shepard took a deep breath. "I've been talking with Sharon Peterson. First, I was shattered by the news of Becca's death. I assumed that it was the result of a preexisting medical problem. Now Sharon tells me that's not the case."

"At this point, it is an unexplained death," said Ray.

Shepard pulled off his scrub hat and dropped it on his desk. He ran his right hand through his thick, steel-gray hair. "As I said, I was devastated by the news of her death. The suggestion that she may have died as the result of some violence makes it so much worse. I am without words."

"How well did you know Becca?"

"How do I explain?" He paused for a moment. "Our families have had neighboring summer homes for generations. Becca was one of the little kids on the beach when I was a teen." Shepard focused on some distant point beyond the walls of his office. "Later, I remember her as a college girl and then as a very sophisticated adult. And then in the past few years, the mature Becca, the neighbor woman with the beautiful child." Shepard looked back at Ray. "She's been part of the landscape for decades."

"We've been talking to the year-round residents of Fox Cove. Your name came up as one of the few people who regularly stays at their Fox Cove home during the winter. We were wondering if you were at your place on Tuesday, and if so, whether you saw anything unusual?"

"Yes, I'm usually there on Tuesday evenings. Monday and Tuesday are my surgery days. I take Wednesday off to recover. Thursdays and Fridays are devoted to my office practice."

"So you were at your Fox Cove address on Tuesday?"

"Yes."

"And what time did you arrive there?"

"Let me think. It was kind of late. I did some hospital rounds and stopped home briefly to get the dog. Then I picked up a few groceries. It was probably around 8:00, maybe a bit later."

"You didn't happen to stop at Becca Sterling's house?"

"No."

"Have you had much contact with her recently?" asked Sue.

"I tended to see her more often in the summer. You know, strolling the beach, that kind of thing. Not so much in the winter."

"But you did see her occasionally in the winter?"

"Yes, her and my other neighbors who are permanent residents. They often ask me to bring things from town, especially when the roads are bad. You know, prescriptions mostly, occasionally groceries. I make it a habit to check on Frances. Sharon Peterson is an old friend. And Becca's asked me to stop by and check on Ava from time to time. Becca is—" he paused and changed the verb, his face reflecting the realization, "—was a very anxious mother. She seemed to panic at every sniffle. I think that's true of first-time parents, especially older ones. Anyway, pediatrics is not my strong suit, but a cold is a cold is a cold. My showing up and listening to Ava's chest had a calming effect on Becca. Sharing a cup of coffee and some conversation also seemed to help."

"How frequently did this happen?" asked Sue.

"Only occasionally. That said, Ava seemed to have her share of colds and whatever else was going around. I remember the same thing happening when my children were small and their immune systems were still developing."

"When did you last see Becca?" asked Ray.

"Oh, I don't know. Maybe last week, perhaps the week before. It's been a busy month."

"The last time you did see her, did she seem anxious about anything? Did she share any concerns?"

"Not that I remember."

"Can you think of anyone who might want to do her harm?" asked Sue.

"No, absolutely not. Becca was sweet and kind. I can't imagine she had any enemies." He looked over at Sue and then back at Ray. "This has to be some random event. No one who knew her could harm her."

"Have you seen anyone in or around Fox Cove recently who shouldn't be there?"

"No. At this time of the year, it's just us locals."

"And, as far as you know, Becca hasn't had any visitors, anyone staying with her recently?"

"Not to my knowledge. She doesn't seem to have much company anymore, even in the summer. Not like the old days."

"Why is that?" asked Sue.

"She had moved on. The old Becca was history. After she became pregnant, she started to transition to a new place in her life, almost a new identity."

"She's a single parent, right?" asked Sue.

"Yes. As far as I know, Becca wasn't married or in a relationship."

"Do you have any idea who Ava's father is?"

Shepard's mouth twisted with irritation. "That seems like a strange question. Why do you ask?"

"We are trying to develop a complete profile of Becca Sterling's life."

"The parentage issue, that's none of my business. And, in truth, it never came up. While we were friends, the friendship was more a physician-patient relationship."

"And the subject never came up in your conversations with Sharon Peterson or any of the other people in Fox Cove?"

"No, not with me. I know people like to speculate about things like that. But I was never a party to the gossip."

"I take it you're married?" said Ray, letting his eyes rest briefly on Shepard's wedding band.

"Yes, thirty years."

"Does your wife ever go with you on these Tuesday trips to the cottage?"

"No. Olivia's a musician. Her chamber group meets at our house on Tuesday. They make an evening of it, playing music, having a late potluck supper. Nice people, but they get a bit loud, and things run late. So I escape up there for a bit of peace and quiet."

"Sir, was your wife a friend of Becca's? We're trying to talk to anyone who might know something that could help us with this investigation," explained Sue.

"Not particularly. Olivia isn't too fond of the cottage. She only shows up in the summer, mostly when the kids come home for a visit. She has this idea that there's mold in the cottage because it's so old, and that supposedly causes her allergies to flare. I can't dissuade her from that, or get her to go to an allergist, or even to try taking antihistamines. In truth, she's much more comfortable staying at our house in town. Anyway, she thinks we should tear down the cottage and replace it with a modern building."

"You spent Tuesday night at your cottage?" asked Sue.

"That was the plan. When I got there, the place was quite cold, less than sixty degrees. I discovered that the furnace was out, so I called my heating guy. He was out on a job and couldn't get out there till the next morning. I was worried about the pipes freezing. He assured me that the house wouldn't cool that much overnight."

"Who do you use?"

"Northshore Mechanical Systems. Dale, the owner, he's a patient of mine. Dale might have been just blowing smoke. Given the weather, maybe he didn't want to drive until morning."

"So you didn't stay the night?"

"No, I checked things over, then headed back to town."

"What time did you get home?" asked Sue.

"Around 11:00. It was slow going. Heavy snow."

"Were the musical activities over for the evening?" asked Ray.

"They were in the potluck phase. I said my hellos and headed off to bed."

Ray looked over at Sue for a moment, then said, "This past Tuesday, the same night the furnace went out in your cottage in Fox Cove, did you see Becca Sterling or communicate with her in any way?"

"No, absolutely not. I've answered that question already. Are we finished? My workday is far from over."

"Yes, for now," said Ray, sliding a copy of his card across the desk. "If you think of anything that might be useful to us, please call."

"What's your take on this guy?" asked Sue once they were back in her truck.

"He's been talking to Sharon Peterson, so he probably knew we'd be contacting him. I think his answers seemed a bit rehearsed. Your impression?"

"Ditto. He made sure that there was no dead air, no silences. And 'shattered and devastated.' Shepard said they were not close friends. Shattered? Devastated? Isn't that over the top?"

"It depends. Maybe the man uses superlatives. There's a lot of that going around."

Sue started the engine. Ray could practically hear her mind ticking over the details of the interview. "Given your familiarity with the chamber music scene, do you know his wife?"

"No, not by name. That said, there's a violist in one of the local string quartets who would be about the right age."

"And?"

"Well, if I have the right person, she's somewhere in her fifties, probably pushing sixty, pleasant looking, a bit matronly. She plays with great verve."

"Does she play with the blood?"

"Verve, yes, the blood, no," said Ray.

"Maybe she's more interested in her viola than her husband," said Sue, arching one eyebrow. "And Becca was a pretty woman. And, if your assessment is correct, close to twenty years younger."

"There is that. Shepard didn't answer your question as to whether his wife and Becca were friends. And he's one more interview subject who didn't take kindly to us asking about the father of Becca's child." Ray considered Dr. Shepard's self-described role in Becca Sterling's life, then said, "New subject: the prescription bottles."

"Yes," said Sue.

"What's happened with them?"

"I made a list of the meds and sent it to Dr. Dyskin. He was going to check with an epileptologist about the choice of drugs and the doses. You know, do these meds fit the current standard of practice? The bottles are locked away in the evidence room."

"Check the dates on the bottles to see when the prescriptions were filled. And what's on tap for tonight?" Ray asked.

"Yoga with the girls. I haven't been there much lately. Then a long bath and an evening of girl bonding with Simone. You?"

"Quiet evening—reading, listening to music. Probably early to bed."

"You're the life of the party, Elkins. But then, I guess I am, too."

22

Sheriff Elkins started the morning covering the first half of a day shift for one of the patrol officers. Coffee in hand, he watched the sunrise at an ice-covered marina near the tip of the county. Then he started south, going toward the western shore of the peninsula, traveling over familiar highways and lanes, checking road-ends and snow-covered seasonal byways, looking for an old Dodge truck, or at least its burned-out remains.

He was out of his car a second time, standing on the beach near a historic frame building, a century old cannery, when he got the alert from dispatch.

Siren blaring, overhead light bar flashing, Ray guided his patrol car over the snow-covered secondary road. He followed the two deep ruts in the otherwise unplowed lane, coming to a stop at the road's end, a trailhead near the lake shore. Two vehicles stood in the small parking area.

He grabbed the naloxone kit and scrambled out of his car.

"Over here, over here," a woman yelled, waving her arms. She was dressed for cross-country skiing, wisps of gray hair escaping her knit hat.

Ray followed her path through the deep snow. Thirty yards beyond the trailhead, a young woman lay collapsed against a tree. Her head was bare, her close-cut hair dyed pale blue.

"She was still breathing when I found her. Now, I'm not sure. She's got a needle in her arm," the woman explained.

Ray knelt in the snow beside the slumped figure. The young woman was wearing a down vest and a thermal shirt with the left sleeve pushed up around her biceps. Moving in close, Ray reached out and straightened her head, his gloved hand cupping her ear with its many piercings. He could see that her lips were turning blue, and her breathing was shallow and labored. He pulled off his gloves, then removed the hypodermic from her left arm, carefully placing it near the tree trunk. Then he tore open the naloxone kit. He heard Sue's voice in his mind, explaining the necessary steps to administer the drug. He had been reluctant to learn the process, as though putting it off would keep something like this from happening.

Breathing through a surge of panic, he removed the syringe from the package, pulling off the yellow caps at each end. Then he grabbed the container with the naloxone and removed its cap. He slid the nasal atomizer onto the end of the syringe, then screwed the naloxone cartridge into the barrel of the syringe.

"You can help me here," Ray said to the woman kneeling across from him. "Lift her head and tilt it back a bit. We need to keep her airway open."

Ray sprayed half of the contents into her left nostril, then sprayed the remainder into the other.

"What do we do now?" the woman asked.

"We hope," said Ray. He glanced at his watch and moved closer to the victim, observing her and listening to her breathing.

"I think she's gone," said the woman.

Ray didn't respond. His eyes moved back and forth from the victim to the sweep hand on his watch. Finally, he said, "I need to try again."

He tore open the second package and repeated the process, this time with greater confidence. The victim stirred. Her eyelids fluttered as the sound of a siren echoed through the previously silent woods. She was alive! Ray felt a rush of relief bordering on mania. And then his companion was up and moving toward the trailhead, directing the EMS team to the victim.

"I've given her two doses of naloxone," he explained to the EMTs as he rose and moved back, giving them access. He watched as the team quickly assessed the victim's condition, placed her on the stretcher, and hurriedly carried her toward the waiting ambulance.

"Thank you for your help, Ms.—?" said Ray as he started to collect the naloxone packaging scattered around him in the snow.

"You will want this, too," she responded, holding the hypodermic between the thumb and forefinger of her gloved hand. "I'm Laura Evans. When I decided to take advantage of the fresh snow, I had no idea . . ." Her voice faded off.

Ray introduced himself. Looking at her closely, he sensed her distress.

"I read about these overdoses in the paper, I see it on the news, but . . ." She went silent and looked away from Ray, wiping a tear from her cheek as she started to collect her skis and poles. "I don't understand. Such a pretty girl. So young. She has a whole life before her. How does this happen? Can it be stopped?" There was a plea in her eyes when she looked at Ray again.

He could feel her eyes burning into him. "I wish I knew," he said. "I wish I knew."

After returning to his car, Ray started the engine and turned up the radio. The public radio host was just finishing an introduction to the Strauss tone poem *Ein Heldenleben*. He sat for a long time soaking in the sound, feeling drained, and on the edge of tears.

23

Ray found Wendy Morrison in the waiting room of the emergency department at the regional medical center. She stood and gave him a quick embrace. When she pulled back, she said, "Thank you. You gave her one more chance." Tears rolled down her cheeks.

Ray had known Wendy since high school and had always viewed her as thoughtful and wise. He had lost track of her during college and beyond, but when he moved back to Cedar County, he learned that she had become one of the area's most respected psychotherapists, who often provided consulting services to the county prosecutor's office.

Sadly, he reconnected with Wendy when her youngest daughter, Cara, then only fourteen or fifteen, was arrested for driving under the influence of alcohol and marijuana and being underage. It was the first of many incidents that brought Ray and Wendy together again. At the time of Cara's first arrest, Wendy had just been widowed and was rearing three girls. While Cara's older siblings flourished, Cara stumbled from one crisis to the next. Wendy had taken Ray into her confidence. He knew how much time, energy, and money she had spent trying to find an intervention that would help Cara gain control over her substance abuse. Finally, Wendy enrolled her daughter in an out-of-state residential treatment program, and during that time Ray was out of contact with the mother and daughter.

"I didn't know Cara was back in Cedar County," Ray said.

"She was gone for two years. She made real progress. That special school did things for her that I could never have done. I thought we were finally beyond this. She wanted to go to Arizona State. But I'm out of money. Her two years in the addiction program burned through all of her college fund and most of my savings, too. And, in truth, I wanted her closer to home so I could continue to monitor things. She was furious with me, just furious.

"Finally, we reached a compromise. Cara would go to the community college, but she could live in the dorm, and she would see a therapist on a weekly basis. Everything seemed to be going well for the first few months. We had lunch once a week. I did all I could not to be intrusive. And now this. I don't know how many more chances she'll get."

Fresh tears started in her eyes and she dabbed at them with a tissue. "Is she under arrest?" she asked.

"She will be treated and released. I don't think there is any evidence that she committed a crime. We can try to question her as to where she got the drugs. I doubt if she will cooperate. People seldom do in these cases."

Wendy nodded, "Well, she's an adult now. I can't force her into a residential treatment program. I'll talk to her therapist, but beyond that, I'm out of answers. I'm running out of energy. Her sisters are coming home for a few days. We will try to work through this."

"Where are they living now?" asked Ray, trying to fill the silence.

"Reese is through college and the master's degree. She's teaching special education, working with troubled teenagers. Haley is in her second year of medical school, and I think there will be an engagement announcement during the holidays. Another medical student. A young man I like enormously." She sighed heavily. "I just don't know what happened. Cara was so much like her sisters until she hit her teens. And then, it wasn't like she just fell in with the wrong crowd—she went looking for them. I don't know what more I can do."

Ray held out one of his business cards and Wendy took it. "I hope you won't need it. I hope she'll rebound." Even as he said it, a shadow passed like a ghost across his mind. "But if you or Cara need anything at all, just call."

"Tough morning," Sue said later, peering into Ray's office.

He beckoned her in with his hand. "Thanks to you and your good instruction, I was able to administer the naloxone."

"Everything go okay?" she asked.

"Yes. I fumbled my way through it the first time. The second dose went smoother."

"Cara is lucky that you were close by."

"She is lucky she was found, lucky the woman called it in. You know, I didn't recognize her, Cara. She's not a skinny little kid anymore. Dyed hair, lots of piercings."

"How did you ID her?"

"I found her driver's license in her purse. It was on the car seat."

"Anything else easily observable?"

"McDonald's bag with trash, cigarette butts in the ashtray, and textbooks and papers in the backseat. Nothing more," said Ray. "They will try to hold Cara overnight for observation on the pretext that there may be an underlying health problem they want to look into.

"I told her mother that you would stop by and chat with Cara. I warned Wendy Morrison that her daughter was unlikely to provide us with any information on where she got the drugs. I'd like you to do that as soon as possible in case the kid decides to check herself out."

"This seems to have knocked the wind out of you."

"These deaths, it's just a kick in the chest every time it happens. We go after the dealers…with limited success. People want these drugs. That's the problem. What's going on? I don't understand. I feel helpless."

"Lighten up, friend. You saved a life."

"This time," Ray said.

"Are you okay?"

Ray thought about the question. "Not really."

"We can only do so much. You've pointed that out to me over the years. Anyway, I'm off to see Cara, and without great expectations." Sue stopped at the door and turned back toward Ray. "Isn't Hanna coming home this evening?"

"Sometime tomorrow, depending on the weather."

"Has she made a decision? Is she California bound? It's lovely out there. Palo Alto. San Francisco. I'm sure you could find something interesting to do, maybe go back to college teaching."

"I don't know what her plans are. We haven't discussed it."

"Ray, you two look like a couple. Your relationship has to be an important factor in her decision. What are you feeling about it? Don't be so damn cognitive."

"It's Hanna's choice. It's her life, her journey. If you walked in tomorrow and said you were leaving—going back to school, taking a new job, getting married and moving away—I would do nothing to dissuade you. I would miss you intensely as a colleague and as a friend, but I would know you were taking the next step in your life."

Sue gave Ray a playful smile, "If I ever tell you I am going back to Chicago to hang out with a certain lawyer known to both of us, please do everything you can to dissuade me, up to and including the use of handcuffs." She sobered. "If you love this woman, Ray, you have to let her know. That matters. Anyway, cheers."

24

It was late Saturday evening when Ray pulled into the short-term parking lot at the airport. He walked through the nearly empty facility, joining a group below the arrivals and departures board at the entrance to the airport's only concourse. He could hear hushed complaints about an additional delay to the inbound flight from Detroit. He wandered away from the group to a small lounge just off the corridor and looked through the several piles of abandoned newspapers and magazines, finally extracting a wrinkled but current copy of *The New Yorker*. He was part of the way through a lengthy treatise on the looming environmental crisis when the world slipped away. When he next opened his eyes, Hanna was calling his name and gently brushing his cheek with her hand.

"Oh, Ray. I am so sorry. I could have gotten a cab. Just one delay after another."

Ray looked up at her and smiled. "Glad you're here," he mumbled through an uncontrollable yawn. Then he slowly pushed himself out of the chair. As he stood, she slipped into his arms.

Ray wasn't wholly awake until they confronted the arctic wind and blowing snow as they crossed the parking lot. He opened the rear hatch and helped her load her suitcase. Then she handed him the large Styrofoam cube that she had been carrying. The package was held together by four bands of skillfully applied packing tape.

"What's this," he asked, "body parts?" As soon as the words were out of his mouth, he could read a change in Hanna's demeanor. His sarcasm had dulled her enthusiasm.

"A special gift for you. You get to open it if you're nice." She gave him a half-hearted grin. "I think I'd better drive. You're tired and grumpy."

"Your place or mine?" Ray asked.

"Yours, if that's okay. I was hoping to spend the weekend with you." Hanna started the engine, then got out and began brushing the snow off the car and scraping the ice-covered windshield.

Ray climbed out to help.

"I can do this. Stay inside."

He collapsed into the seat, turned the defroster on full, and then closed his eyes.

"You feeling okay?" asked Hanna as she buckled her seatbelt and headed toward the tollbooth.

"Just exhausted. Everyone in the department seems to have something, and so far I've escaped the bug. But we who remain ambulatory have been covering for the people who are too sick to come in."

"So both you and Sue are doing road patrol?"

"You know, we're a small agency. We don't have any extra resources, and I can't cut the jail staffing. Hopefully in the next few days, we'll start getting back to normal. This has never happened before."

The conversation dropped off. Ray sat silently. He was apprehensive about what Hanna might soon be telling him.

Eventually—after Hanna had slowly crawled through the city streets and reached the highway on the north edge of town—she said, "Ray, I've sent you messages and emails. You've barely answered. When you did write back, your responses were laconic at best. I don't know what's going on. You were very supportive of me looking at this opportunity. Now I feel like you've shut me out."

Ray said nothing. He just sat there, his eyes focused on the road ahead.

"Aren't you going to ask me about the job?"

"I'm sorry. I am just exhausted. Tell me about the job."

"I met the team. Tony, the head, the person who invited me to interview, is someone I met during my residency and later crossed paths with when I was in the military. I think I've told you about him. He and some of his colleagues at Stanford have major funding to research the genetics of inherited coronary disease. The team members come from a variety of disciplines. They are looking for someone with extensive surgical experience."

"Interesting people?" asked Ray.

"Intense group, lots of experience, everyone appears to be very bright. There's a real sense of mission. They think they can make some significant breakthroughs and develop new treatment approaches."

After an extended silence, Hanna continued. "I got a complete tour of the facilities, the university, and Palo Alto. They also showed me areas where I might want to live if I joined the team. I had one-on-one meals with each of the team members. It was the most intense interview process I've ever been through. That said, it was the most informative."

"So, did they offer you the position?" asked Ray.

"The team let me know there were three other candidates. Tony took me to the airport. As we were saying our goodbyes, he indicated that the job was mine if I wanted it."

"So, this Tony, is he a former love interest?"

Hanna took her time answering. "Nothing like that, Ray, not ever. He's married, has three little girls. I had dinner at his home, met his wife and children."

"Are you going to take the job?"

"I don't know. They would like an answer not too long after the first of the year." Hanna let her answer hang, then said, "Remember when you said you wouldn't ever leave Cedar County? Did you mean it? Have you thought about it at all since I told you about this job?"

Ray didn't respond.

"Ray, I feel closer to you than anyone I've ever known. You're a friend, a lover, a partner who can actually keep up with me in a kayak. I know I haven't been easy, especially in the beginning. You helped me deal with the PTSD I thought I'd never shake."

Images flashed across Ray's memory—Hanna struggling with alcohol; Hanna paddling out into almost impossible conditions as a way to push back her demons; Hanna waking in the night weeping uncontrollably, saying it was just a nightmare.

"Remember when that woman referred to us as a cute couple?" Hanna said. "I loved that. Up until that moment, I had always been the isolate—the only child, the striver, the surgeon with ice water in her veins. And because of that, because I spent so much time alone or just hooking up for sex, I'm not good at talking about feelings. I'm just beginning to learn what a relationship is about. What it means to be part of a couple. And I want us to be a couple, you and me. I don't want to go to California without you. I want to think about it as something we might do together. Would you even consider it?"

"I don't know," said Ray. "My life is so connected to this place. I can't promise you anything, but I'm willing to consider the possibility."

"Really? Okay, wow. I can work with that."

Ray could feel the relief, the joy in her voice.

Hanna parked close to Ray's front door and rolled her bag in as Ray followed with the Styrofoam container.

After he deposited it on the counter, she asked, "Aren't you going to open it?"

Ray cut through the tape with a paring knife and separated the two halves of the foam cube. Then he extracted the carefully wrapped packages.

"You seemed to be very down the last time we talked on the phone," Hanna explained. "I thought a pastrami sandwich kit from Zingerman's would lift your spirits. Sandwich therapy."

"How did you make this happen?" asked Ray. His admiration for her had grown exponentially in the past few minutes.

She smiled slyly. "When I knew I was going to have a long layover in Detroit, I called and asked if I could pick up a kit at their airport store. No problem. It was waiting for me."

"You know how to play to my weaknesses," said Ray, taking her into his arms.

25

Ray awoke to the sound of the grinder, the low hum of the espresso machine, and the high-pitched screaming hiss of milk being steamed. He started to stir as the scent of the coffee wafted in through the open door of the bedroom.

"You want your first cappuccino in bed or in the kitchen?" Hanna called.

"I'm on my way," he answered.

As he stirred some sugar into the foam he said, "I didn't hear you get up."

"You were out cold. Are you all right? I've been puttering around for more than an hour."

"Aren't you running on Pacific Time?"

"Boats are on my car," she responded.

Ray looked through a window toward the drive. He could see the kayaks strapped in the racks.

"And the weather?" he asked.

"It's about seventeen degrees, going up to a steamy twenty-two sometime this afternoon. The waves are one foot or less this a.m., starting to build in the afternoon."

"How much?"

"Well, ah, three to five coming from the south south-west. My thought is we launch at the Cannery, so we're protected, then head south. When it starts to get bumpy, we turn around and have the wind at our back. We can probably get a couple of hours on the water."

Hanna turned off the road onto the snow-covered lot. She maneuvered around the deepest drifts and parked facing the water.

"It's starting to look bumpy already," Ray observed.

"Then we better hurry," Hanna responded.

A few minutes later they were in their kayaks, bows facing the water. Hanna pushed off first, sliding down the gentle slope into the icy water. Ray followed.

They paddled west past the headland, then turned south, moving through the tall swells that danced across a shoal near the beach. As they pushed out into deeper water, the surface flattened a bit, and the heavy gray overcast parted briefly. A wedge of sunshine moved across the lake and over the dunes, and then quickly disappeared. Snow rushed in behind it, the shoreline soon disappearing behind the swirling flakes.

"Was there snow in the forecast?" Ray yelled over the roar of the wind and waves.

"Possibility of some lake effect. Scattered."

"Let's head back," said Ray.

Hanna nodded and swung her bow around. Ray followed. He peered at the compass at the front of his ice-covered deck and guessed at a heading. Then he glanced at his watch. They quickly retraced their route, aided by a following wind. The snow started to decrease before they reached the headland, providing a clear course to their takeout point.

They were securing their boats to the top of the car when Hanna said, "I'm still totally geeked. I need a walk. Aren't you glad I packed the snowshoes?"

Ray was tired, but Hanna's energy inspired him. "Have I ever taken you to the ghost forest?" he asked as they stood near the hatch of Hanna's car, securing snowshoes to their hiking boots.

"You've mentioned it, but no. What's the story?"

"Wait till we get there," said Ray. He led the way to the trailhead, where the terrain rolled gently for a mile or so before giving way to steeper slopes in the interior of the dunes. They climbed through deep drifts, moving forward one careful step at a time. Then they crossed ice-covered hillsides, the steel teeth on the snowshoes cutting into the glaze. Finally, Ray stopped on the crest of a ridge above a wind-swept plain overlooking a steep dune that ran down to the water. Whitecaps marched toward the shore. The Manitou Islands were obscured by the blowing snow.

"Not much left now," said Ray, pointing to the weathered remains of a cedar forest randomly scattered across the side of a dune.

They moved in among the ruins—branchless gray trunks, the bark and softer wood stripped away by eons of blowing sand. A few of the trunks remained vertical. The rest were bent at odd angles or strewn across the slope.

"When I was a kid," said Ray, "there really was a forest here, long dead, but mostly intact. Hundreds of years ago the cedar flourished in a patch of soil. Then the trees were covered with sand. Eventually, the sand was blown away again, and only the skeletons remained. And slowly the forest has almost disappeared, rotting away or being carried away by summer people for beach fires. This is a place I've always loved, and now it's just a ghost of what it was. In a few more years the forest that once existed here will just be a memory, a curiosity that only exists in yellowing photos."

"A surf and turf day. I could tell you were tired after kayaking. Thank you for putting up with my hyperactivity and taking me up to the ghost forest," said Hanna as she scurried around the kitchen preparing a meal. Ray opened a bottle of red wine, poured two glasses, and watched.

"How do these look?" asked Hanna as she plated the two pastrami sandwiches.

"Without a side-by-side comparison of one just off the grill in Ann Arbor, I can't be exactly sure. The taste is the most important criterion."

"Well, sit and have a bite," she said, carrying the plates to the table.

Ray followed with the wine, settling across from her and cutting the thick sandwich in half.

"I think you've nailed it," he said after carefully chewing his first bite.

"You're smiling, Ray. I haven't seen you smile since I got back."

"Thanks for this," said Ray.

"Twice today, first this morning and then after our nap, I beat you out of bed. That's a personal best for me. That's never happened before. This morning I got you moving with the promise of coffee. And just now I think the promise of pastrami pulled you from the sheets."

"Pavlovian on your part," said Ray.

"Eat," Hanna directed. "It's only hot from the pan for so long."

Hanna held the conversation to small talk for the rest of the meal. But as they worked to clear away the dishes, she said, "I've never known you to be a slugabed."

Ray didn't respond.

"You sent me a message about administering naloxone."

"Did I?"

"Well, not much of a note. A sentence or two."

"I guess I forgot. I was unnerved. We've been struggling with the drug epidemic for a long time. But kneeling there, hoping that this young woman would start breathing again . . ." A mild echo ran through him of the surge of panic he'd felt wondering if he would be able to administer the naloxone properly. "I don't know how to explain it. Suddenly this girl's life was in my hands. I guess I was lucky. I managed to help her get back. At first, I had this kind of rush, seeing her breathing and finally opening her eyes. But that didn't last long. After it was all over, I sat in my car for awhile feeling hopeless and empty."

"I understand," Hanna responded.

"I know you do. Better than most people."

Hanna inhaled deeply. "For me, some of the nightmares never go away. You've held me in the night. You know that I still see those young soldiers. Some days we had miracles, but too often they were damaged beyond repair. I don't know any of their names, those who lived or died, but I do remember their faces. Maybe just composites, filled with agony, dread, and fear. Too young, too fragile.

"The way I keep going, Ray, is that I push that back. Most of my patients now walk out, even if they arrived by ambulance. I see how they're connected to a family. Even if I've only helped them get a few more years, I know what I do is essential.

"And that's what you do, so much more than just protecting a community. You're a social worker, a psychologist, and a friend."

Ray cut her off. "Did you get some Zingerman's brownies?"

"Elkins, you're impossible."

26

"How was the weekend?" asked Sue, carefully arranging her laptop, a stack of folders, and a plastic evidence bag on the conference table before settling in a chair across from Ray. "Hanna get back all right?"

"After a fashion. Her plane was delayed. The scheduled arrival was at 8:00. The flight came in way after midnight. She found me sleeping in a chair in the waiting area."

"Any decision on her plans?"

"The job is hers if she wants it."

"So did you and Hanna talk about it, Ray, or did you kick the can down the road?"

"Quiet Sunday. Heavy snow. We slept in. Then went to the big lake." Ray looked over at Sue. He was still noodling things over. In his mind, nothing had been resolved.

"How was kayaking?"

"The waves were just too big for a long paddle. We snowshoed across the dunes for a while, too."

Ray held up a clipboard. "And a quiet weekend here, too. Other than fender benders, people in ditches, and a few DUIs, nothing much happened, according to the reports from the shift commanders."

"What I was asking about was whether you and Hanna managed to talk about her job interview?"

"Not much."

"Elkins," she said, shaking her head.

Ray moved the conversation forward without responding. "So I have this note from you rescheduling our meeting to 11:00 because you are going to be in town to meet a UPS driver. What's that about?"

"This weekend I was reading your interview notes with Frances Adams. She mentioned that the UPS driver comes late in the day. As you know, I've started doing background checks on anyone who was regularly in the Fox Cove area. When I went through the recycling bin in Sterling's garage, a high percentage of the boxes came via UPS. So I thought I'd start there. I was at the regional distribution center well before 8:00 this morning. I wanted to meet the driver before he was on the road. I started with the supervisor, explaining that my questions were part of a murder investigation. The woman, Jill, got all upset, saying that she'd have to clear things with corporate before she could share any delivery records or let me talk to the driver involved. After she gave me a spiel on their corporate commitment to confidentiality, I assured her that I wasn't interested who the shippers were, and I didn't even want the name of the recipients. All I need to know was if a package was delivered to Sterling's address last Tuesday, and if so, could I chat with the driver. I reminded her again that this was part of a murder investigation and the driver might have seen something that could be helpful in solving the crime. She finally relented. First, she checked to see if there had been a delivery to that address. Yes, a package was dropped off at 7:23 p.m. Then Jill walked me out to the terminal area and introduced me to Earl Hawkins. He's the regular driver on the route that includes Fox Cove. Jill explained why I was there. Hawkins seemed shaken by the news."

Sometimes Sue got caught up in the details of a story. "And?" Ray asked impatiently.

"Ray, I know you've seen this man over the years. Big mirrored sunglasses in the summer, sandy hair, starting to go gray. The guy always seems happy. I've driven by him or seen him out of his vehicle making deliveries hundreds of times."

"Okay."

"Hawkins said he often delivered to that address. It is near the end of the route. I asked him about last Tuesday. Jill, who stayed with us the whole time monitoring our conversation, verified that he had dropped off a package on Tuesday at 7:34 p.m. He said his typical pattern is to park at the foot of the drive, carry the box to the porch, scan it, and ring the bell before starting down the hill.

"I asked him if he noticed anything special about Tuesday. Hawkins was slow in answering, like he was pondering the question. He said during the winter the drive was usually empty. He assumed the woman's car was in the garage, but he remembers a car parked near the door on Tuesday. I pressed him as to make and model. He thought it was black, fairly new, and foreign. Maybe a small SUV or a crossover. Of course, I asked him about the plate. He didn't notice."

"Did you learn anything else from this man?"

"He said he saw Sterling a lot during the warmer months. She and her daughter were often outside and greeted him. He commented on the beautiful child, the friendly woman, and the tragedy of it all. Seemed sincere. Nothing inappropriate."

"So how does this fit?" asked Ray.

"I spent the weekend at home with Simone and a laptop. I had uninterrupted time to organize everything, carefully study the autopsy report, read interview notes, and try possible scenarios. And then there's some new info. The DNA samples from the scene's bed sheets, the victim's panties and the material recovered at autopsy went to the Michigan State Police lab on Thursday. It's been processed. There were two distinct DNA profiles found on the sampled materials. Obviously, one was identified as Becca's. The second DNA profile was submitted to the Combined DNA Index System. There were no hits. Becca's lover has not been arrested for a felony, at least not in Michigan." She considered what she'd just said. "There's something sort of grubby about this. Messing with someone's privacy."

"Agreed," said Ray. He leaned forward as if he was going to add something, then sat back. His thoughts were conveyed without being articulated.

"But you will find this interesting," continued Sue, opening the top of a plastic bin. After rummaging around for a moment or two, she extracted a clear plastic bag containing an amber prescription bottle. She passed it over to Ray. "Remember how you asked me to check Becca Sterling's prescription bottles?"

Ray held the bottle in front of him and carefully read the label. "What's Macrobid?"

"It's an antibiotic."

"What's it used for?"

"Bladder infections, according to WebMD. So Becca probably had one. But that's not the point. Look at the label carefully."

Ray held it at arm's length to read the fine print. "Prescribed by Brian Shepard, MD. And it's written for Brian Shepard."

"The date, Ray."

"That was last Tuesday, wasn't it?"

"Yes. So the good doctor who occasionally brought out prescriptions for some of his neighbors seems to have forgotten that he stopped by Becca's with the one you're holding. I checked her smartphone. Seems she and Shepard very occasionally messaged one another. Nothing incriminating. No Xs and Os. But let me read the last message."

Sue looked down at her notes. "I'm quoting here. 'Old problem seems to be back. Please pick up meds for me.' The message was sent on Tuesday at 10:34 a.m. The message was read at 4:47 p.m. He told us he stopped for some groceries. Maybe he did, but while he was there, he wrote a script for Macrobid in his name and probably ran it through his prescription plan. Then he stopped by to deliver this to Becca." She looked across at Ray. "Go ahead, say it."

"I don't need to say it if you know what I'm thinking. You assume that DNA matches Shepard's."

"You've taught me to assume nothing. But I think it's a strong possibility. If Shepard was in the military at some point, we might try to get a match in the DOD DNA Registry. I've investigated that route. It's complicated, slow, and we'd need to get the blessing of a federal court."

"How slow?"

"Probably months."

"The rest of the messages on her phone, the ones to or from Shepard. No hint of romance?" asked Ray.

"Like I said, there were only a few and all were very businesslike. Most were related to Ava."

"Did she have Snapchat or similar apps?"

"No," answered Sue. "Nothing like that."

"How about her computer?"

"I've just started looking through it. Dr. Shepard is in her contacts file with his email and iPhone. I found nothing when I searched on his email address. That said, there was another phone number, a landline with an extension number. I called the number and it's Shepard's office number. And, interestingly enough, Becca also has a landline in addition to her cell."

"Where are you going with this?" asked Ray.

"If you were involved in an extramarital affair and had a suspicious wife, why not use the landline in your office rather than taking a chance of having her find something on the iPhone you've carelessly left around the house? But, going back to Earl Hawkins, UPS, and the black car. I did a quick check. A black Series 3 BMW Sports Wagon and a Honda Odyssey van are registered to Brian Shepard. We need to check out his alibi with his wife. Then we have to sit down with the good doctor and see if he can be a bit more truthful."

Ray nodded. "Did you get a chance to talk with Cara Morrison?" he asked.

"Yes," Sue said, "but our encounter was brief. Cara was in the process of checking herself out."

"Did you learn anything?"

"Yes, to a limited degree. Cara is a complicated young woman. She was totally tuned into me. I suspected she was trying to figure out how to play me. I was in mufti, but I might as well have been in uniform. She was wary of me. At times she was a victim.

Occasionally, she was an almost perky college kid. It was interesting watching her flip from one persona to the next."

"Any word on where she got the drugs?"

"The usual disinformation. She bought the drugs somewhere downstate at a party. Thinks the guy's name was Keith or George and can't remember what he looked like. Cara was pleasant enough until that point. Then she suddenly got very hostile, said she didn't have to answer my questions, and told me to leave." Sue inhaled deeply. "I did my best, Ray. I've thought about the interview a lot. I don't know what triggered the anger."

"I'm sure it had nothing to do with you."

Sue sat quietly for a moment. "You know I would like to have kids. Then I look at Cara. I can't imagine what it would be like to have a child with an addiction."

Ray recalled the slump in Wendy Morrison's shoulders. What was the nature of a force strong enough to make a parent give up on her own child?

27

Sue slowed and turned off the highway onto a long circular drive that ran to the large home above the lake.

"When is your replacement vehicle coming?" asked Ray.

"A few more days. Then it will take a day or two to transfer over the extra equipment from my wrecked truck."

She pounded her fist against the dash. "'The Dodge that refuses to die.' That's what they call this beast at the county garage. I sensed that there was absolute delight among the good old boys that this was the only vehicle they could offer me."

"Well, they did a terrific job prepping up a beautiful new vehicle for you. And then, a couple of weeks later you totaled it."

"Yeah. Sure," Sue responded, parking near the front entrance.

As they moved under the columned portico, the front door swung open, and Ray took in the dark-haired woman in the running suit, noticing the tight impatience of her mouth. Her voluminous garb was filled by her ample physique.

"Mrs. Shepard?" said Ray.

"Olivia. Most people call me Liv. We'll take coffee in the kitchen."

Shepard led the way across an expanse of white carpeting in a formal living room toward the lakeside of the house. A carafe of coffee and three mugs were already set up on a long granite island in the kitchen. Ray settled on one of the stools at the side of the counter and ran his fingers over the smooth, cool stone. The ebony surface stood in marked contrast to the stainless steel appliances and white floor, walls, and drapery. His eyes searched the room for hints of color. He found none.

"Mrs. Shepard, this is Detective Sue Lawrence," said Ray.

"Thank you for agreeing to meet with us on such short notice," said Sue.

"I'm happy to help. Brian told me about his conversation with you. He said he thought you might want to talk to me also."

"Yes," answered Sue. "As you know, we're investigating the suspicious death of Becca Sterling. We've talked to the winter residents of Fox Cove, including your husband. You're the only one we haven't had a chance to chat with yet."

"Well, I'm sure Brian told you that I hardly ever go out there during the winter. Our place, it's an old drafty barn," she said as she poured coffee into the three mugs. "Cream and sugar?" she asked, pointing to the cut-glass containers.

"Have you been out there in recent months?" asked Sue.

"No, I haven't been there since late August. That's when Lindsay—she's our youngest, lives in New York—showed up with her current boyfriend. Lindsay attaches all kinds of romantic ideas to that old place. I'm terrified that when the time comes she's going to want one of those dreadful beach weddings—mosquitoes, flies, people drinking and smoking on the perimeters. I've played way too many of those . . . Pachelbel's Canon versus the roar of jet skis. And I can't imagine how we'd ever get that decrepit old shed ready for a wedding." She looked toward the floor-to-ceiling windows that overlooked the bay and then mused, "I guess we could bring in lots of those beautiful tents. Let the caterers use the cottage as a staging area."

"So you never accompany your husband on his Tuesday night trips to the cottage?" asked Ray. As she had been talking, he'd been noticing her meticulously applied makeup: carefully painted fine black lines around her eyes, eye shadow shimmering on her lids, plum colored lip liner and lipstick.

"No. As I'm sure he told you, that's chamber music night. I don't violate his need for a respite at the shore, and he doesn't infringe on my music. Besides, he doesn't particularly like chamber music, and I think he finds my friends loud and silly. His heading out to the hermitage with his dog is a good thing for both of us."

"How well did you know Becca Sterling?"

"Oh, hardly at all. I've seen her over the years, of course, but I've seldom talked with her in any depth, if there was any depth, indeed, to plumb. If I ran into her on the beach or at Art's, we exchanged greetings. Other than that, I had little contact with her." She paused for a moment and carefully made eye contact with each of them. "Brian's dowry included the family cottage and his college debt. I should add the cottage came with all its mythical connections to that sandy patch of beach and all the characters who ever walked those shores. So Brian has lots of memories of Becca and her family and all the other inhabitants of Fox Cove, living and dead. Over time, Becca certainly has provided the neighborhood with some interesting gossip."

"Such as?" said Sue.

"This goes back a few years, to when she was, I guess, a fairly well-known fashionista. During those summers her compound was crawling with, I don't know what to call them, a strange collection of people. Exotics, that's what they were. People you'd find in summer communities on the East Coast or Europe. And over at Becca's, the bar was always open. On beach days, the women were in string bikinis, and the guys were in those thongy contraptions. Everyone seemed to be holding a drink. The summer Becca was pregnant, I mean like really pregnant, she continued on in her bikini.

"I'm an enormously open-minded person, but I thought her behavior and the behavior of her friends was inappropriate to our summer colony. Most of the people I talked to held similar views. I don't know much more about her other than a few rumors. And I don't engage in those kinds of conversations."

"The gossip that you did hear, was any of it malicious? Do you know if she had any enemies or was involved in any controversies, whether in Fox Cove or anywhere else?" asked Sue.

"No, nothing like that. About all I know was conveyed to me over glasses of white wine. Postmenopausal women sharing scandalous tidbits, sometimes with a sense of longing, if you get my drift. I don't think I have anything more to tell you, and my

Nabokov reading group is coming for lunch. So, if there's nothing else … ?"

Olivia Shepard gestured toward several platters arranged along a counter, one with small sandwiches, another with an array of petite cupcakes, and a third with chocolates. Wine glasses were lined up at one side.

"One more thing," said Sue. "Your husband told us he didn't spend the night at your cottage last Tuesday evening, that there was some problem with the furnace. Could you verify what time he returned home that night?"

Olivia Shepard's eyes hardened. "You don't suspect him of being involved in . . . ?"

"We're trying to determine who was in the area near the time of Becca Sterling's death. We're hoping that someone saw something that could lead us to her assailant," answered Sue.

"I can't say exactly. We were having a late supper, as we usually do. It was probably around 10:30 or 11:00 when he and that dog of his came marching through. I invited him to join us, but he just gave us a wave. He seemed out of sorts, maybe because the furnace foiled his plans. He and Bo slept in the guest room at the other end of the house. I didn't see him again until the next morning."

"And there's no possibility he might have gone out again?"

"I didn't check on him, if that's what you're asking."

"One more thing," said Sue. "You haven't been in contact with Becca Sterling in recent months, have you?"

"Oh, heavens no. Like I said, I haven't even seen her since summer, late August, probably. That's the last time I was out to Fox Cove."

Sue engaged the key, the starter motor groaned, the engine sputtered briefly, and then stopped. She looked over at Ray. "Do you think Mrs. Shepard has jumper cables?"

"Even if she did, I can't imagine she would tolerate our interrupting the Nabokov luncheon preparations. Did you check out the snacks?"

"Quickly. I knew you would give me a complete report."

Ray gave her a long look. "Give the beast another try. I'll cross my fingers."

The engine started, and Sue said, "You brought us luck. Thanks."

They sat for a few moments as the motor warmed up.

"It was difficult for me to picture Mrs. Shepard playing the viola with verve," Sue said.

"Yes, she is somewhat stiff," said Ray. "I didn't see a hint of affect in our conversation. She talked about Becca but didn't mention that she was dead. Her husband was 'without words' and 'shattered.' Nothing like that from Olivia. Granted, he spent a lot more time in Fox Cove over the years than she did."

"Maybe she has suspicions about her husband and Becca," Sue suggested.

"I was wondering about that. She did give him an alibi."

"Yes," agreed Sue. "But if he was off sleeping somewhere in the hinterlands of that gigantic house, he could have slipped out unnoticed."

"Yes. I was looking for a video security system. There's a camera over the garage and one above the entrance door. I wonder how long the video is archived."

"I loved her line about him bringing the old cottage and his college debts to the marriage. Given that their city house is on four or five hundred feet of the lakefront, I wonder what she brought to the marriage?" Sue looked over at Ray. "I bet you'd like a kitchen like that."

"No. It was too perfect. It looked unused. I'm more comfortable with my collection of battered pots and pans, and scarred cutting boards."

"Everything about the house seemed too perfect. Even Olivia's makeup," said Sue.

"I noticed the makeup, too. Maybe we're beginning to understand the good doctor's need to hang out at his old cottage in the company of a dog."

28

W ith the heavy automatic rifle strapped to his back—barrel up, stock down—Toby Osmann crept laboriously up the steep incline, poles providing leverage, snowshoes compacting the deep drifts that covered the long-abandoned slopes of the shuttered ski resort. He stopped from time to time, pulling in the cold air, waiting for his breathing to slow. Then he trudged on, each step becoming more strained as he crawled toward the summit, the thick leather sling cutting into his chest and shoulder.

Finally, he reached the top of the slope and slowly took in his surroundings. The wind howled across the bare branches of the oaks and maples and the skeletons of the derelict machinery. Lightning pulsated through the dark, dismal overcast. Thunder followed—low rumbles in the distance, sharp percussive claps up close.

"Thundersnow, thundersnow, here we go, thundersnow," Toby chanted hoarsely as he struggled to move from the west-facing slope he had ascended to the steep terrain on the other side of the ridge. He stopped under the monolithic bull wheel of an old chairlift, a ring of dark steel balanced horizontally on a thick vertical shaft. The occasional lightning flashes gave form and dimension to the decaying structure.

Toby moved forward, stopping at the top hut of the lift, next to the decaying ramp where skiers had once come off the chairlift and set off down the slope again. He slid the strap from his shoulder and cautiously leaned the rifle against the hut. Releasing his snowshoes, he explored the higher end of the ramp, carefully probing the downward sloping surface with a ski pole to see if the deck would hold his weight.

After scooping out a cavity in the blanket of snow covering the ramp, he crawled, on hands and knees, into the hollow and peered at the valley below. The occasional flashes of lightning made the chairlift, the buildings beyond, and the forest at the perimeter of the ski area visible for a few seconds at a time.

Toby retrieved the rifle and returned to the ramp. Kneeling, he pulled off his gloves and worked to open the two-legged stand at the front of the barrel, a clumsy mechanism requiring the loosening and retightening of four wing nuts. The cold and darkness slowed his progress, his fingers quickly stiffening as he struggled with the corroded apparatus. Finally, he brought the rifle parallel to the surface of the deck and pushed the bipod stand forward, down the ramp, bringing the barrel in line with objects below.

Toby rubbed his hands together vigorously, then retrieved a cartridge clip from an interior pocket of his jacket. After pulling back the operating rod, he turned the rifle ninety degrees counterclockwise, the barrel rotating in a sleeve on the stand. Shivering, he struggled to push the clip into the receiver at the front of the trigger guard. Finally, the clip clicked into place. He rotated the rifle back to firing position and pushed the operating rod forward, loading the first round from the clip into the chamber. Then he lifted the rear sight into a vertical position. Yanking his gloves back on, Toby rested for a few moments, his hands tucked into his armpits, his body rocking back and forth as he tried to warm himself.

"Thundersnow, thundersnow, thundersnow. Here we go, go, go."

Sliding into a prone position, he pulled the stock tight against his shoulder, positioned his index finger on the trigger, and waited.

Dull light fluttered in the distance followed by low, rumbling thunder.

Minutes ticked away.

Again and again, flickering lightning, distant thunder.

Toby fought back the cold, tried to keep from shivering.

Then, suddenly, the blazing white light flashed around him. The earth shook. He breathed in the metallic ozone scent. Then the landscape went dark again as a fierce percussive wave echoed across the rolling terrain.

Toby focused on a dark shape beyond the bottom lift hut, a gray rectangular shadow. He squeezed the trigger—a short burst, sparks flying as hot brass ricocheted off cold steel. He relaxed his finger before the thunder diminished.

Drunk with joy, panting, he waited for another lightning strike. The storm intensified overhead. With each powerful rumble, a burst or two of bullets collided with unseen targets.

Then the weapon went silent. He extracted the clip and inserted a second, carefully pocketing the first. Shifting his body to the right, he swung the barrel toward the target. With each new clap of thunder, he fired a burst, giggling and chanting until the gun went silent again.

"Toby, Toby, Toby is done, done, done," he sang over and over as he packed up the ammunition, hefted the gun, and slowly retraced his steps off the summit and back down the slope, falling forward a few times during his descent. Once on the flat ground again, he unclipped his snowshoes and headed toward the van waiting in the shadows on a two-track.

"I done good, good, good. Getting even is so much fun. Firing Toby was really dumb."

"I knew you would, would, would," answered the hunched over figure at the wheel.

He collapsed into the passenger seat. The driver pulled the dilapidated vehicle onto the highway, switched on the headlights, and headed south on the deserted road.

29

Ray sat in the passenger seat, cell phone to his ear. Finally, he clicked off and turned toward Sue.

"New destination."

"Something more important than lunch?" asked Sue.

"We're going back to the scene of the crime. The great snowmobile heist. Head toward Mount Ski-no-more."

"What's going on?" asked Sue.

"Dispatch just took a call from a Howard Rankin. That's the guy that leases the old equipment barn, the original resting place of the truck and snowmobiles. Rankin reports gunfire hit the building. Rather than sending road patrol, dispatch thought we might want to check it out."

"They got that right," said Sue as she pulled to the side of the road, waited for a few cars to pass, and then made a U-turn. A few hundred yards down the road, she pulled onto a secondary road and headed west toward the big lake.

"There's no hurry," said Ray, peering out at the snow-covered road.

"I just want to find that perp and nail him."

"Hell has no fury—" Before he could finish his sentence, Sue jerked the car violently to the right, trying to avoid a deep pothole.

The Beast shuddered violently as the right front tire dropped into the deep crater and then climbed out of it. Sue slowed and moved toward the side of the road. She was standing, looking at the tire, by the time Ray extracted himself from the vehicle and climbed over the snow bank next to his door.

"Don't say anything," she said, staring at the flat tire.

"We don't want to get run over changing a tire halfway in the road. See if you can get it to limp over to that driveway," said Ray, pointing.

"I wonder if this crate even has a spare or a jack," said Sue, climbing back into the car. She turned the key, and the worn engine begrudgingly sputtered to life, now emitting a loud, syncopated roar. She looked over at Ray, shaking her head.

"Muffler," he said. "I wonder what else has shaken loose."

Fifteen minutes later, after struggling with a cumbersome jack and rusted lug nuts, they were on the road again, the unmuffled engine bellowing as Sue accelerated, rumbling and backfiring when she took her foot off the pedal.

Ray looked over at Sue. He could feel her frustration. "Cheer up, kid. We've been able to get outside and enjoy the first sunshine in weeks."

"Sure, boss."

As they approached the old ski area, they could see two men on snowmobiles near the large pole barn on the perimeter of the property. Sue parked near them.

"You better get that thing fixed. You can get ticketed for excessive noise," said the older of the two, chuckling as he extended a hand first toward Sue, then Ray.

"I'm Howard Rankin. This here is my son, Jack."

Ray glanced down at his notes. "You're the man who leases this building?"

"Yes. I talked to one of your deputies a few days ago when I noticed my truck and some old snowmobiles had gone missing. And now this," he said, leading them toward the large open door at the front of the building.

Rankin crossed the threshold and stopped. After they came to his side in the gloomy interior, he pointed toward the back wall of the building. "Look at all those holes. Some are clustered, others are, well I don't know."

"When did you first notice this?" asked Sue.

"Just this morning. I called you guys as soon as I saw the damage. My son is visiting for a few weeks. We were out riding, enjoying the sunshine. I just stopped by here to check on things given what just happened."

"Any other damage?" asked Ray.

"Yes. Let me turn on the lights," said Rankin as he walked back toward the door. Then they followed him around the interior. "As you can see, there is damage from bullets here and there. A window was hit on the tractor over there. There are a few holes in the sheet metal of that piece of equipment. I don't know if there's damage to the mechanics. There's also a deflated tire. The shooter couldn't possibly see what he was hitting. So why shoot randomly through walls?"

"Any idea when this happened?" asked Sue as she started to photograph the damage.

"Sometime in the last few days. I haven't been back since the day the truck disappeared."

"Do you live nearby?"

"About a mile and a half. My farm is just on the other side of the next ridge."

"Anyone live closer than you?" asked Sue.

"No, not anymore."

"Have you heard any gunfire in recent days?"

"No," said Rankin.

Ray looked up at the wall, counting the places where daylight was showing through the steel siding. "There are fifteen or so holes in that wall. Wouldn't you have heard that much gunfire?"

"That's the interesting thing about our place, Sheriff. Even in the old days when this place was open, with all the speakers on the lift towers blaring music during the ski season, we couldn't hear it. That ridgeline is plenty steep, sends the noise straight up. It must work like those concrete walls you see along expressways."

"Where do you think the shots came from?" asked Sue.

"Well, you can sort of guess from the angle. The shooter had to be somewhere high on that hill on the other side of the building. We were going to go up there and explore, but we didn't want to mess anything up. We decided to wait for you."

"Let's go and have a look," said Ray.

After exiting the building, they walked to the slope side of the building. Ray turned to Rankin. "I see what you mean. They had to be high on that hill."

"My best guess is that they were up there somewhere near the top of the lift," Rankin said. "We can run you up there, unless, of course, you want the exercise." He looked at Ray. "The snow is kind of deep, even with the current thaw."

"We'll ride," said Sue.

With Ray on the back of Rankin's sled, and Sue holding onto Jack, they circled halfway around the hill and started their ascent on a long gentle slope that meandered to the top. Ray and Sue climbed off the machines and slowly followed a trail to the lip of the east-facing slope, Sue studying the impressions made in the snow. They stopped under the bull wheel and looked at the unloading platform of the lift with the sloped ramp at the front lip.

"You can see it all, can't you?" said Ray.

"Yes," answered Sue. "I want to record some video here. You can visualize the shooter's movements. The snow tells the story. And you can see his field of fire—the chairs, probably the lift house at the bottom, and that storage building."

"Brass?" asked Ray.

"There will be lots of it," Sue said, tucking her mittens into her jacket. She pulled some rubber gloves from a plastic bag and then passed the bag to Ray. "Time to do some digging."

Sue started raking the snow with open fingers on the right side of the indentation made by the shooter's body.

"Bingo," she said, pulling a shell casing from the snow. She held it so Ray could see the brass cylinder.

".30-06."

"Exactly," she responded, dropping it into an evidence bag.

They worked their way through the snow on the right side of the platform.

"Where are we?" asked Ray a few minutes into the dig.

"We've got a dozen. That's enough to get started on for prints. I'll come back with a metal detector and look for the rest."

"And while you're doing that . . ."

"Yes, go back to the Lake Michigan shore and see if there is brass like this at the place the duck hunters pointed out," said Sue. "Thirty ought six. I wonder what type of weapon."

"Semi-automatic, hunting rifle. Just speculation, but the shooter ran through a lot of ammo. Let's go back down. I want to see if there was any damage to the area around the lower lift house."

Ray and Sue, accompanied by Howard Rankin and his son, walked around the lift house and machinery at the bottom of the hill, noting the numerous fresh penetrations to wood and sheet metal on the lower lift house.

"Looks like the shooter was just spraying bullets, hoping to hit something," observed Rankin. "And in the process, he managed to hit most things."

"Yes," agreed Ray as the two of them started walking back toward the storage building.

"Are you the sole tenant of the storage building?" asked Ray.

"Yes."

"And you farm some of the fields around here?"

"Yes. I mostly have orchards—cherries and apples," said Rankin. "I started doing field crops when that property came available." He motioned toward a large covered plateau to the northeast. "It's another income stream, insurance, of sorts, on bad fruit years."

"Is there anyone unhappy with you or what you're doing?"

"Not at all. I bought the property from an estate. It had been lying fallow for years. The heirs were happy to unload it. I leased the pole barn from the bank that holds the paper on the area. I needed someplace to store some extra equipment."

"So you can't think of anyone who might be doing this as a way of harassing you?"

"No, not at all. I've never had any kind of vandalism."

"And you didn't run any deer hunters off your property during the last month or so?"

"No, never," laughed Rankin. "Don't want to mess with those people. They tend to be armed. In truth, Sheriff, the only hunters I've seen in years are my neighbors, and only a few of them hunt. I think this is vandalism of some sort, mindless stuff. In the summer there are kids around quite often, teenagers. Abandoned places are magnetic. You probably know better than me. But once winter settles in, there's no one about, except for occasional snowmobilers."

"Mr. Rankin, given the damage to your equipment stored in this barn, this is a case of malicious destruction of property, a felony. The shell casings we found at the top of the lift are .30-06. This damage was not caused by some teenager taking potshots with a .22. These cartridges," Ray held up one of the evidence bags, "were designed to cause death and destruction. The pole barn you use has been broken into, your truck has been stolen, and now this. I'm concerned, and I think you should be, too. Is there anything more you would like to tell me?"

Rankin's eyes met Ray's. "No, Sheriff. I am baffled. I live in an isolated spot. I have known my neighbors for decades. I can't think of another case of vandalism happening to any of us."

"I'll make sure our road patrol officers roll through here on a regular basis. They've already been alerted to watch for your truck. If you see anything that concerns you, please call immediately. And alert your neighbors. Let us know if you see any vehicles or people around who shouldn't be here."

"Will do, Sheriff."

"One more thing, this building is a crime scene. Sue will need access to make a photographic record of the damage and collect additional evidence if possible."

Rankin pointed toward an entry door on the southeast corner of the building. "That's how they got in. They kicked that side door and then opened the main door."

Ray could see Sue talking to Jack near the road. He gave her a wave and watched the two of them start in his direction.

After exchanging handshakes with Howard Rankin, Ray settled into the car and started checking his messages. A few minutes later, Sue ended a conversation with Jack and slid into the driver's seat.

Sue keyed the ignition. The engine turned over once, then went dead.

As they emerged from the vehicle, Jack asked, "Need a jump?"

Sue nodded sheepishly.

"No problem," Rankin said with a smile. "I'll run to my place and get some cables and a truck."

Ray went back to his messages and Sue drifted off with Jack in the direction of the pole building.

As he hooked up the jumper cables to the Beast, Rankin joked, "I'm going to remember this the next time the county requests a tax hike."

On their way back toward the county government center, Ray said, "You seemed to be having some intense conversations with Jack."

"Interesting man," said Sue. "His mom died this past August. Jack said at the time he was only able to get away for a few days. He's been keeping in touch almost daily with his father since then by phone. He said he could tell his dad was really in the dumps, so he arranged to spend most of December up here. I guess he can do some of his work via computer."

"What does he do?"

"What does every nice-looking, unmarried, interesting man that I meet do? He's a lawyer, of course. And he lives in New York City."

"Maybe it's in the stars."

"Sure, in the stars. Elkins, I bet you don't even know what your sign is."

"Sagittarius rising?"

"Not even close, buddy," she said.

"Did you suggest to Jack that having one's property shot up with a high caliber rifle is not the norm for vandalism up here?"

"I didn't have to. Jack picked up on that immediately and was very concerned."

"Did he have any ideas about possible suspects?"

"No, he said it was inexplicable. That was the word he used, 'inexplicable.' He wondered if we were holding back information. What did you learn from his dad?"

"He's never experienced anything like this, and I think it's safe to say that he doesn't think it's directed toward him. He's never been on our radar, has he?"

"Not during my time."

"Don't head back just yet," said Ray. "Circle to the northwest side of the area. Let's see if we can find the place where the shooter made his ascent."

Once they were back on the highway, Ray said, "Watch for a two-track coming up on your left. If it's possible, park, and we'll hike in."

"No mystery here," said Sue looking at the tracks left by snowshoes and poles on the hillside.

"They had to park over there," said Ray, heading toward the end of the trail with Sue on his heels. "Anything worth casting?"

"Not that I can see," said Sue. "Everything is pretty much obliterated by rain and snow."

They sat in silence for short time. Finally, Sue asked, "What are you thinking?"

"Heavy weapon, .30-06 brass. I don't know. I have these nightmare scenarios." Ray fell silent.

"So what do you want to do?"

"Let's go back to the office. I want to get three things in place. First, make sure all the patrol officers know about this incident. I want everyone to be reminded to use extreme caution. Then I want a press release that details the vandalism here and asks for help from the community. Also, I want the patrol officers in this sector to give the ski area and Rankin's place special attention every shift until further notice. And remind people to call for backup if they encounter anything suspicious."

"Anything else?"

"Yes, see if Rankin is on the radar. It's curious that he's been the recipient of two acts of vandalism in the last week. I'd like to know what that's about."

Okay. How about lunch?"

"Let's do a drive-by so we can eat at our computers. And there's one more thing. See if the motor pool has something that starts consistently and has a muffler. I want to see if I can catch Dr. Shepard at his office this afternoon. I want you with me. And it would be nice if we didn't have to ask him for a jumpstart after we leave."

"While I'm driving, why don't you get started with the report."

30

"I'm sorry we have to impose on your time again, Dr. Shepard," said Ray as he and Sue settled across from him in his consultation room. Ray wasn't actually sorry, since the doctor was the one wasting people's time, and he felt a small sense of satisfaction when Dr. Shepard's face reddened.

"Well, I know you talked to my wife yesterday," Dr. Shepard said. "I thought that would've more than adequately substantiated my earlier answers."

"As we obtain new information, we often have additional questions," said Ray. "It's a process of connecting the dots. I imagine it's a bit like medical diagnosis."

"Well, then, what new symptoms merit this intrusion, to use your metaphor?" said Shepard.

"Doctor, with your permission, I'd like to record this interview. This is such a complicated case. I want to make sure that we have an accurate record of the information you provide us with," said Sue.

"And if I refuse?"

"Well, sir, you certainly have the right to do that. Unfortunately, then we will have to ask you to come in for a formal interview. We know time is at a premium for you, so . . ."

Dr. Shepard rolled the nails of his right hand on the desktop several times. "Okay," he finally said.

As Sue set an iPhone on the table, Ray began, "You told us that you went out to your cottage last Tuesday and that you didn't stay the night because of a problem with your furnace."

"Yes. And I know my wife corroborated that for you. So what's the problem?"

"You also said that you did not see Becca Sterling that evening," said Ray.

"Yes. That's what I told you. The facts don't change."

Ray looked over at Sue and nodded. She slowly looked through the small soft nylon backpack she carried, retrieving an evidence bag containing the plastic medicine bottle. She passed the evidence bag to Ray, and he held it in front of him as if reading the label. "Macrobid, the bottle contains Macrobid. Could you tell us about this medicine, Doctor."

"Macrobid, that's an antibiotic. It's used for bladder infections."

Looking again at the bottle, Ray said, "We found this among Becca's meds. Interestingly enough, Dr. Shepard, you're the prescribing physician."

"Am I?" He looked away. "I do that for friends, occasionally. You know, they can't reach their physician. They tell me what they're taking, and I order enough to get them through. Never opiates, of course. Just things like run-of-the-mill antibiotics. It's probably not the best practice on my part, but I think you'll find most physicians do that from time to time for friends and family."

"Thank you," said Ray. "That clears things up. There's one more thing, Doctor. The prescription was dated last Tuesday. You wrote it, and it appears that you are the intended patient. Becca's name is not on it, and yet we found it at her house. Did you have a bladder infection last Tuesday?"

"Look, Sheriff, like I told you, I was heading out of town. I got a message from Becca saying she had a bladder infection. I didn't know what pharmacy Becca usually used. It was easier for me to run it through my insurance plan." He looked over at Ray. "I know I shouldn't have done that. But I know the pharmacist there, and that's the way he did it. I guess he thought it was for someone in my family. It would've taken extra time to have him cancel it out and, well, you know. The drug is inexpensive. I'm not cheating anyone out of a lot of money."

"So how did Becca end up with the prescription on Tuesday?"

Shepard reddened and inhaled deeply. He looked down at the surface of his desk and said softly, "I dropped it off at her house. I'd forgotten to tell you that. I was just at her place for a minute. You know, passed it through the door."

"And you're just now remembering this detail?"

"Well, in truth, I remembered it some time after our first conversation. Late at night, I think."

"That's an important bit of information. I can't help but wonder why you didn't share it with us as soon as you remembered. Doctor, this is a murder investigation."

"It's about the optics, Sheriff. How would it look if I suddenly changed my story? I didn't want to get involved. I mean, it was innocent enough. I am busy. Lots of things going on. I see many sick people every day. So I forgot that I took a few moments to drop off some meds. I was helping a friend. What's the phrase? Let no good deed go unpunished."

Ray pointed to one of the framed diplomas on the wall behind Dr. Shepard. "I see you were in the military."

"Yes, that's where I did my residency." His eyebrows crinkled in confusion. "I don't see how that's—"

"Doctor, we collected multiple samples of DNA at the scene from the bed sheets and the victim's underwear, and additional samples were obtained during the autopsy. We have Becca Sterling's DNA and the DNA from a sexual partner." He moved his eyes from the diploma to Shepard's face. The doctor held his gaze.

"I guess there was more going on in Becca's life than I knew about," Shepard responded.

"Is there anything more you want to tell us?" said Ray.

"Sheriff, I think your imagination is running wild. If I'm going to be subjected to any more questions like this, I want a lawyer present."

"That's a good idea," agreed Ray. "As you may or may not remember, there is a Department of Defense DNA database. We're going to apply to a federal court to see if there is a match with the DNA we collected at the scene. You certainly should have an attorney at your side if we find evidence that you have obstructed our inquiries in a murder case."

"Are we done?" asked Sue.

"Yes," said Ray, "unless, of course, the doctor has something more he would like to tell us."

"Hold on a minute. Let me collect my thoughts," said Dr. Shepard. "I know how things look. But it's not what it seems. It was just a sometime thing."

"What was a sometime thing?" pressed Ray.

"You know what happens sometimes, two lonely people," said Shepard. "I mean, consenting adults. It's not right, that's for sure. But it happens. It's just natural. I'm not proud of it. After our kids grew up and went away, we drifted apart, Liv and I. Happens to a lot of couples."

"Would you please tell us exactly what happened on Tuesday?" said Sue.

"Haven't we been over that already?" Shepard said.

"You have given us several scenarios, Dr. Shepard. Now we need you to walk us through Tuesday evening again. This time, please give us a chronology of everything that happened. Including approximate times."

"I'm pretty rattled now. But I'll try. As I told you, I left my office sometime after five, ran by the house to pick up my dog, Bo, and stopped at the store to get some groceries."

"And the prescription?" said Sue.

"Yes, the prescription, too."

"What store?" asked Sue.

"You know that already. It's on the bottle."

"Just answer the question, sir," she responded.

"Meijers."

"Then what?"

"I drove out to Fox Cove and stopped at Becca's to drop off the prescription."

"And?" said Ray.

"She invited me in for a glass of wine. And then one thing led to another."

"Would you be more specific, please?"

"We ended up in bed. Is that specific enough?"

"Where was her daughter, Ava?" asked Sue.

"She was napping. Anyway, afterward, well, Becca made me a quick dinner, salmon and rice. And then I left."

"What time was that?"

"Maybe eight or a little later."

"Your dog, where was he all this time?"

"I had dropped him off at my place. He doesn't get along with Germaine."

"So you went to your place first? And you didn't notice the problem with the furnace when you dropped your dog off?"

"No. I always turn the heat down before I head back to town. When I get to the cottage again, I turn up the heat and leave the dog."

Ray exchanged a glance with Sue. Dr. Shepard's Tuesday visits to Becca Sterling's house were not a sometime thing, after all.

"So you dropped the dog off, went over to Becca's, you made love and had some dinner, then you went back to your house?" Ray asked.

"Just like I told you before, I went to my place, discovered the furnace wasn't working, and then drove back to town."

"And you never returned to Becca's house that evening?"

"Correct."

"Was that your normal pattern?" asked Ray.

"Your meaning?"

Ray leaned toward Dr. Shepard and asked, "The two of you spending only a few hours together. Why not spend the night?"

Dr. Shepard was slow in responding. "Yes, well, we did our best to be discreet about things."

"And how long has this . . ." Ray cleared his throat, ". . . affair been going on?"

"I don't know, a few months."

"Your best guess, Doctor?" asked Ray. He felt his lip curling and worked harder to hide his irritation with the games Dr. Shepard insisted on playing.

"Sometime last winter. Becca asked me to stop and check on Ava. She had a cold at the time. And after I checked the baby over, we had a drink or two, and it just happened."

"Did the two of you have an emotional relationship?"

"Not at first. But we grew more attached to one another over time, and recently I saw her most weeks."

"And was Becca seeing anyone else that you know of?"

"Absolutely not. I mean, I never asked, but I don't think she was."

"And you two were getting along? There were no major arguments or conflicts?"

"None. It was so different from my marriage. Becca seemed to like me. It was mutual."

"Did you think about pursuing a more permanent relationship with her?" asked Ray.

"The topic came up occasionally. Becca's view was that we shouldn't mess with a good thing."

"And your view, Doctor?"

"For the immediate future, that was probably a wise course."

"Last Tuesday evening, did Becca say anything that would suggest she was expecting any other visitors?"

"No."

"Was Ava's paternity ever a topic of conversation?" asked Sue.

"No, not ever. But we've been through that. Why do you keep coming back to Ava?"

"It might be important to this investigation," answered Sue. "I take it you're not the father."

"No, I am not. Like I said before, I didn't ask, and she didn't tell me. Are we done? I've got things to do."

"There is one more thing. If you allow Sue to get a sample of your DNA, it would speed things up for us. We're attempting to tie names to all the DNA we've found at the site."

As he was talking, Ray could see Sue out of the corner of his eye pulling on sterile gloves and then breaking the seal on a DNA collection kit. Then she moved forward, "Dr. Shepard, please open your mouth."

Shepard, startled, looked up and complied as she quickly guided the swab into his mouth. Seconds later she sealed it back inside the kit.

"Thank you for volunteering your help," she said, dropping a single piece of paper on the desk: *Contract for Provision of Exculpatory DNA to Cedar County Sheriff's Department.* "It's all outlined there, sir. We will be protecting your privacy."

Shepard scanned the single page document, then looked up. Ray watched the man trying to control his rage.

"Is there anything else?" Shepard demanded, his voice rising.

"That's it for now. Again, thank you for your cooperation," answered Ray, looking directly into the other man's eyes. "Unless there are other things you forgot to mention."

"I don't think so," said Shepard. His face reddened again. "My wife doesn't have to know about this, does she?"

"It's not our intention to share this information. That said, things come out during a murder investigation. People talk, the press sometimes gets involved. If you want to head off that possibility, perhaps you should sit down and have an honest conversation with your wife."

Ray stood. "If anything else occurs to you that might be helpful in this investigation, please contact us immediately."

When they were settled back in the Dodge, Ray asked, "That move with the swab, where did that come from?"

"Eight years of ballet with a bit of Taekwondo thrown in, in case things went south."

"Ballet. What happened? Was it your mother's thing?"

"No. I just realized I wasn't destined to remain 101 pounds."

"And the *Contract for Provision of Exculpatory DNA to Cedar County Sheriff's Department,* shouldn't I have known about that before I saw it . . . ?" Ray could hear the irritation in his voice as he asked the question.

Sue looked abashed. "Sorry, I planned to run that by you—and the prosecutor's office, too. You and I have talked about it."

"Yes, but . . ."

"I know. I've been pulling things together. I used the current draft. It was only in my bag because I meant to show it to you during our travels. I couldn't help myself when the moment arrived." She paused. "You are ticked. I can tell."

31

Ray's attention was suddenly diverted from the rows and columns of figures on the screen in front of him by Simone's attempt to climb into his lap. He pulled the small wiggling dog up with one hand. Seconds later, Sue came through the doorway.

"Sorry for the interruption. I couldn't hold onto her, Ray. She was determined to see you."

"A welcome relief," said Ray.

"Revising the budget again?" asked Sue.

"Yes, I'm trying to figure out how we can keep you supplied with trucks."

Sue made a hissing sound before breaking into a smile.

"What time did you come in this morning?" she asked.

"Early. Jan's been piling up all the things that require my signature. And then there is the Sisyphean task of staying within budget. How are the roads?"

"Not getting any better." Sue placed her backpack and a coffee mug on the conference table as she looked over the notes on current cases that covered the whiteboard.

Ray tucked Simone under one arm and joined Sue at the table.

"So you want to start with Rankin?" she asked.

"Sure."

"I think he's okay. I looked at his LinkedIn account, read an article in the *North Coast Business Insider*, and scanned the usual databases. He was an exec in the auto industry who cashed out early years ago and came up here to grow fruit. He's been active in local agricultural groups and at one time served on the township board. There was also a recent obit on his wife's passing. So when he told us that he couldn't imagine why this vandalism was happening, I think he is completely believable."

Ray stroked Simone meditatively as he looked across the table at Sue. "It makes no sense. What's the motive? If the vandalism wasn't directed at Rankin . . . ?"

"I'm with you. It makes no sense. Maybe it was just an act of random violence."

"I guess that's possible. The problem is that random violence with a weapon of that caliber makes me exceedingly nervous, especially considering it might be the second occurrence. How about Rankin's son?" he asked, changing tack. "Did he merit a background check, too?" asked Ray.

"I looked at his LinkedIn page," answered Sue, blushing slightly. "He, too, seems genuine."

"You didn't happen to look for his profile on Match.com?"

"No," she responded. "I only use TrainWreck.com. The only dating site that is honest about possible outcomes. Can we move on to Dr. Shepard?"

"Sure."

"I listened to our interview again as I was driving home last night."

"And?"

"Everyone lies about sex, but there is so much more than that going on, so many layers of meaning. I'm having the interview transcribed. I want to reread it, slowly. I think you would term it an 'overly nuanced narrative.'"

"He didn't want us to tell his wife, but what are the chances she already knows?"

"If she doesn't, I'd bet she has strong suspicions. She didn't strike me as either incurious or daffy," said Sue. "Maybe she's developed other passions also."

"And she corroborated her husband's alibi. But what if Olivia herself had some reason to drive out to Fox Cove for a conversation with Becca after her husband and Bo had settled in for the night? What if she'd had enough of their fooling around?"

"Possible, she could have snuck out unnoticed," said Ray. "The paternity issue might be an important element. Remember how Shepard danced around the issue? He said that they became lovers last winter sometime, but is it possible it was earlier, and he's lying to detract from the possibility that he is actually Ava's father? And given what we know, the pregnancy might have happened at a time when Becca had several lovers. Perhaps there is some truth to the story she told Frances Adams. Maybe Becca didn't know who the father was for sure."

"Princeton, Williams, or Wayne State?"

"Wayne State?"

"You didn't look at all the diplomas on Shepard's wall," said Sue.

"See if Sharon Peterson will permit you to get a sample from Ava for DNA testing. If Shepard is the father, we have a new line of questioning. Still, we'd have to find a hole in his alibi. Too bad Bo can't testify as to his human's whereabouts on the night in question."

"Don't you think Shepard's dog would lie for him?"

Ray looked down fondly at Simone curled up in his lap. "No, I think dogs are without guile."

"Let's say for the moment that Shepard's alibi collapses," Sue said. "What might his motive have been?"

"How about another man suddenly coming into the picture, someone who would engender jealousy and rage? Remember, it appears that Shepard has fallen for this woman. An older man, a beautiful younger woman, a new rival. Shakespeare, Chaucer, Updike, pick an author. It's an old plot line. Maybe a late-night lovers' argument went out of control."

"Or what happens if his wife shows up and confronts the other woman?" Sue went quiet for several moments. "Too bad Becca didn't have a close woman friend with whom she shared important information. Then again, there's Sharon Peterson. I'm beginning to think she knows more than she is telling us."

"We should talk to her husband, too," added Ray. "He's less protective of Becca than his wife. What's happening with the financials?"

"I'm currently looking through her bank records. I can tell you this much, money was not a problem. More than adequate funds in her checking and savings accounts. There are regular monthly deposits of five thousand dollars into her checking account. I have yet to determine the source of those funds. I need some uninterrupted time."

"Make the time. Delegate what you can. Let's move on the paternity issue and see if we can learn anything from the Petersons. Also, check and see if there are any allegations of spousal abuse against Shepard—or his wife, for that matter."

32

"Do they ever plow this thing?" asked Sue as she navigated through the deep ruts on the road leading into Fox Cove.

"We need a few days without lake effect snow so the road crews can catch up," Ray responded.

"It looks like we got a dog walker," said Sue, slowing.

"This is perfect," said Ray. "Let me out. I'll have a chat with Chuck Peterson and you can go up to the house and talk to his wife. I'll meet up with you later."

"Hey, Chuck, mind if I walk with you a bit?" asked Ray.

"Happy to have the company, Sheriff," said Chuck as Ray greeted the dogs, first Thor and then Germaine.

"My sergeant needs to have a word with your wife. I'm glad to get the opportunity for a walk."

"Would you like to hold onto one of the dogs? The two of them are a bit much at times."

"Sure."

"Any preference?"

"Mox nix."

"Here, take Thor. He's controllable. Maturity is a good thing. Germaine, she goes crazy at the hint of anything wild in her woods. I'm always afraid she'll break loose and run off."

"This is always the toughest part of the winter," said Ray.

"I'm with you on that. Fortunately, these dogs keep me moving, even on the darkest days. They insist on their walks. And the nice thing about dogs is they never seem to be bothered by, what's that called, seasonal disorder something. They are always enthusiastic about going on a hike. Look at those two, happy as can be. I have a hell of a time turning them around. They want to keep going."

They walked on in silence for several minutes, then Chuck asked, in a pained voice, "Are you any closer to figuring out what happened to Becca?"

"We're moving forward. No breakthroughs, yet. There is one thing you could help me with."

"I'm happy to," Chuck said.

"Brian Shepard. Any chance he and Becca might have had more than a casual friendship?"

"Interesting that you should ask. I've wondered about that myself. I didn't want to say anything to you about it, though."

"Why's that?"

"Brian is a very decent sort. He certainly wouldn't have been involved in Becca's death. If I had brought him into the conversation, I would have put him under suspicion, and that wouldn't have made any sense. I've known him for years. Brian is a true gentleman." Peterson looked over at Ray. "I wouldn't have wanted to waste your time."

Ray focused on his breathing and marched silently along behind the dogs.

"So what made you wonder about Brian Shepard?" asked Ray.

"Well, I guess it's Becca as much as Brian."

"I'm not following," said Ray.

"I don't know quite how to explain this. I don't want you to get the wrong idea. It's just that Becca was a lot like her mother, Monique. Beautiful women, the two of them. Both of them were, what should I say, earthy. Maybe sensual would be a better word. Monique might not have had much of a marriage, but Sharon and I had a sense that she maintained an active love life, nevertheless. Not that she flaunted it. She was very discreet. With Becca, the fruit didn't fall far from the tree. By the time she went to college, there was always someone special around. Celibacy was not her modus operandi. This past year, Brian seemed to become much more attentive to her and Ava. I asked Becca about it, and she just blew me off. She referred to Brian as her drive-by pediatrician."

"Did you share this observation with your wife?" asked Ray.

"Sharon was very protective of Becca. In a marriage, some things are best left unsaid."

"Is there anyone else with whom Becca might've been involved romantically at the time of her death?"

"No, not that I can think of. We're relatively isolated in the dead of winter."

They trudged on for a few more minutes. Then Peterson said, "This is where I usually turn around."

"Perfect," said Ray. "My sergeant has probably finished talking with your wife. She will be waiting for me."

"Anytime Ava wants a nap, I'm happy to put her in her crib. I need a break," said Sharon Peterson as she served coffee to Sue and settled across from her with a cup of her own.

"How are things going?"

"We're used to having Ava, but before there were always parameters. She would be with us for a few days, and then we'd go back to normal. Now there's a new normal. That's taking some getting used to. But Ms. Lawrence—"

"Please call me Sue."

"Sue, Ava is very easy. Easier than my own, as I remember it." She looked up and smiled. "But you probably didn't come to talk about child-rearing. Are there any new developments in Becca's case?"

"We are working on several leads. An investigation like this often takes a long time to resolve." Sue stirred some sugar into her coffee. "We collected several samples of DNA from Becca's house, and we're currently trying to match them with the people to whom they belong. Would you permit me to take a sample from Ava? I will swab the inside of her mouth. Nothing invasive or painful."

"I understand. I have no problem with that. The other DNA, what can you tell me about it?"

Sue hesitated. "At this point in the investigation, I can't say very much. It does appear that Becca had a male lover. Would you know anything about that?"

Sue watched Sharon's face closely as the older woman struggled for the right words. "I think she got very lonely for companionship," she said finally.

"And when she got especially lonely, did she turn to anyone in particular?"

Sharon shook her head, "Not really."

"We've talked with Dr. Shepard. He's mentioned that he's occasionally stopped by to attend to some of Ava's medical needs."

"Brian's a good man. He and Becca have been neighbors and friends for a long time. Are you trying to suggest something?"

"I'm looking at possibilities, all the possibilities. That's what we do."

Sharon toyed with her coffee cup, then met Sue's gaze. "As I said, Brian's a good man. That doesn't mean I condone his actions or Becca's. They were two lonely people. That's what sometimes happens."

"So you knew what was going on?"

"I had a sense of it, not that Becca told me explicitly."

"Could you please tell me what you know about their relationship?"

"Olivia, Brian's wife, is a friend of many years. She confronted me about a possible affair. I wish I could say that I was startled. I wasn't. As I said, I had a sense of it." She stalled by taking a long sip of her coffee. "Olivia was angry, accusatorial, said that I should have told her, that I owed her that much based on our long friendship."

"Do you know what triggered her anger?"

"I do. Olivia said she learned from Brian's accountant that he was giving Becca a substantial amount of money every month. She demanded to know what I knew, specifically whether or not Brian was Ava's father. I told her I had no idea. My answer further inflamed her anger. She got in my face—I thought she was going to slap me.

She demanded that I find out. When I told her it was none of my business, she stormed out. I haven't talked to her since."

"When was this?"

"Earlier this fall."

"How about a month?"

"Late October. She just arrived one afternoon out of the blue."

"Did you tell Becca about your conversation with Olivia?"

"I did. I told her to be careful."

"Did you bring up the issue of payments from Shepard or paternity?"

"No."

"Why am I just finding this out?" Sue said, unable to keep the frustration out of her voice. "Sharon, this is a murder investigation."

"Sorry. I know now that I should have told you. The confrontation was long past. I didn't think it was important."

"Are there other things that you didn't bother to mention?" Sue asked tersely. "Did Becca have other romantic interests, besides Dr. Shepard?"

"No, nothing like that. We got used to the idea that Brian would be around on Tuesday evenings. We knew not to drop in." Sharon looked away momentarily. "Not telling you about Brian, that was dumb on my part. I can see that now."

Sue didn't respond.

"My children are coming this weekend. I need their help."

"Your husband told Sheriff Elkins about planning a memorial service."

"Yes, that's on the agenda. I think we're going to push that back. Legal and financial things are of a more immediate concern. My daughter, Yvonne, the lawyer, she's reviewed the will, the trust, and other legal issues having to do with Becca's estate. She's going to explain it all to Chuck and me and her siblings. Then we're going to have a family council to plan for Ava's future."

"Becca's financial affairs," said Sue, "I'm just starting to work on that part of the case."

"How do you get access to that kind of information?"

"Some of it, like wills, is public record, and trusts become public at probate. We get search warrants to access bank records and other financial information."

Sharon stood and retrieved a thick gray folder from a stack of folders on a nearby desk. "Here are all of Becca's legal and financial documents: her will, trust, power of attorney, and I don't know what all. I collected all these documents and had copies made so we could go over them this weekend. You can take that if you like. I made extra."

"That would be helpful. Thank you."

"I hear Ava fussing. Should we get the DNA sample done?"

"That would be perfect," agreed Sue.

As they drove south, Ray gave Sue a summary of his conversation with Chuck Peterson. Sue followed, her version less condensed. Then she said, "I wish we had recorded these two conversations. I'd like to get transcripts of each, put them side by side, and pinpoint the differences."

"That would be interesting," agreed Ray. "Things that people share and don't share in a marriage."

"I was talking with my grandmother once. This was after my grandfather had died. Like they had been married close to sixty years. She said, 'All those years, and I hardly knew the man. But I didn't tell him everything either.' At the time, Ray, I thought she was losing it. Maybe not. Perhaps she was trying to tell me something important."

33

"Ray, your secretary said that it was okay if I wandered in."

Ray looked up. Wendy Morrison, Cara's mother, was standing just inside his office.

"Wendy. Please come in," said Ray, gesturing toward the chairs at the conference table. He pushed back from his desk, held Wendy's hand briefly, and sat down across from her at the table.

"I was hoping that you might have a moment. You said one of your people would stop by to talk to Cara while she was in the hospital."

"Yes, Sue Lawrence chatted with her briefly on Saturday. Cara was not forthcoming with any information about the source of the drugs." Ray paused for a moment. "This is almost always the case. There is not much more we can do at this point. Sorry."

"I'm not surprised about her response. Cara has been shutting me out for years. I keep hoping she will have a breakthrough, that this nightmare will end."

Ray nodded his understanding.

"Regardless of how this all works out, I will never forget what you did for her. You gave her one more chance. And thank Ms. Lawrence for her efforts, too."

"I'll pass that along. Wendy, are you still playing the cello?"

A smile spread across Morrison's face. "Where did that come from?"

"It's something else I'm working on."

"I am still playing the cello. Not as much as I'd like to. I always thought once the girls grew up, I'd get back into it. But you know how it is. You work a long day, and you don't feel like going out in the evening. I have occasionally played in a couple of chamber groups the last several years. I'm not a regular member, but people know I'm available as needed. I take part in a few concerts and play weddings during the summer with one of the groups."

"Is Olivia Shepard part of any of these groups?"

"She's one of the major organizers and supporters of chamber music in the area. She opens her house every Tuesday night for anyone who wants to come and play. I've gone a few times. After we play, she wines and dines us. Why do you ask?"

"It has to do with the Becca Sterling murder." Wendy shook her head to indicate she hadn't heard about the case. "We've been talking to the residents of Fox Cove. The Shepards have a cottage there."

"Olivia isn't under . . ."

"Not at all. How well do you know her?"

"We have a casual friendship. It's all about music, nothing beyond that."

"Does she ever talk about her marriage?"

"Oh, I see where this is going. You want to know about Brian. Reading between the lines, I take it the victim was an attractive woman."

"Yes."

"You know Ray, up here the medical community is pretty small. You hear things. And I want you to know that none of this came from any of my clients. What little I know is mostly based on rumors."

"I hear your discomfort. Is there anything you can share?"

Wendy sighed. "I heard a long time ago that Brian told people he and Olivia had an open marriage. I never heard that Olivia was a participant in the arrangement. The consensus was that the marriage had been falling apart for years. Some people laid the blame at his feet, and others held her responsible. I have no idea where the truth lies. Is that what you wanted to know?"

"Yes. Anything else?"

"Well, there is a story going around in the music group that he and his dog have been exiled to one end of the house, sort of a subterranean level, and she lives at the other end, overlooking the bay. I don't know if he is a cave dweller by choice. Of course, that story is nothing more than speculation. The narratives people construct are often more interesting than reality."

Wendy held Ray in her gaze. "Ray, are you okay?"

"I'm fine," Ray said.

"Ray, I may not be able to understand my kid or do anything to change her behavior, but I'm quite successful with adults. You don't look okay. You don't sound okay. Are you overworked? Exhausted? Too many gray days in a row? Or is your world just out of control at the moment?"

"I think it's the weather. Too many grey days." He looked across at Wendy. He could tell she wasn't buying his answer.

"What's happening with the pretty woman I've seen you with?"

"She's looking at a fellowship at Stanford."

"How do you feel about that?"

"It's a great opportunity for her."

"That wasn't what I asked you." She glanced at her watch. "Unfortunately, I've got to run. But please know, I'm happy to talk. Sometimes, just laying it out, just articulating things helps you work through your feelings. You can come in and see me or call me on the phone." Wendy stood. "Ray, this community appreciates your professionalism and humanity. Every day, you make a positive difference. That's the best any of us can do. Thank you."

Ray nodded. He appreciated the gratitude, he did, and yet somehow it beaded up and ran off of him without sinking in, rain on a slicker that he couldn't seem to take off.

34

"Thank you for making time for me on such short notice," said Sue, setting her backpack on Laura Stock's desk at the bank.

"Anything for a fellow yogi," answered Laura. "What can I help you with?"

"I need some information on the estate of Becca Sterling. I believe your bank is handling the matter."

Laura leaned toward Sue across the desk. "Sue, after yoga and over wine, I can gossip about just about anything, but when it comes to client matters, I follow strict confidentiality."

Sue withdrew a stack of folders from her backpack and pulled a document from the top folder. She passed it to Laura across the desk.

Laura carefully looked over the search warrant. Then she looked up at Sue. "Thank you. All the *t*'s are dotted and the *i*'s are crossed. How can I help you?"

Sue opened a bulky folder. "I have Becca Sterling's will and trust agreement. These documents were provided by Sharon Peterson, Ms. Sterling's aunt. I'm searching for possible motives in this murder. There is a lot of money here, and money is often a key motivator in major crimes. I've looked through these papers. To my layperson's eyes, everything appears to have been done in a manner that best protects Ava, Becca's daughter. I can forward this to the FBI and have a forensic accountant look it over, but that option will take weeks. I noticed your name listed as the trust officer on the estate. What I'm wondering is if you see anything suspicious here."

"I'm very familiar with this estate and the trust," Laura said. "I worked closely with Becca Sterling and her attorney. The trust agreement follows standard practice. It's a highly detailed document with more than ample safeguards to protect the minor child. And it reflects all the recent changes to state and federal law. As a lawyer, I should throw in a few caveats, but I don't think you'll find anything amiss in these documents. The assets in the trust are fully protected. Now, I'm only talking about the trust.

"Ms. Sterling had accumulated a significant amount of wealth for a woman her age. There may have been other assets . . . how do I say this . . . other valuables that could have put her in danger: artworks, jewelry, et cetera. You know, the kinds of things that some people kill for, items that she failed to specify in these documents.

"If you want a forensic read, I encourage you to send them on to the FBI. The Bureau's task is to look for criminality, while my focus is to fulfill my clients' wishes, protect their interests, and comply with the current standards of practice."

"Thank you, that's helpful," Sue said. "I have another question."

"Go ahead."

Sue removed a bank statement from the folder and handed it to Laura. "I've highlighted a deposit in the middle of the page. The deposit is for five thousand dollars. The depositor is WHISNDS, LLC. I've noticed these payments arrive on the fifteenth of each month. Can you attach a person's name to that LLC?"

Stock leaned back in her chair and chewed her upper lip. She picked up the search warrant again and looked at it a second time. Then she said, "Yes, I can do that. It's one of our customers."

Sue watched the reflection from the computer screen on Laura's glasses as Laura tapped at the keyboard, searching through several screens.

"It's an abbreviation for a company called Whispering Sands, LLC. The account holder is Brian Shepard, MD."

"Thank you," said Sue, writing the information on a small note pad, working to maintain a deadpan manner.

"Is there anything else?" Laura asked.

"No, you've been very helpful. Thank you," said Sue as she started to gather up her things.

"Do you have a couple of minutes?" asked Laura.

Sue checked her watch and then said, "Sure."

"I was surprised when you called to meet with me," Laura said, "because I've been thinking about you lately and wanting to have a conversation. I've noticed that you haven't been to yoga much lately."

"There's been so much going on. Some evenings I end up working, and at other times I'm exhausted and want to crash."

"I understand. You do important work. It's got to be hard. It's an interesting time here at the bank, too. Our former management left things in disarray. You remember our former CEO?"

"No, but I do remember seeing some articles in the paper. The feds got very excited about something."

Laura chuckled. "That's one way of putting it. We called him Chef Charley on the sly. He was always cooking up special deals for his personal friends. The feds 'got excited' because his friends were sometimes securing their loans with questionable or nonexistent assets. The FDIC doesn't like to pay off account holders because a bank's management is either corrupt or inept.

"Anyway, I've been thinking of you because I'm part of the executive team now. We are in the process of developing a security unit for the bank. Part of the job would be the physical security of all our branches. A bigger part would be concerned with things like vetting loan applications. We're also increasingly concerned about wire fraud and electronic crime. We're looking for a smart, energetic person to build that capacity inside." She looked expectantly at Sue.

"It sounds like an interesting job. That said, none of what you're describing is part of my skill set."

Laura smiled. "It's a management job, Sue. It's all about leadership and multidisciplinary skills. We're looking for someone who can identify the problems and recruit specialists to deal with the rapidly changing challenges we will be encountering in the future.

"I think you would be an excellent candidate. I can offer you at least twice what you're currently making. It's a forty-hour-a-week job. No evenings, no weekends. Excellent health benefits, a retirement plan, and a stock option. You'll have time to go to yoga. No one will be ramming your car and dropping snowmobiles on you. You'll have time for a relationship, for kids if you want them."

Sue stared silently at Laura. Then she smiled. "I'm nonplussed. I don't know what to say."

"Will you think about it?"

"Yes, I will," Sue promised. "But my immediate objective is getting justice for Becca Sterling."

"That's why we want you," Laura said. "You're that kind of person."

Sue stopped at the door and looked back at the interior of the bank. She couldn't imagine spending eight-hour days in the gloomy surroundings.

35

Sue set a cappuccino with fat-free milk in front of Hanna and placed a coffee and a raspberry scone in front of her own chair. "Are you sure you won't have some of this scone?" she asked as she sat down.

"I've been overeating and getting too little exercise," said Hanna. "That and being wined and dined for close to ten days didn't help things."

"You have amazing willpower."

"One of the downsides of being short is that five pounds on me look like twenty pounds on a normal person. If I gain ten pounds, people start asking when the twins are due." Hanna stirred the foam into the espresso, then asked, "What brings you to town?"

"I needed to talk with a banker about a case we're working on. Since I was going to be just a few blocks from the medical center, I hoped you might have a few minutes. I haven't seen you since your trip. How was California?"

"A nice break, especially the sunshine. It was startling to see a green landscape. Palo Alto is beautiful."

"And the job?"

"It would be fascinating. I liked the people. The project's goals are enticing. The job is mine if I want it. But I didn't say yes. I'm still thinking through things. Has Ray shared any of this with you?"

"A little."

Hanna smiled. "If anyone could get the details of a matter out of him, it's you. It's obvious that you two have a special friendship."

"We do. And I need to talk to you about Ray."

"What's going on?" asked Hanna, her smile disappearing.

"I don't know. Ray has been down, more than I can ever

remember. He seems to feel responsible for things that are beyond his control."

"Anyone with half a brain is upset with the state of the planet," responded Hanna. "Is there something job-related bothering him?"

"At the moment, drugs and the epidemic of drug-related deaths. Based on population, our numbers are similar to other areas of northern Michigan, but he takes this problem personally. He feels that he isn't doing enough. As you have no doubt heard, he successfully saved a young woman's life with naloxone last week. That experience almost seemed to make things worse. Being face to face with the problem seemed to intensify his angst."

"I hear you," said Hanna.

"Day in and day out, we do important work for the people of this county. That's what sustains us. Ray's lost sight of that. He's fixated on things he can't change and calamities he won't be able to prevent."

Hanna looked down at her hands. Finally, she said, "Yes, I know he's down. I have wondered how much I may be contributing to his gloom."

"I didn't mean to suggest . . ."

"I know. Your concern is real. Sue, I wasn't looking for this job. I had begun to settle. Then this opportunity suddenly appeared. To be part of a cutting-edge research team is very appealing. Part of my baggage, Sue, going back to my work as a battlefield trauma surgeon, is a need to fix the unfixable. And how did that work out? I come home with PTSD and the tendency to self-medicate. Maybe the appeal of the California job is the fantasy of being able to do that, fix the unfixable by pushing science forward."

Hanna focused on her coffee for a few moments. "I've tried to get Ray to talk to me about the job. I want this to be a joint decision—I even asked him if he'd be willing to go to Palo Alto with me."

Sue felt a jolt of surprise. She hoped her shock didn't show on her face. "What did he say?"

"He said he'd consider it. That's all I could get out of him. Listen,

I'm not laying blame on him for the trouble I'm having making this decision. I'm just stating the facts. Maybe I've told you before, but I'm not good at relationships. This one is special. I've been working at it. I don't want to screw it up. But I don't know what to do. I'm a surgeon. I'm good at cutting and stitching, the physical side. I'm just starting to explore my emotional side."

"So what can I do? Any suggestions?" asked Sue.

"I'm not sure. But maybe it will help if I stop vacillating about what I want to do. Perhaps if I lay it out on paper, you know, like choices and possible consequences, maybe that would get a conversation going."

"Worth a try," said Sue.

A text alert sounded from Hanna's phone, and she looked at the screen. "Listen, I've got to run. An emergency surgery. Thanks for the coffee. We should do this again soon. I know it would do me good."

36

The small pole building was hidden away in the woods at the end of a long drive. Smoke from a wood-burning barrel stove floated skyward above a metal chimney that jutted through the roof of the structure. Six bare bulbs, in widely spaced porcelain fixtures attached to the rafters, cast a dim glow over the litter-filled interior. Toby Osmann, working below one of the lights, was cutting a piece of steel in two. He stopped from time to time to replace a worn cutting wheel, then filled the interior of the building again with the sharp wail of the pneumatic tool. Red-hot fragments of steel cascaded down onto the dirt floor.

When he was finished, Toby set one piece aside and centered the second one on the sawhorses. Measuring carefully, he marked out two rectangles in the lower half of that steel plate, one rectangle smaller than the other and positioned below it. He used the grinding wheel to cut them out.

Holding the piece of steel so his companion could see his accomplishment, he said, "The gun port and my window."

"You are the master, Toby Osmann. Now let's get your armor welded on."

Using a series of clamps, he secured the piece of steel to the interior frame of the left rear door of the van. Reaching back and pulling down the welding helmet to protect his eyes, Toby carefully tacked the material in place, the MIG welder hissing and throwing sparks each time he squeezed the trigger. After the panel was secured, he removed the clamps that had supported it and added additional spot-welds. He clamped the second piece of steel, the one without any holes, to the inside of the right rear door of the van and repeated the process.

"Will that stop a bullet, Toby?"

"From their Glocks, yes. We'll really rock. Not a scratch on Toby Osmann," he answered.

Working from the interior, using a long bit, he drilled eight holes through the exterior sheet metal of the van, marking the corners of the 'window' and 'gun port.' Then, working from the outside, he used the grinder to cut out the holes.

As the scream of the grinder faded, he became aware of his companion's coughing. "Why are you smoking again?" he demanded.

"It doesn't matter, Mr. Toby."

"Go into the house. Get warm. Have some tea."

"I'm okay," came the answer.

He closed the left door of the van, then struggled to close the right door.

"What's the problem?"

"Sagging hinges, rusting metal," he said, opening and closing the door a few times, trying to get the latch to stick. Finally, he grabbed a giant rubber mallet and pounded the door in place.

His companion watched as he fitted and welded one more piece of steel in place, securing the two rear doors permanently together.

"Did you fix it, Toby?"

"It will never open again, never," he said.

"You are a genius, Mr. Toby. You're the man I depend on. Let's put the gun in place. I want to get this show on the road. We need more practice before the big dance."

37

Ray counted the items in his shopping cart, then moved to the end of the express line. As he waited impatiently, he scanned the lurid headlines of the tabloids and entertainment magazines displayed beside the checkout lane. He was always surprised by how little he knew about the celebrities who gazed back at him from the gaudy covers. A cart bumped him from behind, and he moved forward slightly. The cart nudged him a second time, and he turned.

"I hope you checked that baguette carefully for freshness," said Ben Riley, Ray's former second-in-command at the Cedar County Sheriff's Department. His blue eyes sparkled. "I know you bring special vigilance to that task."

"I do my best," answered Ray, enjoying the ribbing from his former colleague.

Ray looked at the items in Riley's cart. "I see Maureen is trying to help you develop some new skills."

"Yes, it's already posted on my LinkedIn page: Hunter and Gatherer at Lost Acres Cherry Farm. Please, make sure you endorse me for that skill at your earliest convenience, Ray."

Ray moved close to Riley and lowered his voice. "One of your old friends is back in town."

"Who?"

"Rhonda Johnson."

"There's a tragic story," responded Riley, his tone becoming somber.

"I know there's a history," said Ray. "Maybe you can give me some background. Got time for a quick coffee?"

"Being retired and all, I'm on tight time constraints. But, hey, for old times' sake, sure. Meet you next door?"

Ray nodded as the cashier started to run his order. A few minutes later, Riley slid into Ray's booth at North Country Roasters.

"So how much do you know about Rhonda?" asked Riley.

"I just had one encounter with her a few years ago. You probably remember the case. Bad checks, lots of them over a few days. She seemed to be under the influence of drugs and alcohol when we arrested her. We confronted her with the evidence, including video, during an interview. She denied the whole thing, claimed we were making a major mistake. Told the same story to the judge. She ended up getting two years at Huron Valley."

"Yes, I do remember that now. I can't say I knew Rhonda, but I certainly have known about her over lots of years. She's been on the radar since she was in junior high or early high school. It's a long, complicated, tragic story. No kid should have to endure a childhood like hers."

"Do you have time to tell me about it?"

"I will give you a condensed version—I have to get these groceries home and have supper on the table by seven."

"So, you're more than just a hunter and gatherer?"

"Yes, I've become a regular mensch, as my daughter-in-law would say."

"Okay, give me the condensed version."

"Part of it is family background. Her mother was the secretary and bookkeeper over at the lumberyard when I first moved up here. I don't know anything about her father. He wasn't around. Janice, that was the mother's name, was a pretty woman. By all accounts, she seemed to be very competent, but she had a bit of a reputation. You know how that goes, especially in a small town where everyone knows way too much about everyone else. Janice was also a drinker, a sometime girlfriend of her boss, and over the years dragged an assortment of men home."

Ben went on to explain all of the domestic runs to Janice's and how he first learned about one of the darkest sides of law enforcement. He said that most of the time Rhonda wasn't at the scene, her mother pawned her off on an aunt, but on a few occasions when she witnessed fights between her mother and some man, she became a participant in the brawl.

"Then her mother was killed, a rollover on M22 with a drunken boyfriend at the wheel. It was a big old Cadillac convertible, top down, powder blue as I remember it. It was a gory scene, worst I ever worked. I had a new guy riding with me that night. He quit the next day."

"I get the picture," said Ray.

"Rhonda was fourteen or fifteen at the time. Her mother may have been struggling with her own demons, but I think she loved her kid, and Rhonda knew it. Janice was all that Rhonda had to hold onto. With her mother's death, Rhonda's world seemed to spin out of control. We got called to the high school several times. Kids would make jokes about her mother, and Rhonda would lose it. She was a fighter.

"Rhonda dropped out as soon as she could and went feral. Sometimes she stayed with her aunt, but during the warm weather she mostly lived rough. Today we'd say she was homeless. She got picked up shoplifting. She was usually after food and cigarettes."

"So she ended up in the juvenile justice system?"

"You would think. No, Rhonda avoided that. She acquired a couple of—shall I say—mentors or patrons."

"Let me guess, the usual suspects?"

"Yes, it's a hard one, isn't it? The Lowther brothers and Kenny Obermeyer, Sheriff Orville's enablers and keepers. I was so green. It took me years to put things together. The three of them operated on the need to know. They were skilled at keeping the rest of us mostly in the dark. I'm not quite sure when she got snarled in their web. Maybe it was at Sherwood, that hippie commune you were asking about. I know she was living there early on. Lots of runaways ended up there, at least for a while. After the tenants vacated Sherwood and all the buildings burned down, Danny Lowther let her live at an old hunting cabin he owned. He was married at the time—to wife number three, maybe. But there were always other women. He called it the farm system."

"How do you know this stuff?"

"One of my duties early on was dealing with delinquency problems. I was talking to kids all the time, listening to their stories. Once they decided I could be trusted, they told me all kinds of things.

"Anyway, then she disappeared for some years. People said she was living in the UP. Then she reappeared. Her MO was fairly consistent. She was always with a man, some lowlife."

"When was that?" asked Ray.

"Can't quite give you a year, but it was about the time Orville was starting to lose it. You've heard about that. The Lowther brothers and Kenny were running the department. And I was amazed when I learned that they had installed Rhonda as Orville's housekeeper and, for want of a better term, minder. I had to chauffeur Orville back and forth to his house occasionally. It was clear that Rhonda had no domestic skills. His house was a total dump. Given the empty packaging scattered around the kitchen, Orville was fed SpaghettiOs and microwave dinners. There were a lot of pizza boxes, too. And the whole thing was part of a scam."

"I'm not following."

"Truth is, I don't know all the details. Those guys played with the personnel appointments and ran the department books. Years later I learned Rhonda had been on the payroll as a jail matron. But her real assignment was looking after Orville. Finally, after he had a stroke and died, she was left to her own devices again. And then, as you say, she went inside for a couple of years. It's a sad history, Ray."

A silence hung between the two men. Finally, Ray said, "Thank you for telling me all this. She's currently in the Heartbreak Hotel."

"What for?"

"Eluding, assaulting a police officer, possible parole violations."

"How do you fix history?"

"I wish I knew."

"At least we're better at domestics. That said, we still have a long way to go."

"Yes," agreed Ray. "Before you go, there's one more thing."

"I'm all ears."

"You heard about the vandalism at the ski area?"

"I saw the report in the paper. Someone was shooting at lifts and buildings."

"Yes," said Ray.

"Someone with an AR-15 playing at Rambo?"

"No, .30-06. Do you remember anything happening like this before?"

"Vandalism with guns, especially a hunting rifle. Yes, it's part of being up north. Stop signs from one end of the county to the other collect bullet holes from time to time—the more remote the signs, the more numerous the holes. And the No Hunting signs seem to be absolute magnets for projectiles of every caliber. That said, a shooter in one place doing a lot of damage, I don't remember anything like that. But I'm never surprised."

"There's something more," added Ray. "The ammunition used had been around for years, lots of corrosion on the brass. And the bullet fragments Sue collected, full metal jacket."

"Old military issue."

"Some military, not ours. The first response from Sue's contacts at the FBI date the shells to the 1960s, probably manufactured in Pakistan."

"How did they get here?"

"Good question, how and when? Anything come to mind from the past?"

"No. But people come and go, and some of them take their crime waves with them. Like that string of arson cases up on Northshore Headland about twenty years ago."

"I don't know about that."

"There's maybe twenty-five, thirty homes up there, all seasonal places back then. Over a year or two, six burned down. Arson.

Everything pointed to one young man, but there was no hard evidence, just a feeling on the part of many of the cottage owners. The kid's old man was a friend of Orville's, so the possible suspect was treated with kid gloves. Then the man's house goes up in flames."

"What happened?"

"The family bought a new summer home out east, Maine I think. No more suspicious fires around Northshore Headland."

38

"**D**id you get a chance to read the notes I wrote after my conversation with Ben Riley?" asked Ray as he and Sue waited for the prisoner in the interrogation room.

"Yes," she answered. "It was a sad commentary on the way law enforcement operated around here not too many years ago."

They both stood as Rhonda was led into the room. Ray directed her to the single chair on the other side of the table.

Sue switched on the recording equipment, identified the three people in the room, and advised Rhonda of her Miranda rights.

As Sue carefully moved through the pre-interview procedures, Ray studied Rhonda Johnson. He knew from her records she was in her sixties, but today she looked older than that, older than she'd looked at their last encounter a few years before. Dressed in the county's bright orange jumpsuit, Rhonda appeared worn and tired. Her complexion was sallow, her graying brown hair hung in uneven strands. Her face and hands showed little extra flesh. The jumpsuit hung awkwardly on her emaciated frame.

"When am I getting out?" asked Rhonda as soon as Sue finished reading all the required boilerplate.

"Rhonda, you broke the conditions of your parole. As soon as the prosecutor and your parole officer get this sorted out, you'll be back in front of the judge. The prosecutor wants some more information from us. If you cooperate with us, things can happen sooner."

"What do you want to know?" asked Rhonda.

"When you were heading up that two track, you were going to see Bruno Schmidt, right?" asked Sue.

"Can I smoke in here? Will you guys give me a cigarette?"

"Rhonda, you know the rules. You're wasting our time," said Ray.

"What was the question?"

"Bruno Schmidt?" said Sue.

"He's just a guy I met at a bar."

"Where?" asked Ray.

"T'ville."

"Did you go home with him?" asked Sue.

"Who do you think I was out buying breakfast stuff for? There was nothing there. He gave me some money. Look, I needed to get away for a day or two. My aunt was driving me nuts. I'm tired of hearing about the wages of sin. Her preaching and cabin fever, that's what took me to the bar."

"So you have no history with Bruno Schmidt," said Ray.

"I just met him. He bought my drinks. Yeah, I know the terms of my parole."

"Did you see drug-making equipment in the house?" asked Sue.

"Not at first. Do you want me to draw you a picture? I noticed it in the morning when I went looking for coffee. I'm not blind, Sheriff. Look, I was hungry. I got groceries. I was going to cook up some breakfast and get the flock out of there. I'm trying to be good. I don't want to go back in."

"What do you know about Bruno?"

"Like, nothing."

"You must have talked about something," said Ray.

"Look, Sheriff, I learned a long time ago, especially in bars, most guys are just blowing smoke. If you give them an occasional smile and look like you're listening, they never know otherwise."

"The cottage, did he say he owned it?"

"No, he had some goofy tale about staying rent free. Then he said the Mafia was after him. Bruno isn't all there. Too much dope over too many years. Lots of those old shop rats are like that."

"How do you know he was a shop rat?" asked Sue.

"He said he worked at the Buick. Flint, get it? That's all I know."

"We want to ask you about something else," said Sue, taking the lead.

"I don't know anything else."

"New subject, Rhonda. Did you once work for Orville Hentzler?" said Ray.

"What does that have to do with anything?"

"Stay with me, Rhonda. This is another case we're working on. It has nothing to do with you. I just need some background. Sheriff Hentzler, did you work for him?"

"Well, not really for him."

"I'm not following," said Ray.

"Danny Lowther, that's who I was working for, or at least that's who paid me."

"And what were you doing?" said Sue.

"I was taking care of the crazy old coot of a sheriff."

"Tell me about it," said Ray.

"Orville had lost it. Danny and Dirk seemed to be in charge. My job was to feed Orville, do the wash, get him showered, shaved, and dressed in clean clothes once a day so they could take him to the office for a few hours. I also did some housework. I was Orville's caretaker. And—" Suddenly Rhonda went silent.

"And what?" asked Sue.

"With Danny, well you know. He expected something in return. It was handy having me there when he wanted me."

"How long did you do this?" asked Sue.

"Close to five years. Then Orville had a stroke, next day he was gone."

"How much did you get paid?" said Ray.

"In the beginning, I got $250 a week cash and an extra $100 for food and household stuff. Whatever was left was mine."

"Where did the money come from?" asked Ray.

"Danny."

"Was it Orville's?"

"No idea. Not my business."

"Did Orville have many guns around?" said Sue.

"You gotta be kidding. Orville slept with a big old revolver under his pillow and had an arsenal in the basement. Samurai swords, guns, knives, stuff like that. When I started working for him, Orville would sometimes spend evenings down there in his toy box. Toward the end, he seemed to lose interest."

"Do you know what happened to those weapons?" asked Ray.

"No idea. Once he was dead, I was out of there. I hated him. I hated that old house."

"Where did you go?" said Sue.

"Danny bought me a one-way bus ticket to Escanaba. He gave me a fat roll of hundreds, too. Said I should stay scarce for a while. The roll and the money I had saved kept me going for a long time. I worked in a bar and hung with a nice man for a while."

"Did you ever go back to Orville's house after he died?" asked Ray.

"Never. That place was a nightmare."

"You've heard that someone burned it down?" asked Sue.

"Yeah. Wish I had thought of it."

"Rhonda, I'd like to ask you about something else," said Ray. "Did you hang out at Sherwood, the hippie commune, when you were a kid?"

"Like a million years ago. How did you know that?"

"So it's true, you spent some time there?"

"Yeah. I started staying there before my mother died. Maybe I was thirteen. And after the accident, I lived there for a couple of years off and on. It was a sad time, but those people, they were good to me. I'm sorry the place went away. It was probably the best home I ever had."

"What happened, why did the commune go away?" asked Ray.

"I don't know. I was clueless back then about most things. I was only fourteen or fifteen when this all went down. This is what I remember and what Danny told me a year or two later. He said some guy with big bucks was leaning on Orville to close Sherwood down. The reason I heard was that the man's daughter got in trouble there. So Orville had his boys start making trouble. Eventually, they went after Rob. He was the leader, the guy that made things work at the commune. I mean, a whole lot of us didn't know jack shit about anything." Rhonda's voice took on a sorrowful tone as she said, "They killed Rob in the end. Without Rob, there was no Sherwood."

"What evidence do you have that they killed him?" asked Ray.

"No evidence. Just a story."

Rhonda provided a rambling tale of what she remembered of the last days of the commune and how Danny Lowther offered her a place to live when everyone deserted Sherwood. She lived at his hunting camp for a couple of years and he kept her in weed, cigarettes, groceries, and beer. Danny often spent the night with her when he was supposed to be on road patrol. Once when he was drunk and stoned, he said that Orville told the guys that they had to get rid of Rob. Without Rob, the place would fall apart. So Dirk and Danny and the other deputy, Kenny, lured Rob into a trap. Danny said they invited him to some kind of peace talk. Danny said they just intended to beat the hell out of him, escort him to the county line, and tell him never to come back. Rob died on them, and they buried him in a swamp near Otter Lake. Then they got rid of his truck. Danny never said how they did that. When people from the commune tried to file a missing person's report, Orville blew them off. He wouldn't take a report. He told them Rob had been seen in Florida.

"Did you believe that?"

"Not really. It didn't make sense. That's why I worked to get the truth, and maybe I eventually did. Not that it mattered anymore. Danny, he told me more than once that he'd kill me if I ever said anything. Years later when I heard that someone filled that SOB with lead, hey, that was a happy day for me. He hurt me a lot. He did bad things. I was young, Sheriff."

"How old were you when you moved to Danny's hunting camp?"

Rhonda thought about it. "I wasn't sixteen yet."

"Are you sure?" asked Sue.

"Yeah. I wanted Danny to teach me how to drive. He said I had to wait for my birthday so I could get a license. And sometime later, on my birthday, he took me in to get my license. He paid for it."

Silence filled the room. Ray looked over at Sue. Finally, Rhonda asked, "Can you help me, Sheriff? I want to be free. I don't want to go back inside."

"I'll talk with the prosecutor and your probation officer. I'll see what I can do. Rhonda, no one wants you to go inside again. But you've got to continue to work with us, too. You know what I'm saying?"

"Yeah, I hear you."

"What do you think?" said Sue.

"I am almost without words," answered Ray.

"How much of it is true?"

"You remember what a slime bag Dirk was. By all reports, Danny was much worse. In this case, I think I believe much of Rhonda's story," answered Ray.

"Can she ever sort things out and stay out of trouble?"

"There's always hope. It won't be easy putting one's life in order at sixty-something."

"The Sherwood things, you're still noodling around the Orville vandalism?"

"Yes. I wonder if Rhonda's story about Danny and Dirk is true. Did they get away with murder? Does anyone else know that Rob was murdered? Orville's house was torched, his grave vandalized. Those things happened so long ago. Who knows about them and is still filled with rage? Did someone recently get out of the Heartbreak Hotel and come back to get even?"

"No body, and the alleged assailants are all dead. That's a crime too far, Ray."

And yet Ray couldn't stop thinking about it as he lay in bed that night, Simone nestled in the crook of his arm. He stroked her for a long time before finally falling asleep.

39

"I have to leave for an appointment in twenty minutes," said Olivia Shepard as she directed Sue toward a stool at the island in her kitchen. "I've already told you everything I know about Becca Sterling."

Sue noted the edge to the woman's tone.

"Thank you for making time for me," Sue said calmly. "This will only take a few minutes. We continue to gather new information during an investigation. Sometimes that information conflicts with things we learned earlier. When that happens, we need to go back and clarify with the person who provided the information initially."

Sue took out her iPhone and set it on the counter. "With your permission, I'd like to record our conversation."

"I don't see why that's necessary," Shepard huffed, now clearly angry, her porcine countenance reddening.

"It's all about accuracy. It allows me to listen to our conversation again and make sure that I heard everything correctly."

"Whatever," expostulated Shepard.

Sue started a recording app, identified the time, location, and Olivia Shepard and herself. Then she said, "When we talked the other day, you told me that you hadn't seen Ms. Sterling since last summer sometime. Is that correct?"

"Yes, I can't remember exactly when, like a date or anything. But that is essentially correct."

"You also said you hadn't been out to Fox Cove since the summer. Is that correct?"

"Yes. That old building of Brian's is filled with mold and mildew. I only go to the cottage when I can have all the windows wide open. I don't go near the place in the winter."

"You could go to Fox Cove without setting foot in your cottage."

"True, but why would I? You're wasting my time."

"A social visit, perhaps? You have friends there."

"I'm a summer person only."

"Sharon Peterson told me she had a conversation with you sometime in October."

"Possibly, I don't remember. We're old friends. We talk from time to time on the phone."

"Sharon's memory is that the conversation was less than friendly. You accused her of not telling you about a possible relationship between your husband and Becca Sterling." Sue looked across the granite countertop at Olivia Shepard, her words hanging between them for several moments.

"I don't remember the conversation quite that way," said Shepard. "And I'm sure it happened in the summer."

"There was something about money, too." Sue watched Shepard closely as her words landed.

"Look," said Shepard, "that was a conversation between friends. It's not some rumor to be bandied about. I feel betrayed, totally betrayed. Why would she do that?"

"Becca Sterling, her niece, is dead," Sue said sternly. "A murder has been committed. A little girl is without her mother. My job is to get justice for this woman and bring closure to her family."

"I shouldn't be talking to you. This conversation is over."

"That's your choice. But I'd think that you'd want to help. You have information that would move this investigation forward."

Olivia Shepard looked past Sue, out to the swirling snow dancing across the bay. Finally, she said, "The money. Okay, here's the whole sad story."

Shepard launched into a long-winded story about her long-term friend, Emma Doyle, the bookkeeper at her husband's practice. She explained how the two women had bonded over the years as they shared the intimate details of their tottering marriages.

Shepard then detailed a conversation in the early fall with Emma Doyle. They were having dinner at the Cooks' House. As they were finishing their second bottle of wine, Emma told her about the payments going from one of Brian's LLCs to Becca Sterling's checking account.

"Emma's disclosure triggered something deep inside me. All the hurt, all the tears, all the embarrassment, all the suppressed anger came to the surface. I confronted Brian. He laughed at me. He said that I had shut him out of my life years ago. Then he told me that Becca made him feel loved, something he never got from me. He said that Ava was his, that she was more part of him than our children could ever be. He said he wanted to spend the rest of his life with Becca and Ava, and that I could go to hell." Shepard collapsed in tears.

Sue regarded her calmly, although her mind was racing.

"I know what you're thinking," Shepard said, struggling to regain her composure. "I should have broken a wine bottle over his head or something like that. I didn't. First, I blamed myself, like always. Eventually, I went after Sharon Peterson. After that, I destroyed my friendship with Emma Doyle. And at the end of the day, I let Brian skate. I was blaming myself first and my friends. When I told my shrink about this, she just rolled her eyes."

"But you never went toe-to-toe with Becca?"

"No, never."

"I'm not certain I can trust your story now, Mrs. Shepard, since it keeps changing. Why wasn't Becca on your list of people to blame and confront?"

Shepard didn't answer. She hunched over the island, her lips tightly pursed, the knuckles of her closed hands pressed against the hard countertop.

"A week ago Tuesday, in the evening, where were you?" Sue asked.

"I was here. It's my Tuesday night music group. At least ten people, including Brian, can tell you."

"All evening?"

"Look, we play music, we eat food, drink wine, and then some stay late and talk. Eventually, my company left, and I went to bed."

"Your husband had come home earlier that evening. And as far as you knew, Becca was alone. I notice you have a security system. If I got a search warrant to access that video, what would I find on the evening in question? Would the video show your minivan backing out of the garage sometime after midnight, maybe returning two hours later? Or perhaps we'd see your husband leaving. Who is on that video? My bet is it's you."

Olivia Shepard's eyes darted around the room and then returned to Sue's face, panicked. She took several deep breaths, then said, "It was me. But nothing happened. I mean, the three other women in my string quartet—we're very close—went with me. They know what I've been dealing with. They hung around after everyone left. We were drinking wine, probably way too much. Somehow the idea came up that I should confront Becca. You know, like drive out there, get Becca out of bed, and get it over with. As we talked about it back and forth, there seemed to be great clarity that this would resolve everything. I would feel better and finally be able to let it all go, let Brian go. Now it seems like a silly idea, but it made sense then. Anyway, we got into my minivan…"

"Who got in?"

Shepard gave Sue the names of her three friends. "They were cheering me on. As we drove out to Fox Cove, they helped me rehearse exactly what to say. The plan was that when we got out to Becca's, they would march to the door with me. And then she and I would have this dramatic face-to-face."

"So what happened?"

"She has a steep driveway, and I almost got stuck in a drift. I gunned it to get through. As I cleared the crest at the top, a truck was blocking my path. It was facing my way, lights on, blinding me for a second or two. And not just ordinary headlights. There were four lights, extra bright."

"What kind of a truck?"

"A work van, I think. You know, like plumbers or electricians use."

"Color?"

"They're always white."

"Could it have been a pickup truck?" Sue asked, thinking of the elusive black Dodge.

"No, no hood. The windshield was close to the front. It had to be a van."

"Did you see any lettering, any names?"

"Nothing like that. I could only see the front."

"What did you do?"

"I slammed on the brakes so that I wouldn't smash into it."

"Was there anyone in the vehicle?"

"I couldn't tell."

"Then what happened?"

"Suddenly, I was sober. I backed down the driveway very slowly. Thank God for rear cameras. I didn't want to get stuck. Can you imagine having to call for a tow right there? How embarrassing would that be? And then I drove home. No one said much on the way back. Get a search warrant. Look at the video. That's what you'll see."

"Why didn't you tell us about this the first time we talked to you?" Sue asked, barely concealing her own indignation.

"It would have given Brian a perfect alibi. He deserves to suffer, the bastard." Her dark eyes burned. "I swear, I would have let him go to jail for it."

Olivia Shepard stood and reached for her phone, and then recited contact information for the three friends who had been in the minivan with her the Tuesday night that Becca Sterling had died. Sue suppressed the impulse to push out a loud breath, to try to purge the feeling that pettiness was the most dangerous human trait.

Once the interview was over, Sue sat in the Shepards' driveway, vibrating with the excitement of uncovering another clue. She needed to tell Ray right away about the white van. But first, she dialed one of the numbers Olivia Shepard had given her for the other three women in her string quartet. As the phone on the other end of the line rang, it occurred to her that Becca Sterling had most likely been fighting for her life as Olivia Shepard backed carefully down her driveway and drove away.

40

S ue was nearing the law enforcement center after her interview
with Olivia Shepard when she got a call to respond to a possible
B and E at Butch's Guns and Ammo a mile or so off M22 in a
remote corner of the county. She welcomed the opportunity to stay
out of the office and put a few more miles on her new truck.

Sue slowed, then stopped and surveyed the area in front of
Butch's Guns and Ammo, a small frame structure set back from the
road with paint peeling off the siding in patches. To the left of the
building, a deeply rutted drive ran up a steep grade, disappearing
into the woods beyond. The front door of Butch's had been ripped
off. Framing and insulation clung to the open wound.

Sue, taking a camera with her, climbed out of her truck and
photographed the scene. She recorded the tire tracks in the
unplowed parking area in front of the store, standing for a moment
and scanning the tracks, hoping to find a tire print that could
be cast. There was none. Then she circled back, approaching the
structure from the left front. Pausing near the center of the store and
looking toward the road, she could see the remains of the front door
scattered across the snow. She took several more pictures and then
panned from left to right, shooting video of the area.

The snow had stopped. A heavy overcast still enveloped the area.
Then the quiet of the winter's morning was broken by the rumble
of a vehicle. As she turned, a red pickup came down the drive next
to the store and slid to a stop at the base of the hill. A heavily built
man wearing worn Carhartts emerged and waddled toward her, his
tall leather boots unlaced, the tops spread open, barely clearing the
snow. A red knit hat covered the man's head.

"Where's the sheriff?" he demanded, his full beard moving as he spoke.

"I'm Detective Sue Lawrence," Sue said, pulling her ID from a jacket pocket and showing it to the man. "I do crime scene investigations. Are you Butch?"

"Naw, Butch is dead. That was my dad. When I was a kid, people called me Butch Junior. I never liked that much. Eventually, everyone just called me Junior. That stuck."

"And your last name, sir?"

"Wade."

"And you called this in?"

"Yeah."

"So, Mr. Wade, you just noticed the damage this morning?"

"That's right. I was going out to get a few groceries. It was snowing hard. I came down the hill and saw this mess." Wade gestured toward the debris. "I looked around for a couple of minutes, then went back up to the house and called you guys. We don't got no cell."

"So when do you think this happened?"

"It had to be sometime in the night. I went out yesterday for cigarettes just before dark. Didn't notice nothing then."

"And no one called your attention to the damage before you discovered it this morning?"

"In the winter, we're at the end of the line. Just a few summer homes on that puddle of a lake down the lane. That was always old Butch's joke about this place. When he retired from Pontiac, he said he needed something to do. He had been a millwright for close to forty years. He had been thinking about opening a gun shop forever, but he didn't want to be too busy. So when he found this piece of property at the end of nowhere, he thought it would be perfect."

"This is not an operating business?"

"No, not for years, not since old Butch died. That was back in 2003. And even then, he wasn't doing much for maybe ten years before. He never really sold guns, he found out there was too much paperwork. But he was a skilled gunsmith. Word got around. He had some steady business from locals for a while. I think things were petering out toward the end. After he died, I put a big Closed sign on the front. It fell off a few years ago. Didn't seem to matter. Everyone around here knew it was closed."

Sue studied the damage to the front of the building. "Looks like someone hooked on to the security door and pulled it off. Must have been a four-by-four of some sort."

"That was my thought," said Wade. "You can see the marks in the snow. Spun the tires trying to get enough traction."

"And you live up there?" Sue pointed toward the hill.

"Yup. Me and the wife."

"And you heard nothing?"

"Our place is back in the woods, maybe a hundred yards. We never hear nothing from down here. And I don't hear much, anyway. Too many years on the factory floor."

Sue gestured toward the damage. "Have you gone in and looked around?"

"I poked my head in."

"Can you tell me what's missing?"

"Not really. Nothing much in there but junk, old tools mostly. Everything's rusty as hell. Mice and squirrels, they took possession years ago. I hate being in there. Makes my skin crawl."

"So there were no guns of any type in the building?"

"No, ma'am."

"And you're sure there was nothing else of value in the building?"

"Like I said, just a bunch of rusty junk."

"Why would anyone go to all trouble of breaking in?"

"Beats the hell outta me. They must not have been from around here. Or maybe they got fooled by the security bars on the windows and door. Drugs, people do crazy shit."

"I want you to go inside with me. Tell me if anything seems out of place or is missing."

Sue took out her LED flashlight and carefully picked her way through the debris and into the store, Wade following her. A narrow, navigable trail circled the rubbish and machinery that filled the interior. A littered workbench ran along the back wall. A pegboard secured above the workbench displayed the black outline of tools. Sue pointed at the pegboard.

"Butch got excited about organization. He just never could keep it going. I never saw many tools up there after he put them up the first time."

Sue turned her attention to the north end of the building. "How about this area here?" she asked.

"That's where he used to stack ammo when he started the business. He said there was a good profit in ammo, especially early before the big box stores came in. Then, he told me, his sales petered out."

"It appears that there are still a variety of cartridges here," Sue said, holding the beam of light on some stacks of boxes.

"In later years that was mostly his private stock. He was a hunter. The cartridges left here must have been oddball stuff that didn't work in his guns."

"I take it you're not a hunter?"

"No, I never really liked hunting."

"And you no longer have your father's weapons around?"

"No, we have a grandson with behavioral problems. I got rid of the guns when he started spending summers with us."

Sue ran the light back and forth along the wall of shelves, where small stacks of cartridge boxes were widely spaced.

"Can you tell if anything is missing?" she asked.

"I would have no idea. I can't imagine any of that stuff would be usable. I mean, they got to be way past their use date," Wade said, coming to stand beside her.

"Give things a careful look," said Sue, handing him the light.

She watched as he ran the light back and forth over the shelves.

As he handed the light back, he said, "I don't know. I think there used to be more here. I mean, back in the day, he had labels on the shelves, you know that plastic tape stuff that came out of a handheld contraption. As you can see, the labels have mostly fallen off. I mean, it's possible there were more boxes here. But I couldn't say for sure."

Sue carefully scanned the stacks of boxes again. She did find a red plastic label with white lettering reading "30-06" below an empty shelf. A break in the layer of dust suggested that at least one box had recently been removed.

"When were you last in this building?" asked Sue.

"Sometime in the fall. I was looking for a tool, a vise-grip. Thought there might be one here. There wasn't. Not that I could find, anyway."

Sue handed Junior the light. "Sir, please take a careful look around the interior. See if there is anything here that shouldn't be."

"What am I looking for?"

"Anything that shouldn't be here."

She waited patiently as Wade looked around the interior. Finally, he said, "Nothing that I can see. Other than the door, everything is pretty much the same."

"Does anyone else have access to this building?"

"No. I'm the only one to be in here since my dad died."

"Has there ever been a break-in before?"

"Never."

Sue took one more look around the interior and then followed Wade out of the building.

"I'll file a police report," Sue said. "You can get a copy for your insurance company. I think you should get all of the cartridges out of there, so they don't fall into the wrong hands."

Junior shrugged. "I'm not sure what I'd do with them."

"I have a cardboard box in the truck. If you like, I can take the ammunition with me and have it properly disposed of. Would that work for you?"

"Yes, that would be good. One less problem for me. I don't know what to do with this mess." He looked back at the building. "How about nailing the SOBs who did this?"

"We will do our best. At this point, I don't have much to work with." Sue passed Wade her card. "Feel free to contact me. If you see anything else suspicious or think of any details we didn't cover, please call us immediately. I'll get the box for you."

A few minutes later, Sue returned to her truck, stowing the shells in a rear cargo area. After pulling on her seatbelt, she watched Junior Wade's truck disappear up the hill toward his home. Then she turned her attention to filling in the bones of the police report. She thought about the possibility of stolen .30-06 ammunition. *20 rounds to a box, 100 rounds to five boxes, 200 to ten boxes.* She shuddered as she thought about the possible deadly scenarios.

41

Ray pushed the door open at Northshore Mechanical Systems, triggering a tinny brass bell mounted above the frame. As he stood in the damp cold of the converted old gas station, he could hear the sound of machinery running in the back room.

"Dale?" Ray called, but no one answered. "Dale!" Ray shouted, and when even his raised voice drew no response, he opened the door marked "Employees Only" and walked into the workshop.

Dale Huber, the owner, wearing heavy plastic hearing protectors, was cutting a piece of metal on a band saw. He jumped when Ray touched his shoulder.

Dale switched off the machine and removed his ear protectors and safety glasses. "Hey," he said, wiping his hands on a rag before extending one in Ray's direction. He was a slender man about ten years older than Ray, with eyes crinkled at the corners from smiling and squinting into the sun.

"How are things going?" Ray asked, remembering that he hadn't seen Dale for several years.

"Can't complain. My busy season," said Dale.

"How are your parents?"

"They're good—snowbirds now. Used to be they'd stay till Christmas. Now after the first flake or two, they're out of here. I won't see them again until May."

"And the twins?" asked Ray.

"Julie is still at State, working on a master's. Jenna's got a job in Chicago and is thinking about law school. She's also got a man. We don't know where that's going. Kids," said Dale, throwing open his arms and rolling his eyes up toward the ceiling. "What brings you in?" he asked Ray.

"I've got a couple of questions that maybe you can help me with." Ray shifted his weight inside his boots to warm his toes.

"I'll do my best."

"Did you hear that Becca Sterling was murdered in her home in Fox Cove?"

Dale grimaced and rubbed the back of his neck. "Awful. When Ms. Sterling rebuilt the place, I was the sub for the mechanical systems. And the first fall after she moved in I came back to do some fine-tuning—balancing the heat in all the rooms, that kind of thing. I got to know her a bit. And then about a year ago she had me come back to put in a smart thermostat. Her little girl was about a year old then. What a lovely person, Becca. I've been thinking about her since I heard the news. As I told my wife, I don't understand why anyone would want to hurt her. What's going on?"

"My detective, Sue Lawrence, and I have been talking to anyone who was in the Fox Cove area near the time Ms. Sterling died. We're hoping someone might have seen something. First, we talked to all the winter residents, and now we're branching out a bit. Brian Shepard mentioned that he contacted you late that Tuesday, and you couldn't do a service call to his place until Wednesday morning. Is that correct?"

"Yes. Not late-late. Nine or so. I was on the other side of the county on a service call. I knew I was probably going to be there until close to midnight. I told Dr. Shepard that I'd come in the morning. He was grumpy as hell, like I should drop everything and run over. I had to explain I couldn't be in two places at one time. You know, usually he's a good guy, but he seemed to have a burr under his saddle."

"So you were at his cottage the next morning, a Wednesday?" Ray's fingers were growing numb as he clenched his pen.

"Yes, dragged myself out of bed. Could have used a few more hours, but I didn't want his plumbing to freeze. You know, I did a tune-up on that furnace in the fall, like I always do. He's one of my regulars. And I've been telling him for years that the unit is worn out and should be replaced. But he didn't want to hear it. I'm surprised it lasted as long as it did."

"Did you install a new furnace?"

"I'm waiting on my distributor. I cobbled the old one together with some spares I cannibalized from junk around here. I've been running out to Fox Cove every few days to make sure he's got heat."

"Have you seen Dr. Shepard since he called about the furnace?"

"No, I've just talked to him on the phone a few times."

"As you're driving out there, have you seen anything unusual? People or vehicles?"

"Most days I'm just happy to get there without ending up in a ditch. I think Fox Cove Drive is the last road in the county to get plowed. I may need to trade my van for a SnowCat if the winter keeps going like this."

"Dale, you know the area up around Fox Cove. Did you see anyone around there that didn't belong? Same thing for vehicles."

Dale pulled at an ear, then said, "This wasn't at Fox Cove. But I did see a real beater on the curve just before the turnoff to the lighthouse. I don't know anyone that's got a work truck that old."

"You talking a pickup or a van?"

"A van. It was dented and rusting at the seams. But the thing that caught my attention was one of the back doors looked like it was being held together with duct tape." Dale picked up a roll of tape from the workbench. "I said to myself that the driver couldn't be a furnace guy. I'm thinking maybe a drywaller. I mean, the tape was all wrinkled like a bad mud job."

"Do you remember anything about the license plate?"

"It was mostly covered with snow, but I thought I saw a cactus. So what's that, Arizona?"

"Probably."

"That got me wondering what the hell the driver was doing in a snowstorm in northern Michigan. I mean, it's amazing they made it up here in that pile of crap. That got me thinking about being someplace warm. When I got home, I said to the wife, 'We need to go south.' She gave me a long look and said, 'Sure. I can be packed in an hour. By the way, who's going to make all the service calls?' Then she added 'I'll call Julie and say the tuition money for next term is going to be a bit late.' Anyway, Ray, it was a lovely fantasy while it lasted."

Ray chuckled as he jotted a few notes. "Did you only see the van one time?"

"No, I saw it a day or two later. I was on my way to check on Dr. Shepard's furnace. It was off the highway a couple of miles down the road from Fox Cove. No one seemed to be around. I thought it must have died, but it was gone on my return trip."

"Did you notice anything else about it?"

"It had a kangaroo catcher on the front. You know, the grille guards young guys use to pimp up their trucks, to give them the macho look. Why would anyone bother with that pile of junk?"

Ray made another note about the grille guard. "And you haven't seen it since?"

"No."

"Give me a call right away if you see it again, won't you?"

"Absolutely."

Ray was grateful to pull his gloves out of his coat and slide them back on. "What's going on with the heating in here?" he asked.

Dale pointed to the furnace suspended from the ceiling above the workshop. "The shoemaker's children have no shoes."

42

Sue stopped off in Ray's office late in the afternoon.

He looked away from his screen, then stood and walked to the conference table.

"The Olivia Shepard interview—the most recent one—skillful work, Sue. You did such an excellent job moving the conversation forward and finally getting her to tell you the whole story."

"I had a good mentor," said Sue, smiling.

Sue peered at the whiteboard. "Looks like you're going in a new direction this afternoon."

"How can you tell?" he asked.

"Different color marker."

"The green went dry. I must have left the cover off," he explained. "Today's color is bright red. By the way, remind me to order more markers."

"You want me to make that happen?"

"No, Sue, just remind me."

"So what are all the lines and things crossed out?"

"I'm trying to get rid of items that seem extraneous to the investigation."

"Don't take too many out," chided Sue. "We won't have anything left."

"I read your report on the B and E earlier at Butch's," said Ray. "Maybe our shooter needed to resupply?"

"Seems so," Sue said grimly. "I brought the rest of the ammo from the shop in for disposal. Butch, Jr. said if the perps were looking for guns, they couldn't have been from the area. All the locals know the place closed after old Butch died."

"And the locals also know we don't bother to take the signs down when we close a business. It's one of our traditions," Ray added.

"I'm still learning about all these up-north traditions."

"By the way, how's the new truck?"

"Good karma, totally good karma," she said, smiling.

43

~

Ray was awakened before dawn by the tinny sound of the opening bars of a Mahler symphony coming from his phone. A few minutes later, he was in his car, carefully maneuvering the snow-covered roads in the gray dawn, finally turning onto Fox Cove Road. The flames from the fire were reaching into the dark overcast, illuminating the low bellies of the clouds. He parked at the end of a long line of emergency vehicles, their lights pulsating, engines idling. He walked toward the fire, now a familiar pathway, up the hill toward Becca Sterling's house.

Tom Butler, the township fire chief, was standing near a tanker truck.

"It was mostly gone by the time we got here," Tom explained. "The man over there said it was unoccupied. I guess he called it in."

Ray looked in the direction that Tom was pointing. He could see Chuck Peterson talking to one of the other firemen. *Chuck Peterson,* thought Ray, *is always at the center of things.*

"Yes, it is unoccupied and an active crime scene," Ray said.

"This is where that woman died?"

Ray nodded.

"I could see some remnants of police line when we rolled in. Someone had been here before us, Ray. There were fresh tracks in the snow. The garage was torched, too. And I don't think the fire could've jumped to that structure. They are too far apart, no wind. We got a pyro on the loose? Two empty buildings torched late at night. This time the guy left a calling card." Tom walked Ray to the front of the truck. A plastic gas can sat on the snow.

Ray's mind rolled over. It was the same type of gas can they'd found in the snow outside Sheriff Hentzler's blazing house. Was it possible that the two arsons were unrelated? While this type of gas can could be found in 90 percent of the garages and sheds in the area, what was the chance that two different arsonists had chosen not only to use it but to leave it behind? If these two arsons were related, what possible connection could there be between Sheriff Orville Hentzler and Becca Sterling?

"I hustled that as soon as I spotted it," Tom said. "Thought maybe you guys could get some prints off it."

"I'll take it with me when I leave. Thanks," said Ray. "I need to talk to that man," he explained, motioning toward Peterson.

"What's this all about, Sheriff?" Chuck Peterson asked, his eyes wide with anxiety. "I don't understand. This is crazy."

"How did you spot the fire?" asked Ray.

"The dogs were restless."

Ray remembered that Chuck Peterson's dog had led him out into the snow the night Becca was killed. If they'd come out any later, Ava might have been lost to hypothermia.

"Finally," Chuck said, "I got up and walked into the great room. I could see the flames shooting skyward. After calling 911, I got Sharon up. We didn't want Ava to see this. So we quickly packed a few things and hustled Ava into a warm car. They're heading downstate to our daughter's. I'll follow them later today with the dogs. I want to check on Frances first."

Chuck looked at the fire, then back at Ray. "Someone torched the place, right?"

"Probably," he responded.

"Yeah, I know that you can't say anything for sure, but you know it's true. What the hell is going on? First Becca is killed—murdered! And now this! We're scared, Sheriff. Is Ava in danger? Maybe we shouldn't even bring her back here. How about Frances? She must be petrified."

"The fire chief has already evacuated Mrs. Adams," Ray said. "Social services will make sure she is safe and cared for. I'll stay in contact with you and keep you updated."

As they shook hands, Ray could see the pain on the older man's face. He stood and watched Peterson retreat, plodding through the deep snow as he maneuvered around fire engines down the slope toward his home.

Ray stayed at the scene, watching the firefighters work to extinguish the blaze. One group, positioned from a safe distance, focused on the garage, the thick stream from their hose directed toward the vehicle inside, tires burning, glass exploding in the heat, the interior of the car in flames.

He moved toward the beach, out of the smoke, and watched the flat roof of the house collapse in a jagged line as the exterior walls gave way. A few of the interior walls remained, briefly giving the structure a tent-like appearance before they, too, gave way. The fire crews moved closer, smothering the last bits of fire, steam rising into the early morning gray.

Ray stood for a long time thinking about the murdered woman and the world she had created for herself and her young daughter. He remembered Chuck and Sharon Peterson's descriptions of how painstakingly Becca Sterling had rebuilt and redesigned the old buildings to reflect her personality. Now nothing remained. It was as if someone was trying to eradicate any evidence that she had ever lived in Fox Cove. He turned toward the lake and looked out toward the Manitous in the dull morning light, dark shadows on an ebony plane. What was he missing? What was the source of this burning rage?

His contemplation was interrupted by the vibration of his phone. He pulled it from an interior pocket and looked at the screen.

Fire. North Bay. Units dispatched.

44

Simone bounded through Ray's open office door, stopped at his side, gave a commanding bark, and jumped into his lap. Sue and Mike Ogden, the state police arson investigator, followed Simone in and sat down on one side of the conference table.

"Better get over here, Ray, everything's hot," said Sue.

"What's the menu?" he asked, rising with Simone under his arm. He took a chair across from them, Simone in his lap.

"For you, the special vegetarian sandwich of the day. Fried tofu in a Szechuan sauce on a whole wheat bun, kale salad with dressing on the side, and a large green tea."

"And for you?"

"The usual, a burger and sweet potato fries, diet coke with a slice of lemon. And he's having what I'm having," said Sue, pointing her thumb toward Mike Ogden. "The slice of lemon thing I learned from Ray," she explained to Mike. "He's helping me develop a more discerning palate." She threw Ray a smirk.

"You guys always do a working lunch?" asked Mike.

"Mostly," Sue responded. "But Ray doesn't get to work at his keyboard during lunch anymore. I insist that he sits here and talks to me. No more double tasking. I'm trying to make him a little bit less of a workaholic."

"Look who's talking," said Ray, tearing off a small piece of the bun for Simone before taking a bite of the sandwich himself. Sue was, as a general rule, chattier than he, but was she chattier than usual today? Ray looked at Mike. "The fire at Becca Sterling's, the place was destroyed so quickly. But the next fire at Stu Baker's hundred-year-old building—I think it was a hardware or general store along the way—it's still standing."

"It doesn't seem logical, does it?" said Mike, taking another bite of his burger and chewing slowly.

Ray, impatient for answers, wondered if he'd ever seen someone savor a burger so deliberately.

"That surprises a lot of people," said Mike finally. "It's all about materials. New furniture—sofas, mattresses, flooring materials, cabinetry—that stuff is filled with petroleum-based compounds that burn hot and fast. And then you've got all that OSB in the walls and roof. That, too, is highly flammable once it gets started. That second fire, in contrast, the building was built with real lumber, first growth. The wood may be old and dry, but it's dense and slow to burn. It's not as flammable as all those wood chips held together with plastics. And then some good luck was involved, too. The building was mostly empty, firefighters were on the scene very quickly, and they had an adequate source of water. They could knock the flames down fast. Long-term, I don't know if the building can be saved, but the place is still standing."

"Same MO?"

"Absolutely," answered Ogden. "The perp splashed some gasoline and torched the Sterling place, then headed up the road sixteen miles and set the second fire, leaving some empty gas cans behind. This guy isn't worried about getting caught. He's some kind of crazy. He's going to keep torching things until he gets caught. You guys got any possible suspects, motives?"

Sue looked across the table at Ray, deferring to him, and then answered after he nodded at her to go ahead. "No one's on the radar. Our last firebug moved on several years ago. As to motive, unclear. Perhaps some old history, maybe a connection between the Hentzler fire and the Baker fire."

"What's that?" asked Mike.

"Hentzler and his goons—I mean deputies—allegedly harassed people living in a commune in the '70s. There is even a rumor that they might have killed one of the commune's leaders," explained Sue.

Mike nodded. "Stories you don't want to hear. But so long ago. Why now? And what's the connection?"

"Baker lived at the commune," said Sue.

"That's it?" said Ogden.

"Yes," she answered. Then she told Ogden about the damage to Hentzler's grave.

"So all you know is someone is still trying to get revenge on a guy long dead? The connection to the Baker fire seems tenuous, at best. Have you guys talked to him?"

"Just a few words," said Ray. "He was distraught. Said he was lucky. He sells his work from that place in the summer, then moves his paintings to a climate-controlled building in the winter. But I pressed him on possible suspects. He had nothing to offer."

"Any reason for him to torch his own building?"

"I don't think so. It couldn't have been insured for much. It's got lots of rustic charm. It was a perfect venue for displaying and selling regional art. But it is what it is, a century-old structure in need of repair."

"What about Ms. Sterling's cottage? That was an active crime scene?"

"Not really active. I don't think there was anything more to learn there. We were still protecting it on the off chance I wanted to take another look."

"Where are you in that investigation?"

"Still turning the soil," answered Sue. "Nothing definite yet."

Ogden wadded up the wrapper from his burger. "You don't need an arson investigator. You need a profiler. You've got some pyro wacko running loose."

"Any suggestions?" asked Sue, giving Mike a playful punch in the arm.

Ray watched her gesture with interest, then headed toward the ringing phone on his desk, passing Simone off to Sue on the way.

"We have to go," said Ray as he hung up the phone.

"What's going on?" said Sue.

"That was Wendy Morrison. Cara went missing a few days ago.

She'd borrowed a credit card to pay her tuition. Wendy just got a call from the credit card company. Someone was trying to use her card at the Shore and Surf Motel. I'll call dispatch for a backup while you drive."

45

"The sounds of silence," said Sue, looking over at Ray in the passenger seat.

"Hard to tell the engine's running," he agreed. "Do you know how the radio works?"

"The manual, Elkins, it's in the glove box. And before you get engrossed in that, what's our plan?"

"We'll go in and leave Rory in his car with the engine running in case someone decides to do a runner."

Sue drove up the narrow drive that led to the Shore and Surf Motel's parking lot and stopped near the entrance. Ray led the way into the dingy lobby. A frail, tired-looking woman, cigarette clutched in a bony hand, stood up behind the counter and then leaned against it, as though she couldn't stay upright without help. Ray looked down the long dimly lit hallway that led away from the lobby and then said, "I'm looking for Cara Morrison."

"No one here by that name, Sheriff," the clerk said, blowing smoke in his direction.

"Stella, I don't have time for any of your crap."

"See for yourself," she said, slamming the register on the counter.

"Young woman, bluish hair, lots of piercings. What room, Stella?"

"Oh, that kid. She and her man left thirty, forty minutes ago. They wanted to stay a couple more nights. Paid cash last night, tried to use a card this morning. It didn't work. I told them they had to come up with the money or be gone by noon. They left about half past twelve, flipping me off on their way out. The room's a pigsty, I just checked. Garbage people. That's all I get this time of year."

"I'd like to look at the room," said Ray.

Stella reached into a tan metal cabinet on the wall and grabbed a faded maroon plastic fob with a key attached. She tossed it on the counter in front of Ray. "It's number twenty-two, down near the end."

"Let's get a quick look," said Ray, leading the way. He opened the door and peered into the dark interior. The room reeked of tobacco. A wastebasket, on its side, spilled beer cans and crumpled fast food wrappers onto the floor. Ray stood near the door as Sue did a quick sweep of the room.

"Nothing here of interest," she said. "No needles, no roaches."

"Stella, let me see the registration again," said Ray when they returned to the lobby.

Looking at Sue, Ray read the entry out loud. "Manny Tishull, T-I-S-H-U-L-L, Kentwood, Michigan."

"Got it," she responded, recording the information on a notepad.

"Did you check this for accuracy, Stella?" Ray asked.

"Damn straight, picture ID, everything."

"How about the vehicle?"

"I made him bring in the registration. He was pissed about that. Like I care. I know his type. If they tear up the room, I want to try to get damages. I do everything by the book, Sheriff. Don't want no trouble."

Ray held the registration book in Sue's direction. "Toyota pickup."

"How about the color, Stella?"

"Red."

"You sure about that?"

"Yeah. My kid's got one just like it. Red, too. I'm not color blind, Sheriff."

"Thanks for the help, Stella."

"Any time, Sheriff. I'm always on the side of the law."

As they walked toward her truck, Sue said, "You and Stella know each other?"

"I arrested her for running a bawdy house my first winter on the job. It was deer season. I guess she'd been doing it for years. She got six months in the Heartbreak Hotel. And a fine of $750, as I remember it."

"Had Dirk and the boys been getting a piece of the action along the way?" asked Sue.

"Probably," answered Ray. "Literally and figuratively, probably both."

"Elkins."

"Just giving you the facts, Sue. According to rumor, they had all kinds of ways of enriching themselves, and they weren't above extracting a little in cash or services for providing protection."

"Did you know what you were getting into when you ran for office? I mean, you'd been living out-of-state and everything."

"The people who encouraged me to go after the job were clear about the problems. And I knew I could put things right. I had done it before. It's not rocket science. Get rid of the deadwood, recruit good people, provide continuous training, and build a professional team."

He paused for a moment. "Back then everything seemed fixable, but now . . ." His voice faded off.

"What are you talking about?" asked Sue.

"The dope thing. I don't see a way out. We're just going down the rabbit hole."

"Maybe there's no fix at this level, Ray. We're doing everything we can," said Sue, pulling open her door.

Ray nodded unconvincingly as they got into the truck. "Run the Tishull guy while I walk over and talk to Rory for a moment and let him get back to his normal duties."

"Anything?" Ray asked as he climbed back into Sue's truck and pulled on his seatbelt.

"Suspended license and two outstandings," she said, turning the screen in his direction. "That's enough to bring him in. I've alerted dispatch. Maybe they're still in the county."

"Head toward Fox Cove," said Ray. "I want to tie up a loose end."

46

"Glad I caught you before you left," said Ray. Chuck Peterson was standing at the back of a Honda van, trying to cram a small suitcase into the already jammed interior.

"Not easy to get a woman, a toddler, and two dogs packed for an extended stay away from home. I had hoped to be downstate by dark. It's probably not going to happen."

"I don't want to interrupt your packing. I won't keep you long. I do need your help."

"Okay," Chuck said without enthusiasm.

"I need a few pictures. One or two of Becca as a teen, and a more recent one. And one of Becca's mother, from her late teens, if that's possible."

"Sharon's the keeper of the photos. I'll see what I can find."

Ray followed Chuck into the house and then down a half-flight of stairs into the family room.

"Sharon's got everything organized by year. I'll pull the ones that might have what you want."

After fifteen or twenty minutes of looking through albums, Ray slipped four photos into the envelope that Peterson handed him.

"These will be helpful. Thank you," said Ray. "I'll get them back to you as soon as possible."

"Lot of our history there," said Peterson, looking from the albums in his hands to the row lined up on the shelf. "I better see if I can get these back where they came from. You know what I'm saying."

"Yes," Ray agreed.

Sue looked up from her report writing to see Ray leave the house, Chuck Peterson holding his hand briefly before he disappeared back into his home. Phone in hand, Ray stopped near the front of her truck and chatted briefly.

"Important phone call?" asked Sue as Ray climbed back into the truck.

"I was arranging our next stop. Head up to North Bay."

"Did you get what you were looking for?" she asked before starting the engine.

"Yes. Look at these." He pulled the four photos out of an envelope.

"These two, I'm guessing ages here, Becca as a young teen, and later, sometime in college," said Sue.

"Yes," said Ray.

"Beautiful woman, even in the gangly adolescent stage." She looked at the other two photos. "This is probably Becca's mother, mid to late teens in the first, maybe around thirty in the second. Strong family resemblance."

"Mother and daughter," responded Ray. "Monique and Becca, seventeen, eighteen, perhaps nineteen years apart. I know you can get the birth dates."

"That's an easy one."

"You know," said Ray, "we might have this all wrong."

"What are you talking about?" asked Sue.

"Dr. Shepard. We need to bring him in and do a formal interview."

"Okay. What are you thinking?"

"What if Becca's death is somehow connected to Sherwood Forest?"

"I've wondered about that," said Sue. "But the connections seem more like an unhappy coincidence."

"Agreed, but still—"

"So we're going to North Bay to talk to Stu Baker about Sherwood Forest, Monique, and the fire?"

"Yes, all of the above. We're meeting Baker at what remains of his gallery."

They parked down the road from Stu Baker's gallery. Bright yellow tape bearing the message "Fire Line Do Not Cross" in bold black lettering circled the building. The township fire department was still on the scene, the crew in the final stages of collecting and stowing equipment. Stu Baker, tall, hatless, with a full head of white hair, stood on the perimeter watching the process.

Ray walked to Stu's side, and Sue drifted away.

"Sheriff," said Stu, extending a hand.

"Sorry," said Ray.

"Thanks. Thought this place would be standing longer than me. You never know, do you?"

"No," Ray answered. They stood quietly, looking at the badly damaged building.

"It just makes no sense, Ray. It's been here for more than a hundred years, and suddenly . . ."

"What's going to happen?"

"My insurance guy just left. They'll bring in an outside consultant to inspect the building."

"Then what?"

"I don't know. I couldn't nail the guy down. The one good thing is they've hired a contractor to secure the building. You know, get the place boarded up. If the building has to come down, I don't know what I'll do. It can't be replaced, not with current code. Big, empty shell, bare stud walls, lots of character. No heat or plumbing, just electricity. It was perfect, a rustic gallery open only during the tourist season."

Ray opened the envelope he had been carrying and pulled out four photos. He first handed Baker the pictures of Becca Sterling.

"Do you recognize this woman?" he asked.

Baker scrutinized the pictures. "I don't know her. I may have seen her around."

"How about this woman?" asked Ray, handing Baker the second set of photos.

Baker peered at the faded Kodachrome images. "Yeah, the fruit didn't fall far from the tree. Mother, daughter, right?"

"How about the mother, does she look familiar?"

"Yes, I think I told you about her. This photo, where she's younger, that was the girl who hung out at Sherwood. What did I tell you her name was?"

"You said it was Ginger."

"Did I? I don't remember that. This fire. I'm all confused."

"Stu, her real name was Monique," said Ray.

"Monique, I don't think I ever heard that." Stu studied the photo carefully. "Look at this picture. You can see she's laughing. Look at those eyes, beautiful smile, long blond hair. And her tan, even in this washed out photo, you can still see it. And her laughter, I can hear it, joyful. How can I remember all that and not remember her name?"

"But you are sure she was the woman at Sherwood?"

"There were so many pretty girls there. And we were all so young."

"Monique, the woman in the photo. Is she the one who you said might have been involved with Rob Habbers?"

"Maybe." Stu looked confused as he handed the photos back to Ray.

"It's a piece of a puzzle," Ray said. "A puzzle that might have something to do with the person who torched your building. Have you seen or talked to anyone about Sherwood Forest Commune since our conversation?"

"No. Truth be told, I didn't think about it again. In spite of my good intentions, I don't know that I'll ever write it all down like the kids asked me to do. Things are sort of fading away."

Ray was distracted by the message tone from his phone. He scanned the screen and then looked back at Stu. "Sorry, we've got an emergency. I'll keep you in the loop about the investigation. You know you can call me if you have questions."

As he headed for Sue's truck, he could see that she was sprinting in the same direction.

47

"Black ice, whiteout conditions, just perfect," yelled Sue over the scream of the siren.

Ray, holding a phone to his ear, nodded, indicating that he'd heard her.

"What's the story?" she asked when Ray lowered the phone.

"The pursuit started as a traffic stop when the truck blew through a school zone in the village and then refused to pull over. Rory broke it off because of conditions but continued up M22. A couple of miles later, he saw the truck was off the road, in the water, wheels toward the sky."

"Survivors?"

"The driver is out of vehicle, conscious, multiple injuries. A passenger is trapped. Emergency vehicles are at the scene."

Ray sat tight, occasionally glancing at Sue as the world rushed by. *Ujjayi breathing*, he thought as the truck hurtled along the slick ribbon of ice and snow. *Cara needs another miracle*, he thought.

Sue took her foot off the gas as they approached a line of emergency vehicles. Ray was out of the truck as soon as she brought it to a stop. When he reached the lip of the steep embankment, his eyes swept the frantic activity below. Several rescue workers were attending to a man secured to a backboard. A second crew, standing in water beyond the shoreline, hovered around the crushed cab of the pickup.

Ray tumbled down the bank, regaining his footing just before he reached the water. He walked out into the waves and stopped at a place where he could observe the crew trying to free the victim trapped in the truck. He could see a woman's upper torso. A rescue crewmember knelt in the water, her hands extended through the missing side window, trying to support the woman's head and shoulders. Other members of the crew were working with hydraulic tools, the jaws of life, to open the deformed steel so they could pull the victim from the wreckage. Ray moved closer, confirming the identity of the woman.

Suddenly, Sue was at his side. "Is she alive?"

"Don't know," he said.

They stood, in the wind and waves, seconds ticking by, minutes inching forward. Finally, one of the crew signaled to someone on shore. Two EMTs splashed out carrying a backboard. Ray and Sue watched as Cara Morrison was gently freed from the wreckage and secured to the backboard, seven or eight pairs of hands holding it above the water. Then the crew moved toward the shore and passed Morrison to another set of hands that quickly expedited her journey up over the embankment to a waiting ambulance.

"How's she doing?" Ray asked one of the crew members.

"She's still with us. That's all I can tell you."

Sue climbed back up to the road and watched Ray splash back to shore.

"Feet cold?" asked Sue as they walked back to the truck.

"Wet, too," admitted Ray.

"I carry boots for you. I tried to remind you, but you were gone."

"They'll warm up."

"Get out of those shoes, towel off, and put on the boots. Sometimes I think you need a minder."

"Once we get moving, I'll kick off my shoes. Crank the heat. I'll be okay."

"Where to?" asked Sue.

"Medical center. I'll call Wendy Morrison. I'd like to meet her there. She's going to need some support."

The radio blared, "All available units, all available units, active shooter—" and then went silent.

Ray reached over and grabbed the microphone. "Go ahead, Central."

Nothing.

"Why aren't they responding?" asked Sue, her attention fixed on the road ahead.

"Go ahead, Central," Ray repeated.

"Pull over," instructed Ray. He keyed the screen on his phone and brought it to his ear. Sue watched as he listened intently. "Backup power on?" he asked, his question directed to the phone.

"Request SWAT, State Police, and fire," Ray barked. "We're inbound."

"What's happening?" asked Sue.

"Active shooter at the county complex. The building is being raked with automatic fire. Power is out. Vehicles on fire at the rear entrance."

Sue turned on the siren and pulled back onto the road, fishtailing on the icy surface as she accelerated.

"What's our plan?" she asked. She glanced at Ray. He was on the phone again, cupping it close to his ear. She could only hear fragments of the conversation, turning right at the top end of the village and heading west.

"What's the plan?" she asked again.

"Automatic fire continuing. We will be first on the scene. Backup's ten, fifteen minutes away."

"Where's the shooter?"

"Not sure. The berm at the west end of the lot. Maybe a vehicle. Straight back from the entrance. Windows are shot out. Smoke's pouring in. I barely heard her—fire alarms and screaming."

"Ray?" said Sue.

"Circle to the back. That will give us cover and a view."

"The shotgun is behind you near the floor," she reminded Ray.

Sue switched off the siren and lights as they approached the county complex.

"Look," said Sue, pointing to a column of dense black smoke and flames dancing on the horizon.

She continued past the primary drive, turning right onto a secondary road a few tenths of a mile down the highway. Then she turned onto a gravel road that circled behind the complex and connected with the central parking area. Creeping up a steep slope, she stopped near the crest, just as the scene became visible.

"Fire is out of control," she said, pointing to the several blazing vehicles near the Sheriff's Department entrance.

"It's the van," said Ray, pointing toward the far west side of the parking lot. "The shooter's over there, beyond the other vehicles." He rolled down his window. The staccato report from the bursts of an automatic rifle continued to rip into the building and the vehicles in the parking lot.

"We could get them surrounded and try for a surrender," said Sue.

"How long, Sue?"

Before she could answer, Ray said, "The shots are coming from the rear of the van." He turned toward her, and the certainty in his eyes steadied her. "Get up as much speed as you can. Ram them from the side. Try to flip them."

"Sure," she said, but she didn't turn back toward the steering wheel just then, held there by a fear that felt like drowning.

"Go," Ray said. "Now."

The big engine roared as Sue crested the hill and closed on the target. On contact, the push bumper on her truck crushed the side of the van. Staying on the accelerator, she drove the wreck across the icy pavement to the curb at the end of the lot. When the passenger side wheels hit the curb, the van began to roll. Sue braked hard at the edge of the slope. The van continued its violent, tumbling descent, finally sliding to a stop upright on the frozen surface of a retention pond.

Sue and Ray scrambled out of the truck and down the hill, Sue with a shotgun, Ray with a Glock.

Steam poured out of the van's engine compartment, the hood torn off in the violent roll. The driver's side door was ajar and wrenched at an odd angle, drooping toward the ground. Sue couldn't see anyone inside the van.

Weapons at the ready, they cautiously approached the wreckage, struggling for footing on the steep, slippery terrain. Sue froze the instant she saw a handgun appear through the opening in the door. Her whole body started at the sharp bark of the pistol, and she fired at the gun, at the hand holding it. Buckshot ripped into the sheet metal. She shot a second time. A shrill scream filled the air.

Sue glanced quickly back over her shoulder. "Ray!" she shouted as she saw him slump forward.

Looking toward the van, she saw two hands extending beyond the door, lifting the pistol. She pulled the shotgun tight to her shoulder and fired again. The pistol dropped to the snow.

Sue closed the distance, gun at the ready. She stopped at the side of the van, retrieving the pistol and tossing it away.

A painful moan seeped from the van's interior. Sue peered in, then struggled to pull the mangled door open. An elderly woman, small and frail, her eyes filled with fear, hands distorted and bleeding, stared up at her.

Sue grabbed the woman by the jacket and pulled her out of the vehicle. Two men, jail deputies, rushed to help Sue. "We've got her."

She glanced up the hill at Ray. People were attending to him.

Sue handed the shotgun off to one of the deputies and drew her sidearm. She slowly entered the van, gun extended. Peering around the seat, she could see a prostrate form in the gloomy interior. The man, pulled tight in a fetal position on one side of the van, moaned softly. She pulled a flashlight from her belt, checking the man's hands for weapons. There were none. Empty shell casings and clips were scattered around the floor. A military-style weapon rested near the crushed sheet metal on the far side of the interior.

"I've got him covered," said Sue to a voice outside the van, not breaking her gaze. "See if you can get the side door open."

Daylight flowed in as the door was pried open. The man didn't move. Sue held her position until two EMTs secured the crumpled body on a backboard. Then she walked around the van and peered down at the small, feral-looking man.

And then she was alone as the stretcher was sprinted away. Sue walked up the slope, stopping where she had seen Ray go down.

Among the multiple footprints, she could see blood in the snow. When Sue reached the pavement, she stopped and viewed the carnage. Fire engines, EMT units, and other emergency equipment filled the vast parking area behind the government center. Firefighters worked to control the gasoline-fueled inferno, trucks and cars, black smoke rising into the heavy overcast. Small groups of people, employees and visitors, were being guided to safety away from the badly damaged building. A helicopter landed at the far edge of the plowed area and was quickly airborne again.

Sue felt unsteady, dropping to her knees in the snow. And then Brett Carty, a patrol officer, was at her side, gently steadying her, slowly helping her to her feet.

"Are you okay?" he asked as he looked her over for obvious wounds.

She nodded in the affirmative. "I need to go in and get washed up."

"You can't," he explained, eyeing her carefully.

Sue looked toward her truck, doors open, engine still running. "I need to—"

"Someone will take care of it," he explained as he guided her to his patrol car, helped her into the passenger seat, and secured the seatbelt.

Sue remained silent as they journeyed toward the medical center.

48

It was the image that would keep Sue up at night, that would wake her from a deep sleep: Ray falling forward, the blood in the snow. Now she stood in the hallway outside surgery as Hanna Jeffers, dressed in scrubs, pushed out the swinging doors and came toward her.

Sue reached for Hanna and the two women held one another.

"Is he—"

"He's okay," said Hanna. "Bad, but it could have been much worse. He was hit twice."

"Twice?" said Sue. She collapsed into a nearby chair. Hanna took a seat next to her, taking her hand.

"His vest stopped the first bullet," Hanna explained. "He's going to have a big hematoma there, and maybe some bruised ribs. I think that bullet hitting the vest knocked the wind out of him and caused him to pitch forward. As he went down, the second bullet penetrated his torso just above his body armor. The bullet exited through his back, leaving a sucking chest wound and soft tissue damage. It could have been so much worse. From an M15 the wound would have been fatal."

Hanna paused, then asked, "Did you see the weapon?"

"An old pistol of some kind. I saw Ray go down. The van, the gun, I just kept going until they were neutralized." She flashed back to the way she'd frozen when the gun appeared from the inside of the van. "Can I see him?"

"Not yet. He's still in recovery. A couple of more hours, probably."

"You seem so calm," said Sue. She watched Hanna consider the comment.

"I knew a gunshot victim was inbound. When I saw it was Ray

. . ." her voice became almost a whisper, "I froze. Then one of my colleagues nudged me, like, 'Are you okay?' Then I went robotic. I don't know how many times I've confronted chest wounds. You start with chaos and the unknown, but there's a process, an order. I was saying the right things. My hands were steady. I was on autopilot. I treated hundreds of traumatic chest wounds in Iraq. This was an easy one. Anyway, after we had finished up, I walked outside. The sun was out. I collapsed on a bench. One of the nurses brought me some coffee and Kleenex and wrapped a blanket around me. She stayed with me, eventually walking me back inside. What about you? How are you doing?"

"I think I was in shock. I guess I still am. Ray, what happens now?"

"We'll keep him a few days, maybe longer if necessary."

"Then what?"

"I don't know. I'm considering a kidnapping."

"Ray?"

"Yes. I get so fixated on saving the world, I don't notice things close to me. We both know he's been struggling. He desperately needs to be away from the job for an extended period. I'm going to get him out of here, someplace warm, on the water, Florida, Mexico, Spain."

"What's your plan?"

"Do you know if he's okay on sick and vacation time?" Hanna asked.

"He's got plenty. He mostly works. Never gets sick, or at least never stops showing up."

"And contingency plans for leadership are in place if he's temporarily disabled?"

"Absolutely. Ray's arranged for every eventuality. The plans have all been approved by the county board. I would be acting sheriff in his absence."

"How about your job?" Sue asked.

"I have lots of vacation time. And I can get a leave if needs be."

"And California?"

"Not now. Maybe not ever."

"So when is this kidnapping going down?" asked Sue.

"Ray's going to need several more days of hospitalization. That will give me time to get my affairs sorted out. As soon as he's well enough, we'll head out."

"He will protest," said Sue.

"What's his choice—a nursing home or a road trip?"

"You're going to have a fight on your hands."

"I don't think so," retorted Hanna with a wry smile. "I'll have him sedated before he's released. We'll be hundreds of miles down the road before he's fully aware of what's happening."

"Lots of luck," said Sue.

"He's got some painful injuries. He'll be compliant."

"The woman involved. She would have come with police guards."

"This is what I know, secondhand. The woman had multiple wounds to her left hand, wrist, and arm."

"Buckshot," explained Sue.

"They got her stabilized. A hand specialist has been called in for a consultation. Those injuries, however, appear to be the least of her problems. She told one of the ER doctors she had lung cancer. And there seem to be serious psychiatric problems, as well."

"And then there was the man with her. He was unconscious when they removed him from the van."

"He's in a coma," said Hanna. "Serious head injury, multiple fractures, including a femur. It doesn't sound like he's salvageable. Who are these two people, anyway?"

"It's a long, complicated story," answered Sue. "I'm still trying to connect the dots."

Hanna responded to a page, looking at the screen on the device. "Look, I've got to scoot. Let's talk later."

Sue found Wendy Morrison in the visitor waiting area of the emergency department.

"The doctors haven't told me much," Wendy explained. "They

probably don't know. It's a severe concussion. They're going to transfer Cara to the level one trauma center in Grand Rapids. We're waiting on transportation."

"Have you seen her?"

"They let me in briefly. I think they wanted to assure me Cara was still alive. Can you tell me what happened?"

Sue explained the chronology of events initiated by Wendy's call to Ray, starting at the Shore and Surf Motel and ending in the icy water of Lake Michigan.

"And the man she was with, the driver, his name?"

"Manny Tishull. Does the name sound familiar?"

"No, I've never heard Cara mention anyone by that name. Where is he from?"

"Kentwood, near Grand Rapids."

"Doesn't ring any bells," Wendy said. "Where is he now?"

"The State Police have him in custody. He still may be here at the hospital. Once he's well enough, he's going to jail. He has several outstanding warrants downstate. Tishull's going to be off the streets, at least for a while."

Sue didn't say what she was thinking, that there were many more Tishulls out there, many more bad decisions for girls like Cara to make. She shook her head as she walked back to surgery, as if to shake off the thought. Ray's pessimism was starting to rub off on her.

49

Ray was propped up in the hospital bed, an IV in one arm, colored lines on the monitor above him marching from left to right.

"Are you behaving?" Wendy Morrison asked.

"Hard not to," he answered, pointing to the IV line attached to the back of his hand. "I was supposed to be here for a few days, then this infection set in. What's happening with Cara? I'm surprised you're here."

"Her sisters and I are taking turns being with her. It's all good news at the moment. She's awake and responding. There doesn't seem to be any permanent cognitive damage. The radius in her right arm is broken. She came back to the world wearing a cast. She opened her eyes, looked at me, and smiled, then noticed the cast and started swearing—I knew instantly she was getting back to her old self. And there's one more thing."

"What's that?" asked Ray.

"A couple of the nurses in the unit told me that when smokers come out of a coma, the first thing they ask for is a cigarette. Cara didn't. She's been smoking since she was fourteen or fifteen. She hasn't mentioned it, Ray. Maybe things got bounced around in her head in a good way. At least that's my hope."

He smiled at Wendy. *She deserves some good news,* he thought. "Sue said you're doing a psych workup of Marian Patozak for the prosecutor's office. Anything you can share?"

"There will be no prosecution."

"How so?" asked Ray.

"I've talked to her hospitalist and he told me about her oncology consult. Marian has lung cancer, end-stage. She's receiving hospice care."

"How about her psychological state?" Ray asked.

"Confused, disoriented, she's dwelling in the past. It's like she went to sleep 40 years ago and suddenly woke up and got busy settling the score with the people who had done her wrong, but she didn't understand those people were mostly gone. I've been searching the literature, I can't find anything that exactly fits what she's presenting. Dissociative amnesia, fugue amnesia, some similarities, but vastly different. Ray, she freely admits that she came here to kill Sheriff Hentzler. She says that she and her accomplice, who she refers to as Little John, torched Hentzler's house and pulled down his cemetery monument. And then they continued on their rampage as if Hentzler was still alive."

"I'm not following."

"It will take a while to bend your head around this madness," said Wendy.

Sue entered, briefly interrupting the conversation. She pulled over a chair on the other side of the hospital bed.

"Is Wendy telling you about Marian?"

"I'm trying to comprehend this," he responded.

"Sue laid out everything for me," Wendy explained. "She was with me for most of the interviews."

"So Becca's death," pressed Ray.

"Marian said she had been there before, years ago. She was looking for Rob, her long lost love. She thought he might be with that blond girl, Monique. Marian said a door was unlocked, and she went into the house. Some woman started screaming at her, telling her to go away. They struggled and the woman fell down and didn't move."

"How could she remember that place?" asked Ray. "Forty-some years, a different building."

"Marian said she and Little John had come back to the area several times over the years and developed a hit list and identified targets."

"How about the fire?" asked Ray.

"Cleansing," said Wendy. "Marian said Little John liked cleansing."

"The machine gun or whatever. Where did that come from?"

"Orville's. The handgun, too. The automatic was a WWII relic, a Browning automatic rifle. We'd known of the possibility that some weapons might have gone missing after you interviewed Orville's daughter, Gretchen Witherspoon." said Sue.

"I didn't begin to connect the dots," said Ray.

"You couldn't," said Wendy. "Not in a normal way. These people were living in an alternate reality."

"And the fire at Stu Baker's?"

"Marian said Stu was one of Orville's gang. He deserved to die. She seemed to believe that he lived in his summer studio. I guess he had at some time in the past."

"And the final assault on the law enforcement center?"

"Marian said they were going to die finishing Orville off," answered Sue.

"It's like you can't ask any logical questions," said Wendy. "In Marian's mind, this all made sense. Still does."

"And her accomplice?" asked Ray. "What's his condition?"

"We've ID'd him as Toby Osmann," Sue said. "He was concussed with multiple fractures and internal injuries." She looked toward Wendy.

"As to his mental state, I've had a few brief conversations with him. He's still highly sedated. That said, he seems to be occupying the same planet as Marian. He's disoriented. No sense of time or place. My guess is that Marian completely controlled him. She gave his world shape and context, and he doesn't seem to know much beyond that."

"So Becca Sterling is dead, and Ava will grow up without her mother because of some evil that took place more than forty years ago," said Ray.

"Yes," answered Wendy. "It's a level of chaos that's almost beyond comprehension."

50

Sue Lawrence slowly piloted the vehicle along the path cut in the deep slush by earlier traffic.

"Thank you for doing this, especially at this ungodly hour," said Hanna.

"No problem. Besides, Simone needs the time with Ray. She doesn't understand why he's disappeared from her life the last few weeks." Sue glanced back over her shoulder briefly to the back seat. "You guys okay?" she asked.

"We had a few minutes of bonding," Ray answered. "Now she seems to be fast asleep."

The conversation dropped off, the only sounds coming from the slap of the wipers against the heavy snow and the drone of the heater and defroster.

Sue paused at the flashing stoplight for a snowplow to pass in the opposing lane. Then she followed a gentle curve that opened to the front of the terminal, stopping at the end of a line of vehicles near the entrance.

Ray glanced over at the aircraft waiting in a circle of light, a de-icing truck parked by its side. He could see a person in the bucket above the truck spraying the plane with a steaming liquid.

Sue pulled forward and stopped again.

"This is close enough," said Hanna. She got out and opened Ray's door. "Say your goodbyes."

Ray held the sleeping dog for a few more moments, scratching Simone's ears and petting her head, then he positioned her on the seat as he slid out of the car, Hanna holding onto Ray's right arm, guiding him over the curb and onto the walkway. He was enveloped by the sound of jet engines and the smell of their kerosene-tinged exhausts.

"Do you want a wheelchair?" Hanna asked.

"No," he responded, slowly moving his head from side to side.

The two women ushered him through the double set of automatic doors and into a chair. Then they disappeared again, returning with two rolling carry-ons. After pulling Ray to his feet, they headed up to the concourse toward the security checkpoint.

Ray saw Sue lean toward Hanna. He heard her ask, "When are you going to tell him?" He saw Hanna answer, only a word or two, but he couldn't quite make out what she said.

Then Sue moved in close and held Ray for a long moment. After giving Hanna a quick hug, she moved away from the jumble of sleepy-eyed travelers awaiting their turn to enter the security gate.

Once they were at the front of the line, Hanna passed Ray off to a TSA agent who guided him to a seat in the departure area. A few minutes later she settled at his side.

"How long am I going to feel like this?" he asked.

"I made sure you had enough meds to be comfortable on the trip. You'll probably be sleeping much of the way. Don't worry, Ray. I'm going to wean you off the drugs as quickly as possible. After a few days of warm weather, sun, and exercise, you'll start feeling better."

"Exercise, a forced march up Kilimanjaro?" he asked.

"Something a bit less strenuous. Walks on tropical beaches at the beginning. In a week or two, you'll be in a kayak for some leisurely paddling."

"Food?"

"Caribbean, eclectic. Everything fresh. Lots of seafood."

He pointed to his bag. "How did you know what to bring?"

"Sue helped me," Hanna said. "Just some essentials. I grabbed your journal, too. Thought you'd want to do some writing. And I tossed in a couple of books from your nightstand."

"Clothes?"

"Like I said, the essentials, Ray. Don't worry. They sell clothes in every corner of the globe. Birkenstocks, too."

"Can I see the tickets? Where are we going?" he asked, groggily.

"Detroit, then points south." She gave him a wry smile.

Ray started feeling around his jacket. "My phone?"

"I gave it to Sue when we picked you up at the hospital. There is little or no cell service at our final destination. You're in recovery mode."

"Can I use your phone?"

"It's in my bag. I can't get to it."

Before Ray could protest, a gate agent pushing a wheelchair stopped in front of his chair.

"We need to get you boarded, sir."

Ray acquiesced, riding the wheelchair to the end of the jetway, then being assisted to a seat in the first row in the cabin.

"I thought you'd like a window seat. If you want a view of the bay, you'll have to keep your eyes open for at least a few more minutes."

Ray nodded, reaching over for her hand.

"What are you thinking?" she asked.

"Thinking? No, just muddling. I just can't make sense of any of this. I've just been lying in that bed the last few days trying to get some clarity. Perhaps it's the drugs. Maybe when I get all this junk out of my system, I'll be able to sort it all out. What do you think, doctor?"

Hanna leaned into him. Over the roar of the revving turbines, she said, "Maybe."

Ray peered out of the window in the darkened cabin as the plane lifted off the runway and circled north over the bay before heading south. He could briefly see some of the streetlights as the aircraft climbed into the heavy overcast.

"Maybe," he repeated, closing his eyes.

Author's Note

The writing and rewriting of *The Center Cannot Hold* took more than a year. Over that time I received help and encouragement from so many people, some of whom wish to remain anonymous.

My thanks to my writing group: Marietta Hamady, Peter Marabell, and Winnifred Simpson for their thoughtful feedback and bonhomie.

I am grateful to so many people in law enforcement and medicine, active and retired, who have patiently shared their expertise and time.

Special thanks to Professor Rhett Diessner of Lewis and Clark State College for our email conversation on psychological disorders. My thanks also to Laurie Lapp who emailed me a newspaper account that proved seminal to the creation of this story.

As always, I'm indebted to Heather Shaw for her story editing skills, cover design, and interior layout. The ten books in this series wouldn't have happened without Heather's support, friendship, and strong work ethic.

I am also indebted to the independent local booksellers in northern Michigan who have been stocking my novels and inviting me for signings and book talks for almost two decades.

Also, to my readers, a special thank you. Your good words in person or by email have kept me buoyed up during the struggle of moving forward from a few concepts and ideas to a finished draft.

And, finally, continued thanks to my wife, Mary K, who provides support, friendship, and wise counsel to a madman who is trying to write yet another book.

Books in the Ray Elkins Series:

Summer People

Color Tour

Deer Season

Shelf Ice

Medieval Murders

Cruelest Month

Death in a Summer Colony

Murder in the Merlot

Gales of November

The Center Cannot Hold